P9-CQA-776

HERO UNDER COVER

*Recent Titles by Suzanne Brockmann
from Severn House*

NO ORDINARY MAN
UNDERCOVER PRINCESS

HERO UNDER COVER

Suzanne Brockmann

This first world hardcover edition published 2016
in Great Britain and in the USA by
SEVERN HOUSE PUBLISHERS LTD of
19 Cedar Road, Sutton, Surrey, England, SM2 5DA,
by arrangement with Harlequin Books S.A.
First published 1994 in the USA in mass market format only.

British Library Cataloguing in Publication Data

Brockmann, Suzanne author.
  Hero under cover.
  1. Bodyguards--Fiction. 2. Love stories.
  I. Title
  813.6-dc23

ISBN-13: 978-0-7278-8583-8   (cased)

All Severn House titles are printed on acid-free paper.

Severn House Publishers support the Forest Stewardship Council™ [FSC™],
the leading international forest certification organisation.
All our titles that are printed on FSC certified paper carry the FSC logo.

Printed and bound in Great Britain by
TJ International, Padstow, Cornwall.

For those fabulous Kuhlmans—
Bill, who's been trying to teach
me simply to be happy, and Jodie,
who's been showing us all how
to be happy for years

HERO UNDER COVER

CHAPTER ONE

"YOU'RE GOING TO DO *what!*"

"A strip search," the FBI agent said, heading for the door. "Please follow me."

Dr. Annie Morrow crossed her arms and planted herself firmly. She wasn't going anywhere, that was for damn sure. "You've gone through my luggage with a fine-tooth comb, you've X-rayed the hell out of my purse, and now you want to do a *strip* search? This is harassment, plain and simple. You've held me here for nearly five hours without letting me contact an attorney. My civil rights are being violated, pal, and I've had damn near enough."

On the other side of the one-way mirror, CIA operative Kendall "Pete" Peterson stood silently, watching Dr. Anne—nickname Annie—Morrow, renowned archaeologist and art historian, professional artifact authenticator. According to her file, she was thirty-two years old, and one of the world's foremost experts on ancient metalworkings—coins, statues, works of art, jewelry. The daughter of two archaeologists, she'd been born on a dig in Egypt. She'd lived in thirteen different countries and participated in nineteen different excavations, and that was *before* she'd even attended college.

What the file *didn't* tell him was that she was filled with a seemingly limitless supply of energy. During the course of the five hours he'd been watching her, she had sat still for only a very short time. Mostly she paced; sometimes she stood, she leaned, she tapped her foot, but generally she moved around the small interrogation room like a caged animal.

The file also didn't describe the stubborn tilt to her chin, or the way her blue eyes blazed when she was angry. In fact, the photo included hadn't managed to capture much of anything out of the ordinary, except maybe her long, shining brown hair, and her almost too-sensuous lips.

But in person, in motion, she was beautiful....

"So that's our little Dr. Morrow," came a voice at his shoulder.

Peterson turned to look at Whitley Scott, the man in charge of the FBI side of the investigation. Scott smiled at him, his eyes crinkling behind his thick glasses. "Sorry I'm late, Captain," he said. "My flight was delayed."

Peterson didn't smile back. "We've been holding her for hours," he said. "She's pretty steamed."

Through the speaker system, he could hear Dr. Morrow still arguing with FBI agent Richard Collins.

"I've told you nine million times, or is it ten million now? I was in England to pick up an artifact—a gold-cast death mask from the nineteenth century—for a client. I wasn't out of the U.S. long enough to do whatever illicit crimes you're trying to accuse me of. The shipping papers for the death mask are all in order—you've admitted that much," she said. "What *I'd* like to know is when you intend to let me leave."

"After the strip search," Collins said. He was a good man for this job, Peterson thought. Collins could outargue anyone. He was solid, steady and extremely patient. And he was absolutely never fazed.

"She's just your type, Pete," Whitley said, with a sideways glance at the taller man. "Something tells me you're going to enjoy this job."

Peterson didn't smile, but his dark brown eyes flashed in Scott's direction for a microsecond. "She's too skinny," he said.

In the interrogation room, Annie Morrow had had enough. She slammed her hand down on the table, pulling herself up and out of the chair she'd recently thrown herself into. "You want to strip-search me?"

she said. "Fine. Strip-search me and let me get the
hell out of here."

She shrugged out of her baggy linen jacket,
tossing it onto a chair as she kicked her sneakers off.
A quick yank pulled her loose red shirt over her head,
and she quickly unbuttoned her pants.

"Umm…" Collins said, rattled. "Not *here*…."

"Why not?" Annie asked much too sweetly, her
eyes bright with anger as she stood in the middle of
the room in her underwear. "Oh, relax. I have bathing
suits that are more revealing than this."

A slow grin spread across Peterson's face. Man,
she'd managed to faze Collins. She knew darn well
he had wanted her to follow him to a private room
where she'd be searched by a female agent. Yet she'd
undressed in front of him, simply to upset him. He
felt a flash of something, and realized that he liked
her—he liked her spirit, her energy, her nerve. He
frowned. She was a suspect, under investigation. He
wasn't supposed to like her. Respect, admire even,
but not like. But, man, standing there, looking at her,
he found an awful lot to like.

Annie turned and gestured toward the mirror,
hands on her hips. "Don't you think the rest of the
boys want to get in on the fun?"

She knew they were watching her. She was really
something, really sharp. Her file said she'd had a 4.0

average throughout college, graduating with a Ph.D. in half the time it normally took. He liked smart women, particularly when they came wrapped in a package like this one.

Her bra and panties were both black and lacy, contrasting the smooth paleness of her fair skin. Her breasts were full, her waist narrow, flaring out to slender hips and long, beautiful legs. "I take it back," Pete said to Whitley Scott. "She's *not* too skinny."

She seemed to be looking directly at him. He could see the pulse beating in her neck. Each ragged, angry breath she took made her breasts rise and fall.

"Do you intend to harass me every time I leave and re-enter the country?" she said.

Pete glanced at Whitley. The older man shrugged. "She's looking right at you," Whitley said.

"You know she can't see me," Pete said, but he motioned for the mike to be turned on. "The Athens investigation," he said, raising his voice so the mike would pick him up, "hasn't been closed."

Annie threw up her hands and began to pace. "Well, there we go," she said. "We're finally getting somewhere. You *are* trying to harass me. You don't give a damn about this death mask. You still think I have something to do with the jerks that bombed and robbed that museum."

Pete tried to keep his attention on her words

instead of her body. But it wasn't easy. She moved like a cat, the muscles in her legs rippling....

"How many times do I have to tell you that I am *not* a thief?" she continued. "Shoot, I wish I were. It would make this a whole hell of a lot easier. But I'm not about to confess to crimes I didn't commit."

She stopped pacing, coming back to stare directly up at him again. It was eerie, as if she really could see him through the glass.

"There was an explosion and a robbery at the gallery in England two hours after you left it," Peterson said, his voice distorted over the cheap speakers. "This time, people died."

Peterson watched Annie's face carefully as a range of emotions battled through her. Anger finally won.

"So, naturally, you believe *I* was involved. That's great, that's really great. Innocent people die, and the best you guys can do is to give me a hard time as I get on and off planes. You should be over there chasing the creeps that did the bombing, not playing peekaboo with somebody who gets queasy when she cuts her finger, pal."

"Doesn't it seem a little strange that you should go to European art galleries twice in five months, and within hours after you leave, each of them is hit by a bomb and a robbery?" Peterson had been in this business long enough to know that when there was smoke, somebody was trying to hide a fire. He wasn't buying the indignant act. "How do you explain the fact that you left the Athens convention hours before anyone else?"

"I don't!" Annie countered, eyes aflame. "I've already told the FBI, *and* the CIA, and everyone else who's asked, that I left because I'd seen everything at the exhibit and I wanted to catch an early flight home." She was pacing the floor now, clearly upset. "What ever happened to innocent until proven guilty? Huh? Just what the hell is going on here?" she shouted, right through the glass at Peterson.

There was silence. Big fat silence. It disarmed her as Pete knew it would. Dr. Anne Morrow was low on patience, and impatient people didn't like being made to wait. She turned, gathering her clothes. "If we're through..." she said pointedly.

"But we're not," Pete said. "It's called a strip search for a reason."

What little remained of her patience snapped. "Oh, give me a break," she said, throwing down her clothes and striding over to the mirror. She came up really close—close enough for Pete to see the details of her thick, dark lashes and the streaks of lighter color in the deep blue of her eyes. Close enough for him to see that her skin was as smooth and soft as it looked. If the glass of the window hadn't been between them, he could have lifted his hand and touched her.

Peterson felt Whitley watching him, and somehow he managed to remain expressionless. But, man, it had been a long time since he'd looked at a woman and wanted her this badly. It had been a real long time.

"I assure you that everything I'm hiding in my underwear is attached, pal," she said. "No removable parts."

"Sorry," he said. "I'm being paid a lot of money not to trust you."

"What exactly are you looking for?" she asked. "Maybe if you tell me, I can check and see if I've got it on me somewhere."

"You ever hear of mules?" Pete asked.

She froze.

He'd managed to shock her, but somehow he didn't feel triumphant about it. "Mules are people who smuggle illegal substances into the country inside their bodies," he said.

"I *know* what a mule is," she said. "Tell me honestly, do you really think I've swallowed the crown jewels? Whole?"

"Not swallowed," he said, and then was silent, letting her figure it out for herself.

"Oh, Christmas," she said. Her face paled slightly

beneath her tan, and her freckles stood out. "We're really trying to go for total humiliation here, aren't we?"

"Just going by the book," Pete said. "And the book says that you'll be searched—completely. We have a physician waiting in another room."

"Oh, you mean you don't want to do it right here?" Annie said. She was furious. He could almost see her pulse accelerating as he watched the vein in her neck. "You sure you trust this doctor to do it right, pal? I would've thought you'd want to watch."

"I'd love to watch," he said, his voice coming out low and intimate, even through the tinny speakers. "And by the way, the name's not *pal.*"

"I prefer to personalize the disembodied voices that talk to me," she said. "It helps me feel more human. But you wouldn't know about that, would you?"

She turned away from the window suddenly, but not before he saw the glint of tears in her eyes.

Pete felt ashamed of himself. What was wrong with him? Why did he have to be so rough on her?

He was rough on her because he felt for her, because he found himself believing her. And he had absolutely no facts to back him up, just gut instinct. *Gut,* thought Pete, *yeah, right. Aim a little lower....* He couldn't let himself forget that Dr. Anne Morrow was a suspect, quite possibly a thief, connected to people who wouldn't think twice about killing to satisfy their greed.

He watched her pull on her pants and then her shirt as the female agent led her from the room. With a nod, he ordered the microphone connection cut.

Whitley Scott was watching him.

"She's gutsy," Pete said to him. "You've got to give her that much."

"I think she's hiding something," Scott said. "We've got to find a way to get closer to her. But how?"

"Good question." Pete leaned against the back wall of the room, crossing his arms in front of him. "I'm not exactly qualified to work in her laboratory. Or even on one of her digs."

"Client?" Whitley asked. "You could bring her some rare artifact to authenticate. One thing leads to another—a little dinner, a little who knows what, and she's telling you her deepest, darkest secrets."

"Perfect," Pete said expressionlessly. "Except she never dates her clients as a rule. No exception."

"Next-door neighbor?"

"She lives over her lab in a restored Victorian house up in Westchester County," Pete said. "Expensive neighborhood. Way out of our budget. It would cost us close to half a million to buy one of the houses next door—provided someone was even willing to sell. And I've already checked—no one wants to rent."

Whitley nodded, turning toward the door. "Well, keep thinking," he said. "We'll come up with something sooner or later."

CHAPTER TWO

ANNIE PULLED HER LITTLE HONDA into the driveway and turned the engine off. Damn, she was tired. Damn the CIA and damn the FBI and damn everyone who was working so hard to make her life so miserable.

Five months. The harassment had been going on almost nonstop for five months. And now, after the bombing in England, it was only going to get worse. Already everyone in town knew that she was the subject of an FBI investigation. The agents had talked with everyone she knew, and probably a lot of people she didn't know. Her college roommate had called last month to say that even she'd been questioned about Annie. And it had been five years since they'd last gotten together....

Damn, damn, damn, she thought. And particularly damn that horrible man who'd spoken to her from behind the one-way window. Somebody had referred to him as Captain Peterson. If she ever ran into him, she'd let him have a good swift kick where it counted. Except she didn't have a clue what he looked like. She wouldn't even be able to recognize him from his voice, not from hearing it over those awful interrogation room speakers.

She stepped out of the car and went around to the other side to pull the package from England from the passenger seat. *Damn these gold artifacts, too,* she thought, as she barely lifted the crate. *They always weigh a ton.*

Her assistant's car was still in the driveway, so instead of going up to her apartment on the top floors of the house, Annie went into the lab. She could hear the sound of the computer keyboard clacking and followed it to the back room, where the office was set up.

Cara MacLeish was inputting data at her usual breakneck speed. She didn't even stop as she looked up and grinned.

"Welcome back," she said. Her short brown curls stood straight up in their usual tangle, and her eyes were warm behind her horn-rimmed glasses. "I thought you'd be here sooner. Like six hours ago."

Annie lowered the crate holding the gold death mask onto her desk top, then brushed some strands of hair back from her face. "I was detained," she said simply.

Cara stopped typing, giving her boss her full, sympathetic attention, swearing imaginatively.

"Took the words right out of my mouth," Annie said, smiling ruefully.

"FBI again?" Cara asked.

"FBI, CIA." Annie shrugged. "They all want a piece of me."

"Well, look on the bright side," Cara suggested.

They both fell silent, trying to find one.

"They haven't been able to make any charges stick," Cara finally said.

Annie pulled a rocking chair closer to the computer console and sat down.

"And you haven't lost any business because of this," Cara said, warming up to it now. She stretched her thin arms over her head, then yawned, standing up to get the kinks out of her long legs. "In fact, I think business has picked up. We had a ton of calls while you were away."

Annie watched her assistant cross to the telephone answering machine. Next to it, a stack of little pink message slips were held by a bright red wooden duck with a clothespin for a mouth.

"Jerry Tillit called," Cara said. "He's back from South America, and he's got some Mayan stuff for you to look at."

"Did you talk to him, or get the message off the machine?" Annie asked.

Cara blushed. "I spoke to him."

"Did he ask you out again?" Annie grinned.

"Yes."

"And...?"

"We don't date clients, remember?" Cara said.

Annie corrected her. "Jerry's not a client, he's a *friend.*"

"He's also a client."

"So he's also a client," Annie admitted. "But just because *I* don't want to date clients doesn't mean *you* can't, MacLeish. Will you please give the man a break?"

"I did."

"You... What?"

The taller woman grinned, pushing her hair back from her face and sitting down on top of the desk. "I told him I'd go out with him. He's coming up to drop his finds off this Saturday. We're going out after that."

Annie glanced around the cozy office. The room was really quite large, but with two desks, two computers, a fax machine, a copier and all sorts of chairs and bookshelves, there wasn't much room even to walk. But Cara MacLeish was an essential fixture here. "Don't you be going and getting married, MacLeish," she said sternly. "No running off to South America with Jerry Tillit."

Cara grinned. "I'm only going to the movies with him," she said. "The next logical step might be a dinner date. Not marriage."

"You don't know Tillet as well as I do," Annie muttered. "And that man has a definite thing for you…."

"Speaking of marriage," Cara said, flipping through the phone message slips. "Nick York called—five different times. Something about a party down at the Museum of Modern Art sometime this month."

Annie released her hair from its ponytail, letting it swing free in a gleaming brown sheet. She leaned back in the rocking chair, resting her feet on top of the computer desk. "Shame on you, MacLeish. You know the words *marriage* and *York* cannot be uttered in the same sentence," she said. "York wants only two things from me. One of them is free lab work. And the other has nothing to do with marriage. Who else called?"

"The freight guy at Westchester Airport said a package from France will be in Saturday."

"Great." Annie sighed. "Like I've got any chance of getting to work on it in the next decade." She closed her eyes. "Okay, so I pick it up on Saturday. What else?"

"A guy named Benjamin Sullivan called," Cara said. "Ring any bells?"

Annie's eyes popped open. "Yeah, of course.

He's the owner of the piece I just picked up. What did he want?"

"He left a message on the machine, saying that we should ignore Alistair Golden if he calls," Cara said. She laughed. "I didn't recognize Sullivan's name, but it seemed kind of mystically, cosmically correct to get a message from a stranger telling us to ignore Golden. I always ignore Alistair Golden. Ignoring Golden is one of the things I do best."

Golden was Annie's chief competitor, and he usually handled all the U.S.-bound artworks and artifacts from the English Gallery.

"And sure enough," Cara said, snickering, "the little weasel called. He was in a real snit, whining about something—I'm not sure exactly what, because I was working very hard to ignore him."

Annie laughed. "I think I know what the bug up his pants was," she said. "When I got to the gallery, Sullivan's package was already crated and sealed. Golden had assumed he'd be doing the authentication job, so he'd already done the packing work."

"Golden packed the crate for you?" Cara said with great pleasure. "No wondering his whine was set on stun. He wanted you to call him back, but unless you want to subject yourself to a solid forty-five minutes of complaining, I wouldn't. I give you my permission to use the 'scatterbrained employee didn't give me the message' excuse for the next time he catches up with you."

Annie smiled. "Thanks. Did Ben Sullivan want me to call him back?"

"He said something about going out of town," Cara said, glancing back at the phone message slip. "Who is he? How do you know him? Come on, fill me in. Height, weight, marital status?"

"As far as I know, he's single," Annie said, then smiled. "But he's also seventy-five years old, so get that matchmaking gleam out of your eyes."

Cara made a face in disappointment.

"Ben's an old friend of my parents." Annie leaned back in her chair, breathing deeply. "I don't think I've seen him since, wow, since I was about fifteen. Apparently, he was talking to Mom and Dad recently, and they told him about me—you know, that I opened this lab a few years ago. When the offer to buy came in on this death mask, he requested that I do the necessary authentication."

"Instead of Golden," Cara said.

Annie grinned. "Instead of Golden." She sat forward, stretching her arms over her head. "Anyone else call?"

Cara nodded. "Yeah. I saved the best message for last. It came in on the answering machine. Let me play it for you."

Cara slid off the table, handing Annie the message slips, then pushed the message button on the machine. The tape rewound quickly, then a voice spoke.

It was odd, all whispery and strange, as if the caller had deliberately tried to disguise his voice. "The mask you have gained possession of does not belong to the world of the living. It is the property of Stands Against the Storm. Deliver it at once to his people, or be prepared to face his evil spirit's rage. The doors to the twilight world are opened wide, and Stands Against the Storm will take you back with him."

There was a click as the line was disconnected. Cara punched one of the buttons on the machine and the tape stopped running. "So, okay." She grinned. "Which one of your weirdo friends left *that* message? And who the heck is Stands Against the Storm?"

But Annie wasn't laughing. Swearing softly under her breath, she stood up, hoisted the crate containing the death mask off her desk and went down the hall toward the lab. Cara followed, her grin fading.

"What?" Cara asked, watching as Annie locked the front door. "What's the matter?"

"We've got to put this in the safe," Annie said, gesturing to the package in her arms.

"Annie, who *was* that on the tape?" Cara asked, eyes narrowing.

"Some crackpot," Annie said, heading back to the sturdy vault that sat directly in the middle of the house, surrounded by the lab in the front and the office in the rear. It was secure, impenetrable. She would feel a lot better after she locked the gold death mask inside.

"If it was just some crackpot," Cara demanded, "why did you rush across the room and lock the door?"

Annie opened the innocuous-looking closet door to reveal the combination lock of the big safe. She spun the red dial several times before entering the numbers. "Because it would be foolish not to take precautions, crackpot or not." She looked up at her assistant. "You must not have had a chance to read the background info I left you on this project."

Cara shrugged expansively. "I cannot tell a lie. I had about an hour of free time last night, and I spent it watching 'Quantum Leap' instead of reading about nineteenth-century Indian chiefs."

Setting the package on the top shelf of the vault, Annie swung the door shut, locking it securely. "Native Americans, not Indians," she corrected Cara. "In a nutshell, the artifact we're testing for authenticity is supposedly a gold casting of a death mask of a Navaho named Stands Against the Storm. He was one of the greatest Native American leaders. He was a brilliant man who truly understood Western culture. He tried to help the white leaders understand his own people as thoroughly."

Cara followed her back into the office. "How come I've never heard of him?" she asked. "I mean, everyone knows Sitting Bull and Geronimo. Why not this guy?"

Annie sat down behind her desk, frowning at the chaos on its surface. Why was it that paperwork seemed to multiply whenever she went away for a few days? "Sitting Bull and Geronimo were warriors," she said. "Stands Against the Storm was a man of peace. He didn't get as much press as the war party leaders, but not from lack of trying. In fact, he was in England, trying to drum up support for his people among the British, when he died." She shook her head. "His death was a major blow to the Navaho cause."

"If Stands Against the Storm was such a peaceful guy," Cara said, "then why would he have an evil spirit?"

"The Navaho believe that when people die, they become ghosts or spirits," Annie said. "It doesn't matter how nice or kind a person was during his life. When he dies, he becomes malevolent and he gets back at all the people who did him wrong during his lifetime. Chances are, the nicer the guy was, the more evil his spirit would be—the more he'd have to avenge. You know, nice guys finish last and all that."

"But if Stands Against the Storm died in England," Cara said, "then how could his spirit come after you? Assuming for the sake of this discussion that the Navaho are right about this spirit stuff," she added.

"Death is a major problem for the Navaho," Annie said. She smiled. "Actually, I can't think of too many cultures that look forward to death, but the Navaho *really* don't like it. In fact, if someone dies inside a house, even today, that house will sometimes be abandoned. See, the Navaho believe that the place a person dies in, and the things he touches before dying or even after he's dead, can contain his bad spirit. Making a death mask would be a real invitation to disaster. The Navaho would *never* make something like a death mask. But it was the custom at the time in England, you know, to make a mold of the dead person's face and then cast a mask from it to get a likeness. I guess Stands Against the Storm was something of a celebrity—and certainly a curiosity, a Red Indian from the Wild West—so when he died, they made a death mask."

Annie looked over at the answering machine. What she couldn't figure out was how it had become public knowledge that she was working on authenticating Stands Against the Storm's death mask. Unless Ben Sullivan, or Steven Marshall, the purchaser, had leaked something....

"Hey, Annie?"

She met Cara's worried brown eyes. "It just occurred to me," the taller woman said. "That message on the answering machine is basically a... Well, it's a death threat."

"It was just some nut." Annie shrugged it off. "Besides, I don't believe in ghosts."

"You gotta admit, it's creepy," Cara said. "Maybe we should, I don't know... Call the police?"

Annie groaned, dropping her head onto her arms on the desk top. "No more police, no more FBI, no way. I'd much rather be haunted by the spirit of Stands Against the Storm."

ANNIE SAT UP IN BED, WIDE-EYED in the darkness as the burglar alarm shrieked.

Her heart pounded from being awakened so suddenly. She clicked on the light and grabbed her robe. Oh, Christmas! This damned alarm was going to raise the entire neighborhood.

She ran down the stairs two at a time and turned on the lights in the foyer as she crossed toward the alarm-system control panel.

Oh my God, thought Annie. It wasn't a malfunction! The alarm schematic showed a breach in the system on the first floor. A window in the lab was marked as the intruder's point of entry.

Suddenly she was very glad for the shrieking alarm. Across the street, she could see the neighbors' lights go on, and she knew they'd call the police—they always did. She ran back up to her room and opened the drawer on her bedside table. Oh, damn, damn, damn, where *was* it?

She pulled the drawer out of the table and emptied it onto her bed. *There* it was.

She grabbed the toy gun, unwinding a stray piece of string from the barrel, and headed toward the stairs. She ran down and kicked open the door to the lab. She flicked on the light switch with her elbow and the bright fluorescent bulbs illuminated the room.

No one was there—either human or inhuman.

But the window had been broken.

Feeling just a little silly, she put the plastic gun down on the lab counter and stepped carefully toward the large rock that had been thrown through the window. There was a piece of paper attached to it with a rubber band.

Spinning lights from two police cars caught her eye as they pulled into her driveway. She went to the front door and keyed into the control panel the code to cancel the alarm. The shrill noise stopped instantly. Taking a deep breath, she opened the door to the town police officers.

They came inside and looked at the broken window. One of them made a quick survey of the house, checking to make sure all the windows and doors were still locked, while the other radioed in to the station.

Big doings in a small town. Annie sighed. She went into the kitchen and put on a pot of coffee. Something told her this was going to be a long night.

PETERSON WOKE UP INSTANTLY and answered the phone after only one ring.

"Yeah," he said, looking at the glowing numbers of his clock: 3:47. He ran one hand across his face. "This better be good."

"It's Scott. Can you talk?" Whitley Scott said in his flat New Jersey accent.

"Yeah, I'm awake," Pete said, sitting up and turning on his light.

"No, I mean…are you alone?"

"Yeah, I'm alone." Pete rubbed his eyes. "If you check my file, you'll see that I haven't been involved with anyone since last March."

"I've already checked your file," the FBI agent

said easily. "And *it* says you've got something of a reputation as a tomcat."

Pete was silent, thinking about that new administrative assistant in the New York City office. Carolyn something. She had curly brown hair and legs a mile long. And eyes that made it more than clear that she was interested in him, no-strings-attached. She'd invited him out for a drink last night. If he had gone with her, she'd probably be lying here right now, next to him.

But he'd turned her down.

Why? Maybe because, regardless of the fact that he'd be using her the exact same way, he was tired of being the flavor of the month for ambitious, upwardly mobile women.

Even though he wasn't overly tall, he knew that with his black hair and his dark brown eyes, he had the dark and handsome part down cold.

For years, he'd used his good looks to his advantage, but recently it had been rubbing him the wrong way. His relationships, which usually lasted a month or two, were getting shorter and shorter. And when he'd looked at that administrative assistant last night, he hadn't felt the usual heat from knowing that she wanted him. If he'd felt anything at all, it had been disdain.

More than once over the past few months, the

thought of retiring from the agency had crossed his mind. The closer he got to his fortieth birthday, the more aware he seemed to become of an emptiness in his life.

He couldn't figure out what he was looking for. He was far too jaded to believe in true love—hell, he was too jaded to believe in any kind of love. And if he stopped having relationships based on animal attraction, on sex, he was in for a whole lot of cold, lonely nights....

"You still there?" Whitley Scott asked.

"Yeah."

"We've found a way for you to get close to Anne Morrow," Scott said. "She practically handed it to us on a platter."

Pete listened intently as Scott explained. It would work. It would definitely work.

After he hung up the phone and turned the light off, Pete stared up at the dark ceiling, feeling a wave of anticipation so charged that it was almost sexual. In a sudden flash of memory, he saw black lace against pale skin, and a pair of wide, blue eyes....

"THE NOTE SAID WHAT?" Cara's voice rose sharply.

"It was stupid," Annie said, clearing some of the clutter off her desk. "I can't believe the police took it seriously."

"When someone bothers to send a message via a rock through a window," Cara said tartly, "it should probably be taken seriously."

"But, God, did they *have* to notify the FBI?" Annie said. "You know, the Federal agents got over here really quickly. I'm wondering if they weren't somehow responsible. I mean, they've been hassling me every other way imaginable. Why not a rock through a window?"

"With a note saying 'Prepare to die'?" Cara asked. "I doubt it, Annie."

"And *I* seriously doubt that a Native American group, no matter *how* radical or fringe, would resort to this kind of petty threat," Annie said. "The FBI can go ahead and investigate, but they're just wasting their time." She sat back in her chair, her normally clear blue eyes shadowed with fatigue. "I just don't need the FBI's garbage on top of everything else. You know, they wanted to provide me with round-the-clock protection. Surveillance is more like it. I told them I could protect myself perfectly well, thank you very much."

"I don't suppose you told them that the likeliest suspect is a ghost called Stands Against the Storm," Cara said. "Maybe we should've called Ghostbusters instead of the police." She sang the familiar horn riff to the original movie theme.

Annie laughed, searching for something on her desk to throw at her friend. She settled for an unsharpened pencil.

Cara dodged the pencil and grinned. "Of course, if a ghost isn't a freaky enough suspect, there are always Navaho witches."

Annie tiredly closed her eyes. "I see you finally read the background information I gave you."

"'Quantum Leap' reruns weren't on last night," Cara said. "So I had some free time. Fascinating stuff. I particularly liked the part that said the Navaho believe some people—who appear to be normal during the day—are really witches. And if plain old witches who can cast spells and wreak havoc aren't bad enough, these witches can transform themselves into giant wolves at night and roam the countryside. Very pleasant."

"Most cultures have some version of bogeymen that stalk the night," Annie said. "Werewolves are nothing new."

"Yeah, but *these* werewolves are neighbors, relatives even," Cara said. "And they start doing their witchy business when they get jealous of another person's wealth or good luck or— Hey, that's it." Cara grinned. "Call the FBI off. I've figured it out. Alistair Golden is really one of these witches, and he's cast horrible bad-luck spells on you because you're starting to steal away some of his business. Although, actually he'd make a better weasel man than a wolf man."

"There's a big hole in your theory," Annie said. "Golden's not Navaho."

"Good point." Cara's eyes narrowed, taking in the pale, almost grayish cast to her friend's face. "The guy fixing the window won't be done for another hour or so," she said. "Why don't you go upstairs and take a nap? I can hold down the fort."

The phone rang.

"That's got to be my call from Dallas," Annie said. "I called Ben Sullivan but he's out of touch for a while. He's on a dig in Turkey, so my contact for the death mask is the buyer, Steve Marshall."

Cara picked up the phone. "Dr. Morrow's office. MacLeish speaking." She listened for a moment, her eyebrows disappearing under her bangs. "One moment, please," she said. She covered the speaker with her hand as she gave the handset to Annie. "What, are you clairvoyant, now, too? It's Steven Marshall. Calling from Dallas."

Annie smiled wanly as she took the phone. "Hello?"

"Dr. Morrow," came the thick Texas drawl. "My secretary tells me you've been trying to reach me?"

"Yes, Mr. Marshall," Annie said. "Thanks for

getting back to me so quickly. We're having a little problem."

Briefly she described both the threatening phone call and the follow-up note that had come through her window.

"I don't think there's any real danger," Annie said. "But I felt I had to notify you and give you the opportunity to have the artifact authenticated by an establishment with higher security."

There was a moment of silence. Then Marshall said, "But…you're the best, aren't you, darlin'?"

"Well, yes, I like to think so," Annie said.

"I'm more concerned with your personal safety," he said. "Are you frightened? Do you want to get out of this contract?"

"Not at all. It's just that I may not be set up to provide security at the level necessary to protect the piece," she explained.

"Oh, that's just a little bitty problem," Marshall said with the easy nonchalance of the very wealthy. "We can solve that, no sweat. *I'll* provide the security, darlin'. I'll send a man over later this afternoon. He'll be responsible for the safety of the death mask. He'll also act as your bodyguard."

Oh, great, just what she needed. A pair of biceps following her around. She took a deep, calming breath. "Mr. Marshall, that's not necessary—"

"No, no, darlin', I insist."

"But I'm backlogged," Annie protested. "It's going to be weeks before I even get a chance to *look* at the artifact. And the tests I need to perform will take that much time again. My contract states an estimated completion date of mid-December. That's over *two months*—"

"I'll tell the guy to be prepared to stay for a while."

"But—"

"I gotta get back to work now," Marshall said. "Nice talking to you, darlin'. I'll be in touch."

"But—"

He hung up.

"But I don't *want* a bodyguard!" Annie wailed to the buzz of the disconnected line.

"A what?" Cara asked.

Annie hung up the phone with a muttered curse. "I'm going to take a nap," she said, stalking toward the door. "Maybe when I wake up, this nightmare will be over."

"Did you say *bodyguard?*" Cara's voice trailed after her.

Annie didn't answer.

Cara's face broke into a wide grin. A bodyguard. For Annie. This was going to be an awful lot of fun to watch.

CHAPTER THREE

ANNIE STRETCHED, LUXURIATING, enjoying having spent the day in bed. It was a real self-indulgence, particularly since she had so much to do in the lab.

But she wouldn't have gotten a whole heck of a lot done if she'd tried to work. Her concentration would've been way off because of her fatigue, and she would have ended up having to do everything over again. So instead she'd slept hard, and now felt much better. And hungry. Boy, was she hungry.

She pushed back the covers and went into her bathroom to wash her face, deciding against a shower. Why bother? Cara would be leaving for home in an hour or so. And the artifacts Annie had to run tests on didn't care if she worked in her pajamas. She brushed the tangles out of her hair and put some moisturizer on her face.

The sky outside the window was dark, she realized suddenly. It must be later than she thought.

She went down the stairs barefoot, calling, "MacLeish! Are you still here?"

"No, she went home."

Annie stopped short at the sight of the stranger standing in the shadows of the foyer. How did he get in? What was he doing here? Fear released adrenaline into her system and, heart pounding, she stood on the stairs, poised to turn and run back up and slam the door behind her.

He must have realized that he had frightened her, because he spoke quickly and stepped into the light. "Steven Marshall sent me," he said, his voice a rich baritone with a slight west-of-the-Mississippi cowboy drawl. "My name's Pete Taylor. I'm a security specialist. Your assistant let me in. She didn't want to wake you...."

He was not quite six feet tall, with the tough, wiry build of a long-distance runner. His hair was black, and cut almost military short. His face was exotically handsome, with wide, angular cheekbones that seemed to accentuate his dark eyes—eyes of such deep brown, it was impossible to tell where the iris ended and the pupil began. His lips were exquisitely shaped, despite the fact that he wasn't smiling. Somehow Annie knew that this was not a man who smiled often.

He held out his wallet to her, opened to reveal an ID card encased in plastic.

Annie couldn't keep her hand from shaking as she took the smooth leather folder from him, and she saw a flash of amusement in his dark eyes. He thought it was funny that he scared her. What a jerk.

She sat down on the steps as she looked at the ID. Peter Taylor. Age 38. Licensed private investigator and security specialist. The card gave him a New York City address, in a rather pricey section of Greenwich Village. Across from the ID card was a New York State driver's license. She lifted the plastic flaps and found an American Express Gold Card for Peter Taylor, member since 1980, a MasterCard, a Visa and a Sears credit card. He was carrying over five hundred dollars cash in the main compartment, along with several of his own business cards.

She tossed the wallet back to him and, as their eyes met, she saw another glint of humor on his otherwise stern face.

"Do I pass?" he said. As he tucked the wallet into the inside left pocket of his tweed jacket, she caught a glimpse of a handgun in a shoulder holster.

Annie nodded. "For now," she said, working hard to keep her tone formal, polite. "But just so that it's out in the open, I think you should know that I don't want you here. I consider your presence an imposition, and I intend to speak to Marshall about it tomorrow. So don't bother unpacking—you'll be leaving in the morning."

"When I spoke to Mr. Marshall this afternoon, he was adamant that I remain," he said. "Apparently he's concerned for your safety. Somehow I don't see him changing his mind so quickly."

Annie stared at him. His feet were planted on the tile floor, legs slightly spread, arms crossed in front of his chest. His jeans were tight across the big muscles in his thighs. His belt buckle was large and silver and obviously Navaho in origin. Annie couldn't see it clearly, but there was a silver ring on his right hand that also looked Navaho. He wore a necklace, but it was tucked into his shirt. She would bet big money that he was at least half Native American, and probably Navaho.

"Where did you grow up?" she asked.

He blinked at the sudden change in subject. "Colorado," he said. "Mostly."

His shoulders stiffened slightly. So very slightly, he probably didn't even realize it. But Annie noticed. Something about the question had made him feel defensive, wary. Was it that she'd asked a personal question, or did his wariness have something to do specifically with Colorado, or the "mostly" that followed it?

She was instantly fascinated. It wasn't because he was outrageously handsome, she tried to convince herself. Her attraction toward him—and she *was* attracted, she couldn't deny that—was more a result of his quiet watchfulness, spiced with a little mystery. He had something to be defensive or at least wary about. What was it?

"You ride horses, don't you, Taylor?" she asked, head tilted slightly to one side as she looked at him, hooked into trying to solve the puzzle, hoping for another clue from his reaction.

She was watching him, Pete realized, studying him as if he were an artifact, memorizing every little detail, searching for his flaws and weaknesses.

Her hair was down around her shoulders, parted on the side and swept back off her face. It gleamed in the light. She wore a too-large pair of men's pajamas, with the legs cuffed and the sleeves rolled up. There was no makeup on her face, and instead of giving her that naked, vulnerable look most women have without cosmetics, she looked clean, scrubbed and fresh.

Her eyes were a brilliant blue, and she met his gaze steadily, as if she were trying to get inside his head.

"Yeah," he finally said.

"I figured it was either horses or a bike," she said. "Don't you feel odd, carrying around a gun?"

"No."

"What do you know about death masks?" she asked.

"Not much." She was firing off questions as if this were some kind of interview. He decided to play it her way. It might make her start to trust him. It certainly couldn't hurt—he wasn't going to tell her anything he didn't want her to know.

"How about art authentication?"

"Ditto."

"A Navaho leader from the nineteenth century named Stands Against the Storm?"

"Only the information that Marshall faxed me this morning," he said.

"Have you read it?"

"Of course."

She watched him thoughtfully. "Where did you go to school?"

He shifted his weight. While most people would have been loath to admit their ignorance, it hadn't bothered him one little bit to tell her he knew next to nothing about death masks and art authentication. But *this* question about himself, about his background, made him uncomfortable, Annie thought. Now, why was that?

"NYU," he said. The bio the agency had created for Peter Taylor had him attending New York University from 1973 to 1977. Truth was, he hadn't even set foot in New York until 1980. But he'd been Pete Taylor so many times, on so many different assignments, he almost had memories of the imaginary classes....

"Are you aware that I'm currently under investigation by the FBI and the CIA?" she asked, her blue eyes still watching him.

He was caught off guard by the directness of her question and had to look away, momentarily thrown.

"They think I'm involved in some kind of international art-theft conspiracy," she said.

He glanced up at her and saw that her lips were curved in a small smile. "Are you?" he asked.

He made a good recovery, Annie thought. He *had* known about the investigation. She was willing to bet he had done a full background sweep on her before coming up from New York City. It didn't surprise her one bit. Marshall wouldn't have hired anyone who was less than outstanding.

"Are you hungry?" she said, standing and stretching, arms pulled up over her head, ignoring his question. "I haven't eaten all day, and if I don't have something soon, I'm gonna die."

Pete found his eyes drawn to the gap that appeared between her pajama top and the loose bottoms that rode low on her slender hips. "I ate already, thanks," he said. "Besides, I have an expense account that Mr. Marshall is covering. It's not fair that I should cost you money. After all, you don't even want me here."

"It's nothing personal," Annie said, climbing up the stairs, heading for the kitchen.

"I know," he said, following her.

She turned on the light in the kitchen and opened the refrigerator. She pulled an apple from the crisper drawer and took it to the sink, where she washed it quickly, then dried it with a towel.

The kitchen was a small room, just barely large enough to hold a table in one corner and a counter with a sink, stove, refrigerator and dishwasher in the other. It was decorated in black and white, with a tile floor that reminded Pete of a chessboard.

"I'd like to do a complete walk-through of the building," Pete said, watching her take a healthy bite of the apple. "I checked out the first floor and the basement while you were asleep. Your safe location is good. It would take a significant explosive charge to blow it open. But your general security is—" He broke off, shaking his head.

"Bush-league?" Annie supplied, leaning back against the counter, ankles and arms crossed, watching him as she ate her apple.

It didn't rate a smile, but there was a flicker of amusement in his dark eyes. "Definitely. A professional could get into this house without triggering the alarm system—no problem. Don't you read *Consumer Reports?* The system you have is known for malfunctions. It's unreliable. It's easily bypassed, and it goes off spontaneously."

Annie shaved the last bit of fruit from the core of the apple with her teeth, licking her lips as she looked up at him. "I've noticed." She opened the cabinet door beneath the sink and tossed the apple core into a compost container, then rinsed her hands.

His expression changed slightly. Most people might not have picked it up—it was just a very small contraction of his dark eyebrows. But Annie was trained to pay attention to details, and on a face as expressionless as he kept his, the movement stood out. "What?" she asked.

He blinked. "Excuse me?"

"Something's bugging you. What is it?"

She was standing only a few feet away from him, and he breathed in her natural fragrance. She smelled sweet and warm, with a little bit of baby shampoo, some rich-smelling skin lotion and tart apple thrown in for good measure. Although her pajamas were boxy and made of thick flannel, he was well aware of the soft, feminine body underneath. He felt his desire for her sparking, and he tightened his stomach muscles. Man, his entire office believed that she was a thief....

"I was wondering if that's all you're going to eat," he said levelly. Through sheer force of will he stopped his desire for her from growing. He forced it back, down, deep inside of him, willing it to stay hidden. For now, anyway. "It doesn't seem like very much, considering that you were so hungry. You should eat something more filling."

Annie laughed, her white teeth flashing. "This is great," she said. "A bodyguard who gives nutritional advice. How appropriate."

He smiled. It was actually little more than the sides of his mouth twitching upward, but Annie decided it counted as a smile. Shoot, with a full grin, he'd be as handsome as the devil. *More* handsome...

"Sorry," he said. "But you asked."

"You're right," she said, leading the way onto the landing, "I did. Look, I've got to get some work done."

She flipped her long hair back out of her face in a well-practiced motion, and hiked up her pajama bottoms. Pete wished almost desperately that she would put on some other clothes. It wasn't like him to be so easily distracted, but every time she moved, he had to work hard to keep from wanting her.

For a long time now, he'd gone without sex. Not because it wasn't available, but because he simply hadn't wanted it. Didn't it figure that his libido should suddenly come to life again out here, in the middle of nowhere, while he was alone in this big house with this beautiful woman? Man, as soon as he got back to the New York office, he'd have to look up Carolyn what's-her-name, the administrative assistant with the long legs....

"It *would* help if I could take a look at the top floors of the house," Pete said.

Annie shook her head. "Taylor, I don't mean to be rude," she said, "but I'm already two days behind in my work schedule. Frankly, there's no point in my showing you around, because after I talk to Marshall tomorrow, you're going to be catching the next train back into the city."

"I drove up," he said expressionlessly.

"I was speaking figuratively," she said.

"It's going to be hard for me to do my job without your cooperation," Pete pointed out.

She started down the stairs to the lab. "Why don't you use my phone to call your answering machine," she said, not unsympathetically. "Maybe someone called with a different job for you. You can work for them and get all the cooperation you could possibly want."

Annie stayed in the lab until shortly after two-thirty in the morning. She finished all but the last set of purity tests on a copper bowl that had been found at a southwestern archaeological dig site, believed to have been left by early Spanish conquistadors. That last test would take another two hours, and the thought of spending that much more time under Peter Taylor's unwavering gaze was far too exhausting. Besides, even if she finished the testing, she wouldn't have any conclusive evidence until the sample results came back from the carbon-dating lab.

She switched off the equipment and put the bowl back in the safe, turning to find Taylor still watching her.

He was sitting in a chair by the door. He didn't look tired despite the late hour. He didn't look uncomfortable or put upon or…*any*thing.

Christmas, he was making her nervous.

She thought about just breezing past him, out the door and up the stairs, but her conscience made her stop.

"There's a spare bedroom upstairs," she said. "You can sleep—"

But he was shaking his head. "No."

"Oh," she said. "I suppose you want to stay down here, to be near the safe—"

"The safe's secure," he said, pulling himself out of the chair in one graceful, fluid motion. "You'd need a crane to move it, and a ton of dynamite to get into it. If I sleep at all, it's going to be in your bedroom."

Annie stared at him, shocked. In her bedroom…

But his words had been said matter of factly, expressionlessly, without any hint of sexual overtones. Either he had no idea of his physical appeal, or he was so confident, he didn't doubt that any woman would be grateful to share her bed with him. "I don't think so," she said.

He raised one eyebrow, as if he knew exactly what she'd been thinking. "I meant, on the floor."

Annie willed herself not to blush. "You'd be much more comfortable in the guest room," she said.

"But you would be much less safe," he countered. "Your alarm system is nearly worthless—"

"I'll be fine," Annie protested. This was starting to get tiring. Why wouldn't he just accept his defeat and sleep in the guest room?

He was blocking her way up the stairs, his arms crossed stubbornly in front of his chest. "Will you please let me do my job?"

"By all means," she said. "Do your job. Just do it in the guest room tonight."

He wasn't going to move, so Annie pushed past him, starting toward the stairs.

But he caught her arm, stopping her. His fingers were long and strong, easily encircling her wrist. The heat from his hand penetrated the flannel of her pajamas.

Her heart was pounding from annoyance, Annie

tried to convince herself, not from his touch. She tried to pull away, but his grip tightened.

"I *am* going to protect you," he said. His face remained expressionless, but his eyes were like twin chips of volcanic glass.

He had pulled her in so close that she had to crane her neck to look up at him. "Maybe so," she said, and to her chagrin, her voice shook very slightly. "But who's going to protect me from you?"

Pete dropped her arm immediately.

"I don't know you from Adam," Annie said, stepping back, away from him, rubbing her arm. "For all *I* know, you're really the guy who's been making the death threats. For all *I* know, you've done in the real Peter Taylor."

"My picture's on my ID, *and* my driver's license."

"Everyone knows picture IDs are easy to fake—" She broke off, staring in fascination at his necklace. She'd noticed earlier that he wore silver beads around his neck, but until now she hadn't caught a glimpse of the necklace. It was clearly Navaho, with small coin-silver hollow beads, and five squash blossoms decorating the bottom half, along with a three-quarter circle design pendant, known as a *naja*.

Ignoring her trepidation, she took a step toward him, lifting the *naja* in her hand. "This is beautiful," she said, glancing up at him before studying it more closely. Two tiny hands decorated the ends of the *naja*. "Navaho. It's quite old, too, isn't it?"

All of her anger, all of her uneasiness was instantly forgotten as she was caught up, examining the carefully worked silver. She looked at the necklace with real interest, real excitement sparking in her eyes.

Pete laughed, and Annie looked up at him in surprise. It was a rich, deep laugh complete with a grin that transformed his face. She had been right—with his face unfrozen, he *was* exceptionally handsome.

"Yeah," he said. "It's Navaho."

She was standing so close to him, mere inches away, holding the *naja*, but looking up at him. As he gazed into her wide blue eyes, he could feel the heat rising in him. What was it about her that made his body react so powerfully? He wanted to pull her into his arms, feel her body against his. He could imagine the way her lips would taste. Warm and sweet. Man, it would take so little effort....

Pete shoved his hands deep into the pockets of his jeans to keep from touching her.

"Your belt buckle is Navaho, too," she said. "And the ring on your hand, I think... I didn't really get a good look at it."

He pulled his right hand free from his pocket,

glancing down at the thick silver-and-turquoise ring he wore on his third finger.

"Do you mind?" Annie asked, letting go of the pendant and taking his hand. She looked closely at the worn silver of the ring, at the delicate ornamentation. "This isn't quite as old as the necklace," she said. "But it's beautiful."

Her slender fingers were cool against the heat of his. She kept her nails cut short but well-groomed, and wore no jewelry on her hands.

"I thought you were a specialist in European metalworks," he said. "How come you know so much about Native American jewelry?"

She turned his hand over, looking at the other side of the ring. "When I was a kid, I spent about six years at sites in Utah and Arizona, one year in Colorado. Out of all the places we ever lived, my favorite was the American Southwest. When I went to college, I even considered specializing in Native American archaeology."

"Why didn't you?"

"I don't know," she said. "I mean, there were a lot of different reasons." She looked down at his ring again. His hand was so big, it seemed to engulf both of hers. He had calluses on his palm, and two of his fingers had healing abrasions on the knuckles—as if he'd slammed his fist into a wall. Or a person, she realized. In his line of work, it could very well have been a person.

He was looking down at her, making no attempt to take his hand away. Their eyes met, and for the briefest of instants, Annie saw the deep heat of desire in his eyes. Fire seemed to slice through her as her body responded, and she dropped his hand, noticing with rather horrified amusement that he had let go of her with as much haste. What had he seen in her eyes, she wondered. Was her own attraction for him as apparent?

She looked away, taking a step back from him, once again heading for the stairs. "Good night," she said, her voice sounding strange and breathless.

But he was in front of her, leading the way up to the second floor. "At the very least, I want to check out your room," he said. "Make sure all the windows are locked—"

"I can do that," Annie protested.

"Yeah, I know," he said as he went into her bedroom. "But I have to see it for myself."

The bed was still unmade from Annie's afternoon nap, and she saw him glance at her bright blue and green patterned sheets before crossing to the bay windows on the other side of the big room.

He pulled back the curtains and looked at each window carefully, checking to see that the locks were secure and the alarm system was working.

Annie stood in the middle of the room, arms crossed in front of her as she watched his broad, strong back. With his conservatively short black hair, she wouldn't have expected him to be wearing jeans with his tweed jacket, but somehow it didn't look out of place. The jacket was well tailored, fitting his broad shoulders like a glove. His jeans were loose enough to be comfortable, yet managed to show off the long, muscular lengths of his legs. Legs that went all the way up to—

She pulled her eyes away, not wanting to be caught staring at Taylor's butt. It *was* exceptional though, she thought, grinning, glancing back at him. Even with his hair cut so short, Taylor would have no trouble qualifying for one of those hunk-of-the-month calendars....

"What's so funny?" he asked, pulling the last of the curtains closed again and walking toward her.

"Nothing," Annie said, backing away.

"Look," Pete said. "I'd really feel a whole lot better if I could sleep in here tonight." He paused for a moment. "You won't even know I'm here," he added.

Oh, sure, Annie thought. And they're expecting heavy snow this year in the Sahara desert. She forced herself to stay in control of what was rapidly becoming a ludicrous situation.

"No," she said. "Maybe I'd feel different if I thought I was in any kind of real danger. But I just don't buy it."

She walked him to the door. He hesitated before stepping out of the room, but finally he did.

"Feel free to use the spare room," Annie said. "It's across the hall. The bed's already made up."

He didn't say anything. He just watched her from behind his expressionless mask.

"See you in the morning," she finally said, closing and locking the door.

Pete stood out in the hall, listening as Annie got ready for bed. The water ran for a while in the bathroom, the toilet flushed and finally the lamp clicked off.

And still he stood there, just listening and waiting.

CHAPTER FOUR

ANNIE WOKE UP AT NINE O'CLOCK, before her alarm went off. Regardless of the fact that it was Saturday morning, she had work to do down in the lab. And wasn't today the day that Jerry Tillit was bringing in his latest finds from South America? *That* meant that Cara would be downstairs, despite it being a weekend. And there was that pickup she had to make at the airport....

She closed her eyes briefly. Damn, damn, damn. Six hours of sleep *used* to be enough. Five, really— she hadn't been able to fall asleep right away last night. She'd been thinking about...work. Yeah, right. Work. She was so far behind schedule, she had absolutely no time to spend thinking about anything or anyone else.

So why did Pete Taylor's dark eyes seem to penetrate her dreams?

Because his presence was a pain in the butt, Annie decided. And as soon as the sun came up in Texas, she'd give Steven Marshall a call and get this body-guard business straightened out once and for all.

Rolling out of bed, Annie tiredly pulled her pajama shirt over her head, then pushed her hair out of her face as she walked toward the bathroom.

Oh, Christmas, Taylor was sleeping on her floor.

She quickly covered herself with her flannel top, holding it against her body, slipping the fabric under her arms.

He was fast asleep, on some kind of thin sleeping bag with a blanket over him. He'd taken off his jacket and shirt, and even in repose, the hard muscles in his arms and shoulders stood out underneath his tanned skin. His face looked younger, softer, less fiercely controlled as he slept. Annie stared in fascination at the way his long dark eyelashes lay against his smooth cheeks.

He *was* a very good-looking man.

And he was leaving this morning, Annie reminded herself. So why the heck was she admiring his eye-lashes? She should be angry with him—God, he'd broken into her room while she was sleeping. She wondered how long he'd stood watching *her* sleep. He had no right....

She reached out a toe to nudge him awake.

It happened so quickly. One moment she was standing up—the next she was on the floor, on her back, with Pete Taylor's heavy body on top of her, his arm pressed up, hard, against her windpipe, cutting off her air.

Her first instinct was to fight, but he had her so thoroughly pinned down, she could do little more than wiggle against him. He was breathing hard, as if prepared to fight as he pulled his arm away from her throat. Gratefully, she sucked in a breath of air as he stared down at her.

"Don't *ever* do that again," he said sternly, his eyes hard, his face harsh.

"Me?" Annie sputtered. "What did I do? I only woke you up. *You're* the one who tackled me and nearly choked me to death. *You're* the one who was asleep on my floor after I specifically told you I didn't want you in here, pal."

She glared up at him, straining against him, trying to get free.

Although he had taken off his shirt while he slept, he had kept his necklace on. Now it hung down between them, the pendant brushing her neck and shoulders and—

Oh, God, she'd dropped her pajama top.

Annie saw from the sudden flicker in his eyes that he realized it the same moment she did. His bare chest was against hers, skin against skin, hard against soft.

They both froze.

She could feel his heart beating against her. Or was it her own heart? Whoever's heart it was, it was starting to beat faster.

"I think you'd better get off of me," Annie whispered.

Silently Pete pulled back, sliding away from her. Man, she was beautiful, he thought, watching her grab for her pajama top and pull it over her head. Her breasts were soft and full, with large dark pink nipples that had hardened into firm buds at the tips.

Pete sat on his bedroll, leaning back against the wall, glad that he was wearing his jeans, that she couldn't see how badly he wanted her. Man, what a way to start the morning.

"I'm going to take a shower," she said, her cheeks faintly pink. "If that's all right with you."

"Yeah," he said.

"Sure you don't want to check the bathroom out first?" she asked, standing up and looking down at him, hands on her hips. "You never know—maybe there's a bad guy hiding in the toilet tank."

Pete stood up gracefully and walked past Annie into the bathroom.

"I was *kidding,*" Annie said, following him, trying not to stare at the rippling muscles in his back.

The bathroom was decorated in sea greens and blues. There was a claw-footed tub in one corner.

Another corner held a large shower stall. The sink had a marble countertop, and it was cluttered with Annie's makeup, lotions, soaps and shampoos.

There was a small window in the room, with frosted glass in the panes. Pete glanced at it, then tried the lock. It was secure.

He opened the door to the shower stall and looked inside.

"Oh, come on," Annie scoffed. "The window was locked. How could someone have gotten into my shower?"

Pete looked at her levelly. "Last night the door to your bedroom was locked. That didn't keep me from getting in. Hasn't it occurred to you that if I could do it, someone else could, too?"

She stared at him. Well, actually, no, it hadn't....

He went back into the bedroom. Annie followed him to the bathroom door and watched him roll up his blanket and sleeping bag. "If that's the case," she said, "why should I bother locking the door at all?"

Pete used a piece of string to tie the sleeping bag up. "Locks on doors and windows will keep most people out," he said. He stood up then, folding his arms across his broad chest. "And as for the people determined to get in... That's what I'm here for."

"That's very good," Annie said. "You should write that down and use it on your business cards. Just the right amount of macho with a little superhero thrown in. I think it'll sell. Unfortunately, I'm not interested in buying."

She went back into the bathroom, not bothering to lock the door behind her.

THE WATER IN THE TEAKETTLE had just begun to boil when Pete came into the kitchen. His hair was still wet from his shower, and he'd changed into a plain black turtleneck that hugged his muscular chest and was tucked neatly into his jeans.

Annie poured steaming water on top of the tea bag in her mug. "I don't have much to offer you in the way of breakfast," she said apologetically. "I usually don't do much more than eat some fruit myself, and even that's running low—"

"I'm eating on Mr. Marshall's expense account, remember?" Pete said, sitting down at the kitchen table. "But if it's not any trouble, would you mind if I kept some supplies in your refrigerator?"

Annie leaned against the counter, holding her mug in both hands. "In theory, I don't object," she said. "But remember? After I talk to Marshall this morning, you're going to be leaving."

"No, I don't think so," he said.

"Well, I *do* think so," she said.

"Sorry, you're wrong," Pete said, unperturbed.

"Mr. Marshall is very anxious to avoid bad publicity. Did you know that he's facing racketeering charges out in Dallas?"

"Steven Marshall?"

Pete nodded. "Call him if you want," he said. "But I know he's going to insist that I stay. If something happened to you, it would be *very* bad publicity for him."

"But what about *me?*" Annie said, putting her mug on the counter. Her bangs were pulled back from her face with an Alice in Wonderland-like head-band. She wore a bright white sweatshirt over her jeans, and a pair of black lace-up boots. She sat down at the table, across from Pete. "I don't *want* a body-guard. No offense, but...I *like* being alone."

"I'll try to stay out of your way," he said. "You won't even know I'm around."

"Yes, I noticed how well you stayed out of my way this morning, particularly when you pinned me to the floor," Annie said. "I can't wait to see what the rest of the day brings. Maybe a little kick-boxing?"

She noticed that he didn't even have the grace to look embarrassed as she left the room.

She *had* to talk to Steven Marshall.

ANNIE HUNG UP THE PHONE with a crash and an oath, making Cara look up.

"Old Steven M. didn't go for your 'I can take care of myself' routine, huh?" Cara said unsympathetically.

"He is *such* a jerk!"

"Things *could* be worse," Cara said.

"Yeah," Annie muttered. "You could start telling me exactly how they could be worse."

Cara ignored the comment. "You could have been stuck with one of those no-brain, mountain-of-muscles-type bodyguards with a shaved head and equally shaved intellect. If someone told *me* that I'd have to spend the next few weeks with a guy as gorgeous as Peter Taylor watching my every move, you wouldn't hear *me* complaining."

"But I like my privacy," Annie said, sitting down at her desk for about four seconds before popping up and pacing again.

"Hey," Cara asked, "did you catch sight of his necklace?"

"Navaho," Annie said. "Looks like it dates around 1860, maybe even earlier. You see his ring?"

"And the belt buckle? Yeah. You're gonna try to buy 'em, aren't you?" Cara finished clearing the files off her desk, uncovering a paperweight made of petrified wood, three framed pictures of her nephews and nieces and a plastic Homer Simpson doll with his head attached by a spring. She looked up at her friend. "Aren't you?"

Annie shook her head.

"You're kidding. Why not?"

"Because it's none of your business," Annie said crossly, throwing herself down into her chair again. "Since when do I have to justify myself to you? You work for me, remember?"

"You're not going to try to buy it off him because you like the man," Cara said triumphantly, making Homer's head bob wildly. "You like him, I knew it. You don't want to take advantage of him."

Annie put her head down on her desk. "Oh, MacLeish, he's going to be here for weeks and weeks and *weeks*. What am I going to do?"

"At least he's handsome," Cara said. "Imagine if you had to stare at some guy with no neck all day and night—"

Annie stared up at her. "Yeah, terrific. Great. Wonderful. He's handsome. He's gorgeous. To tell you the truth, I'd prefer staring at some guy with no neck. Taylor's so good-looking, it's distracting as hell, and he's…standing in the door, listening to me say this," Annie said, looking over at Pete, who was leaning against the door frame, amusement in his dark eyes.

"We were talking about you," Cara said unnecessarily. She smiled happily. "How embarrassing for us."

"It's not embarrassing," Annie said to Cara. "I mean, the fact that he's gorgeous shouldn't come as big news to him. He knows what he looks like. And the fact that we were discussing him also shouldn't put him into shock. He's invading my life, and I deserve a chance to bitch and moan about it—about *him*." Annie gestured toward Pete.

Still smiling happily, Cara said, "Annie just spoke to Marshall—"

"The bastard," Annie interjected.

"—on the phone," Cara finished. "Looks like you might want to get your suitcase in from the car and put it someplace a little more permanent."

"Oh," Pete said.

"Don't gloat," Annie snapped.

His eyebrows moved a millimeter. "All I said was—"

"I'm *so* annoyed," Annie said. "Marshall—"

"The bastard," Cara supplied.

"—doesn't think a woman can take care of herself," Annie sputtered. "I asked him to hire a female bodyguard—no offense, Taylor—"

"None taken," he said.

"—and Marshall—"

"The bastard." This time Pete interjected, his lips twitching up into a smile.

"—laughed that obnoxious wheezing laugh of his." Annie demonstrated it, sounding an awful lot like a circus seal in mortal terror. "And he said that he'd *still* have to pay Taylor—to protect the female bodyguard! He said being a bodyguard is a man's job! Of all the stupid, chauvinistic things to say! *And* he topped it off by calling me 'little lady'! As if *'darlin''* weren't bad enough. So I told him I quit. I told him he could take the stupid artifact and have it authenticated by a stupid *man*."

"And?" Cara asked, grinning in anticipation.

"Marshall—"

"The bastard—" Cara and Pete said in unison.

"Laughed again and said—" Annie imitated Marshall's heavy Texan accent "—'It's typical of a woman to try to break a written, binding contract.' Then he suggested we talk again when it was a better time of month! I wanted to reach through the phone, grab his nose and twist it—hard!"

"So?" Cara asked.

"So *nothing*. I've still got a contract *and* a bodyguard," Annie muttered, with a black look in Pete's direction.

"You know—" Pete started to say.

"You might not want to be talking right now," Annie interrupted him. "I'm starting to feel the urge to vent some of my hostilities, and you're looking like an extremely attractive target."

"Extremely attractive, eh?" Cara smiled, leaning back in her chair and putting her feet up on the desk.

"That's *not* what I meant," Annie said dangerously. "You're fired, MacLeish. Go make some copies or do whatever else it is that I pay you to do."

The phone rang, and Annie swooped toward it.

"Maybe it's Marshall," she said. "Maybe he changed his mind...." She picked up the receiver hopefully. "Hello?"

She'd pulled her headband out while she was pacing, and now she pushed her hair back from her face with one hand as she used the other to hold the receiver to her ear. As Pete watched, she stared into the distance, her eyes temporarily unfocused as she concentrated on the call. He saw surprise, then shock flash across her face. Then her blue eyes narrowed.

"Who is this?" she demanded. "You want to do those things to me? I *dare* you to try. Why don't you show yourself? Come here in person, instead of hiding behind threatening phone calls and rocks thrown through windows—"

Pete leapt toward her, grabbing the telephone out of her hand, trying to activate the tape recorder the FBI had left behind. But the connection had been broken, and the line buzzed with a dial tone.

"Damn it," he swore, hanging up the phone. "What the hell is wrong with you? Why didn't you record that call? And what the hell possessed you to say those things? You really want this guy to come out here?"

She was shaking. "Don't you shout at me!" she said, her eyes blazing. "I just listened to some crackpot describe some incredibly sick fantasy of his in detail, and I happened to have a major role. You can't expect me not to tell him off—"

"I expect you *not* to goad him on," Pete said, his own eyes glittering chips of obsidian. He stood with his hands on his hips, effectively pinning Annie in against her desk.

She wanted to move, but in order to do that she'd have to push past him, or climb over her desk. So she stayed where she was and tried to hide her shaking hands by sticking them into the back pockets of her jeans.

Pete picked up a pad and a pen from her desk. "You have to tell me what he said to you," he said brusquely. "Word for word."

Annie shook her head. "Sorry, I can't."

"If you don't remember exactly—"

"That's not it," she said. "I can remember. I just…can't repeat what he said. It was too awful."

She tried to meet his gaze challengingly, but her eyes suddenly welled with tears. She swore softly and blinked them back. "I'm having a really bad day," she said.

Pete turned away, shocked at his emotional response to the tears in her eyes. He wanted to pull her into his arms, tell her everything was going to be okay and kiss her until her hands shook for an entirely different reason. He wanted to tell her he'd take care of her, protect her.

But he couldn't tell her that, and he certainly couldn't protect her without her cooperation.

Annie took the opportunity to move around to the other side of her desk and sit down. She wished that Taylor would leave her alone. God, wasn't it bad enough that she'd been subjected to that obscene phone call? She wanted to forget about it. The thought of having to tell him exactly what that creep had said to her made her cheeks burn.

Out of the corner of her eye, she saw Taylor pull up a chair across from her desk. He sat down, then looked over her head, across the room to where Cara sat. Annie glanced at her friend, who was watching them both with unabashed interest.

"Would you mind...?" Pete said to Cara.

Cara stood up uncertainly.

"Set up the final test for that copper bowl, please, MacLeish," Annie said. "I'll be out in the lab in a minute."

Cara hated being left out of anything, but she went out of the office. Pete stood up and closed the office door behind her.

Annie looked up at him as he sat back down

across from her. To her surprise, his eyes were soft, kind even.

"The reason I wanted to record this call," he said quietly, "was to help us track the caller. And I'm not just talking about locating him—most of these people call from public telephones, so that doesn't do much good. But the FBI can use their computers and try to match phrasing or word choice or even sentence structure, in the event that this is a repeat pattern offender." He pushed the pad and pen toward her. "And that's why I need to know what he said to you. As exactly as you can remember. Maybe it would be easier for you to write it down."

For a long time she didn't move. She just stared at him. Then, suddenly, she picked up the pen and paper and began to write.

Pete sat back in his chair, watching her.

Sunlight was streaming in the window, and it lit her from behind, creating an auralike glow around her. Pete remembered the words he had overheard her saying to Cara. He distracted her. *He* distracted *her?* Not half as much as she distracted him, he was willing to bet.

He was carrying around this tight feeling of need all the time now, Pete realized. It no longer was triggered only by her quick smile, or her walk, or her low, sexy laugh. All he had to do was see her....

Man, all he had to do was *think* about her and, whammo, he wanted her. And when he wasn't with her, he sure as hell was thinking about her.... This could turn out to be one hell of an uncomfortable two months.

Annie finished writing, put the pen down on top of the paper and stood up. "I'll be in the lab," she said shortly and left the room.

"Thanks," Pete called after her.

She didn't respond.

He reached across the desk and picked up the pad she'd written on. As he read the words that the phone caller had said to her, his jaw tightened. The threats had a horrific, nightmarish quality to them. They were all violently sexual and graphically explicit.

He read it over and over, each time his sense of uneasiness growing. It was entirely possible that these were not idle threats meant only to frighten Annie. It was entirely possible that her life really was in danger.

He reached for the telephone and dialed Whitley Scott's number.

"ONE OF US HAS TO RUN OUT to the airport," Cara said to Annie as they finished up the test on the copper bowl. "We've got that package from France coming in."

Annie looked at her blankly.

"Remember, the package coming in to Westchester Airport?" Cara said. "The job you aren't going to get to for a decade? Subject of a conversation we had two days ago?"

"Right, right," Annie said. She had put her hair back into a ponytail while they were working, but now she pulled it free, and it swung down around her shoulders. She sat down on one of the wooden stools that were scattered throughout the lab. "MacLeish, when's the last time we took a vacation?"

Cara pushed her glasses up higher on her nose and frowned. "You mean, like a trip to Easter Island and two weeks of crashing through the underbrush and staring at giant rock heads from some distant, ancient culture? Or are you talking about Thanksgiving at the parents' house? *Or* do you mean Club Med—lying on the beach in bikinis while handsome men bring us daiquiris and margaritas?"

"I mean Club Med. I *definitely* mean Club Med."

Cara chewed her lip as she thought hard. "I've worked for you for…how long now?"

"Forever," Annie answered.

"Right. And the last time we took a vacation was… Never?"

"That decides it," Annie said. "We need a vacation. When we're through with what we've got—when's that gonna be?"

Cara shrugged. "End of December, beginning of January?"

"We're taking January off," Annie said. "Don't accept any more work unless the clients can wait until February for us to start the project."

"Thank you, Lord," Cara said to the ceiling. "Club Med, here we come! Bless you, master!"

Annie stood up. "Back to work, slave," she said. "I'm heading for the airport."

She quickly ran upstairs and grabbed her jacket and car keys. "See you later," she called out to Cara as she ran lightly down the stairs.

Outside, the air was crisp and cold, and she buttoned her jacket, thinking it was time to dig her scarf out of her closet—

Pete Taylor was standing next to her car.

"Ready to go?" he asked.

She looked at him blankly.

"I'm your bodyguard," he said patiently. "That means when you go someplace, I go, too."

Annie closed her eyes. *Please, God,* she thought, *when I open my eyes, make him be gone. Make this all just be a bad dream....*

He was still there. Damn, damn, *damn.*

"I'll drive if you want," he said.

"I *like* to drive," Annie said. But her car was piled high with books and papers and empty seltzer cans.

And *his* car was a sporty little Mazda Miata…. Her eyes slid toward his shiny black car.

"We can take mine if you want," Pete said, as if he could read her mind. He held out the keys. "You can drive."

Slowly she reached for them. "What's the deal? Is it rented?"

He shook his head. "No," he said with one of his rare smiles.

"You'd trust me…?" Annie asked.

"You're trusting me with your life," Pete said. "I'll trust you with my car."

Annie got in behind the steering wheel and adjusted the mirrors. She didn't realize just how little the car was until Pete got in and nearly sat down on top of her. He was so close, they were practically touching. Maybe they should've taken her car instead….

She turned the key and the engine hummed.

"I faxed the FBI your transcript of that phone call," he said.

"Oh, great," Annie said sourly. "I'll bet they get a good laugh out of *that*." She eased the sports car out of the driveway, feeling the power in the engine.

"They're checking a number of different leads," Pete said, ignoring her sarcastic comment. "There are a couple of radical groups who have already lodged ownership claims to Stands Against the Storm's death mask. And another group has sent a formal complaint, claiming it should be returned to the Navaho people in New Mexico."

"Don't tell me. None of those groups is actually connected to the Navaho," Annie said, glancing at him, already knowing the answer.

"You're right." A white flash of teeth made her turn quickly back to the road. His smile was a killer. It was a good thing he didn't do it more often. "The Navaho don't want anything to do with the death mask. As far as they're concerned, they were happier with Stands Against the Storm's bad spirit safely across the Atlantic Ocean in England."

"How do *you* feel about it?" Annie asked. "Having the death mask in the house?"

She risked another look at him. He wasn't smiling, but his eyes were lit with humor.

"You don't really think it would bother me, do you?" he said.

"You are at least *part* Navaho," Annie said. "Aren't you?"

"Yeah," he said. "Half. Is it that obvious?"

"Actually, no. But your necklace gave you away. It's so valuable. I figured it must have sentimental value to it, that it must be an heirloom and that's why you wear it. Because if you were just a collector, you'd keep it locked in a case."

"My grandfather gave it to me," Pete said. "His grandfather made it. My great-grandfather made the ring and the belt buckle. They were all made to be worn—not locked away."

She glanced at him again. When she met his gaze, she felt a jolt of warmth that was different from the attraction that always seemed to simmer between them. This was friendly and comfortable. Oh, brother, she was actually starting to *like* this guy.

She pushed the Miata up to seventy.

"So what do you think?" she asked. "Who's really after this death mask? If it's not the Navaho…"

Pete shrugged. "Maybe the FBI's right and it's one of these radical Friends of the Native Americans groups."

"But you don't think so." She glanced over at him. He was watching her, his eyes warm. What would he do, she wondered suddenly, if she reached over and took his hand?

He'd assume she'd fallen for him—the way every woman who'd ever crossed his path had no doubt done. But she didn't want to be just another notch on his belt. No way. If she was going to be stupid enough to fall in love with this man, she was going to make damn sure he fell in love with her, too.

Something told her she'd better work fast. She already liked him, and Lord knows she was attracted to him. Her heart was ready for some bungee jumping. It had been a long time since she'd met a man she wanted to get to know better, a man she could imagine becoming involved with. And she could imagine being involved with Pete Taylor. Oh, baby, could she imagine it.

With very little work at all, she could imagine the way his strong, hard-muscled body would feel against hers. She could imagine his mouth curling up into one of his rare, beautiful smiles before he kissed her. She could imagine him in her bed, his hair damp with perspiration, his naked body slick and locked together with hers. She could imagine his dark eyes watching, always watching, learning all of her secrets, giving away none of his own.

She glanced at him again, then quickly looked away, afraid if he gazed into her eyes too long, he might somehow read her mind.

But he managed to anyway. When she looked up at him again, there was a moment when she could see deep hunger in his intense, dark eyes. But he turned away before she did, as if he, too, were fighting the attraction.

Annie cleared her throat, focusing all her attention on the exit ramp that led to the local airport.

Pete tried to wipe his damp palms inconspicuously on his jeans. Man, this woman disturbed him.

One of these days, he was going to lose the last bit of his control.

Annie was following the signs leading to the main terminal parking lot. She slid the car into an empty parking space and shut off the engine. She turned in her seat and looked at him.

"How much danger am I really in?" she asked him point-blank. "Isn't it true that most of the creeps who make crank phone calls only intend to frighten their victims?"

"Yeah," Pete said. "But even if the odds are one in a million, why take that risk?" And the transcript she'd written from the last phone call had really bothered him. His gut reaction was that there was something to worry about here. It couldn't hurt to err on the side of caution.

"There's better than a one-in-a-million chance that I'll be killed in a traffic accident, isn't there?" Annie said. "But I take that risk every day."

Pete was silent, just watching her as they sat in the car. What was he supposed to tell her? "I got a bad feeling about this," he finally said.

She smiled. "You and Han Solo."

He blinked. "What?"

"*Star Wars,*" she explained. "Didn't you see that movie?"

"Yeah?"

"Well, that was what Han Solo kept saying," she said, then drawled, "'I got a bad feeling about this, Chewie.'" She laughed at the expression on his face. "Lighten up, Taylor, will you?"

"If memory serves me, Solo's premonition was on the money," Pete pointed out. "His ship was tractor beamed into the death star, right?"

"Yeah, well, you win some and you lose some," Annie said with a smile. "And they won in the end, when it really mattered."

Pete was watching her, and she looked back at him, examining his face as carefully. There was a small scar interrupting the line of his left eyebrow, but other than that, his features were the closest thing to perfection Annie had ever seen. His nose was straight and just the right size for his face. His eyes were large, with thick, long lashes that would put any mascara company to shame. They were framed by cheekbones of exotic proportions, making him not merely good-looking, but stunningly, danger-ously handsome. His lips were neither too thick nor too thin, and sensuously shaped. But he held them far too tightly, giving himself a serious, almost grim expression. Although his hair was cut too short, it was dark and luxuriant. If it had been another few inches longer, Annie would have been sorely tempted to run her fingers through it. As it was, its length served to remind her who he was, and why he was here.

But looking into his eyes was like staring into outer space on a moonless night. Dark, endless, mysterious, exciting. With a hope and promise for adventure, and a consuming, beckoning pull.

Annie wondered why he didn't try to kiss her. As soon as the thought popped into her mind, she berated herself. Kissing her wasn't in his job description. She was a job, not a date.

On the other hand, there was no denying this attraction between them. Annie had seen it in his eyes before, just a flash here and there, but enough to make her catch her breath. It was there now as he looked at her—a hint of slow burning embers of desire, ready to leap into flames at the slightest encouragement.

A significant part of her wanted to give him that encouragement. But she'd had a relationship based on sex before, and it hadn't lasted. Shoot, wasn't her aversion to casual sex the reason she hadn't gone to bed with God's gift to women, Nicholas York? Except, as attractive as Nick was, he couldn't hold a candle to Pete. It had nothing to do with physical appeal—Nick was as handsome as Pete, but in a golden blond, blue-eyed way. In fact, with Nick's easy smile and cheerful facade, many women would find him the more attractive of the two men. But Annie could trust Nick only about as far as she could throw him. Sometimes she wondered if deception was a sport for him, or maybe a way of life.

Pete Taylor was mysterious, but her instincts told her that the man was honest. If pressed, he might lie, but it certainly wouldn't be a game to him. Not the way it would be for Nick.

And Pete Taylor wasn't entirely selfish. Or unreliable. Or as unfaithful as they come....

Of course, she hadn't realized Nick was any of those things when she first met him. And even though her instincts told her Pete was good and kind and honest, her instincts had been wrong before.

No matter how strong the chemistry was between them, Annie wasn't going to do anything rash or stupid. At least not intentionally, she told herself with an inward smile. Pete was going to be hanging around for nearly two months. That was plenty of time for them to get to know each other, to become friends. And after they were friends, if she still felt this nearly irresistible gravitational pull toward him, well, that's when she'd do something about it.

"You know what I think?" she finally said.

Silently, still watching her, Pete shook his head.

He didn't try to speak because he wasn't sure he could utter a word. In fact, Pete wasn't sure he could move. Somehow, during the last few minutes, the interior of the car had shrunk. Without either of them moving a muscle, they were now so close that all he'd have to do was lean forward to kiss her.

Pete forced himself to look into her eyes, not at her mouth. Not at her soft moist lips...

He had to get out of this car, or he was going to do something stupid. But he couldn't get out, because just looking into her eyes had turned him on so much, he couldn't even stand up without embarrassing himself. Damn, what was *wrong* with him? He felt seventeen again, and desperately out of control.

"*I* think the FBI is behind this whole thing," Annie was saying. She climbed out of the car, then leaned down, sticking her head through the open door. "I think they made those phone calls and threw that rock through my window. I think this is just more of their intimidation technique."

Pete's face was expressionless. "I guess you think I'm FBI, too."

"Are you?"

He met her eyes squarely. "No," he said. "No, I'm not."

She nodded, her eyes never leaving his face. "This is stupid. You know, I have no reason to, but I actually believe you." A wry smile turned up one corner of her mouth. "I guess I sound pretty paranoid, huh? Come on, Han Solo, let's go inside."

Pete slowly climbed out of the car, and stood looking at her across the roof. He felt as if he were balancing on top of eggshells. So far he was okay, but he had to take a step, and it had better be a careful one....

"It must be rough," he said, "when no one believes you."

"Damn straight," she said.

"Tell me about the whole art-theft conspiracy mess," he said. "Maybe I can help."

She was looking at him, her blue eyes wide and vulnerable. Was she involved? He didn't have a clue. But maybe she'd tell him about it. *Trust me, Annie,* Pete thought. *Trust me, trust me, trust me—*

"Can you help make the FBI believe that I'm innocent?" she asked almost wistfully. Then she shook her head. "I'm innocent, but I can't prove it, so I'm being hounded. Whatever happened to innocent until proven guilty, Taylor? *That's* what I'd like to know."

She glanced at the terminal, then at her wrist-watch. "MacLeish said air freight is only open 'til three. We better hurry."

Pete watched her walk briskly toward the low brick building. Did he believe her? He wanted to.

Slowly he followed her into the airport terminal,

watching the life in her quick step, the unconscious sexiness in the sway of her slim hips.

Yeah, he wanted to believe her, because he wanted her.

Normally he didn't allow sex to complicate things. Sex was...sex.

But he liked Annie. He really, truly liked her. And, strange as it might seem, he didn't sleep with women that he liked. Unless, of course, it was a totally mutual, honest relationship.

Well, they had the mutual part covered—Pete had seen the reflection of his own desire in her eyes. But honest? Mentally, he sounded the loser buzzer. Not much honesty here, at least not on his side of the relationship.

No, there was no way on earth that he was going to sleep with her. Even if she came to him and begged, he wouldn't.

Yeah, and my mother's the queen of England, he thought morosely.

PETE WATCHED ANNIE SIGN ALL the papers releasing the valuable package into her custody. He slid the box closer to the edge of the air freight counter and lifted it. It was heavier than he'd imagined, he thought, frowning, and much too ungainly to carry with only one arm.

"We're going to need someone to carry this out to the car," he said to the man behind the counter.

Annie looked at him in surprise. "It's not *that* heavy," she said.

Pete actually looked embarrassed. "Yeah, well, I have this policy of never carrying anything that ties up both my hands at once. I need to keep at least one hand free, in case I need to go for my gun."

"Good point," Annie said dryly. "You never know when you'll need it to blow away some evil spirit."

"Sam's on a break," the man behind the counter said, unfazed by neither the mention of a gun or evil spirits. "He can help you, but he won't be back for another twenty minutes."

"We can wait," Pete said.

"No we can't," Annie said, exasperated, picking up the box herself. Pete opened his mouth to protest, but she cut him off. "What do I look like?" she asked. "Some kind of weakling? I'll carry it. I would have if I'd picked it up a couple of days ago, before you started following me around."

She started for the exit, aware of Pete's discomfort. He was a gentleman, she realized as he held the door for her. It really, truly bugged him to see her straining to lug something he could have carried easily.

"Okay, look," he said when they were outside. "I'll carry it."

Annie kept walking. "Absolutely not," she said. "You should stick to your rules. You always have, haven't you?"

He nodded slowly.

"That's probably why you're so good at what you do," she said.

"Yeah, but I feel like a jerk."

"The very fact that you feel like a jerk proves that you're not," Annie said with a smile. "So relax. You're a nice guy. Don't beat yourself up for sticking to your guns—no pun intended."

She thought he was a nice guy. Pete felt warmth and pleasure spread through him at her words. Sixth grade, he thought suddenly with an inward groan. He hadn't felt like this since sixth grade.

CHAPTER FIVE

ANNIE LET PETE DRIVE HOME. She sat in the front seat with the heavy package on the floor at her feet. She opened it carefully. There were two silver statues inside, wrapped in bubble pack and newspaper, stuffed into a box filled with big foam beads.

The statues glistened, a mournful shepherd kneeling and a Virgin Mary, both faces decidedly Byzantine. They had been cast from a mold, their seams worn with age, seemingly ancient.

Her heart began to beat faster as she examined them. These could be real. Boy, she loved it when the artifacts were genuine. She loved holding the smooth metal in her hands, knowing that other hands had held these the same way over the course of hundreds, even thousands, of years. She loved wondering about the people who had poured the metal, people turned to dust centuries ago....

Annie packed them back into the box, sighing with contentment, and looked out of the car window.

Traffic on Route 684 was heavy for a Saturday afternoon. Pete had the Miata all the way to the left, moving well above the speed limit. Still, a drab gray sedan pulled up alongside them, in the middle lane of the highway. Annie glanced over at the other car's driver.

He had thick, bushy brown hair that looked as if it hadn't been combed since the late 1980s. A full, shaggy beard covered most of the lower half of his face.

Annie pulled her eyes away, afraid to be caught staring. But the sedan didn't pass or fall back. Instead, it kept pace, right next to them.

Annie looked up again, and this time the driver looked over at her and smiled.

Her mouth dropped open in shock.

His teeth had all been filed into sharp-looking fangs. And his eyes...! His eyes were an unearthly shade of yellow-green.

Like an animal's eyes. Like some kind of cat or... Or a wolf.

Wide-eyed, Annie watched with revulsion as the man made an obscene gesture with his tongue. Then he lifted a bright orange squirt gun to the window and she realized the back of his hands were covered with the same thick brown hair—or fur!—that was on his head. He squeezed the trigger.

A stream of red sprayed the inside of his window, hanging on the glass, thick and bright as fresh blood.

"God!" Annie cried, jumping back and slamming into Pete's hard shoulder. "Did you see that?"

"What?"

"That car!" Annie said. But the gray sedan was already falling back, merging into the right lane. "That guy! He had a gun—"

Suddenly she was being shoved down, hard, her head pushed into Pete's lap, her ribs pressed into the gearshift. "Which car?" he shouted.

"The gray one," Annie said, her cheek against the worn denim of his jeans. She tried to sit up, but his arm was pinning her down.

Taylor swore. "I don't see it. Are you sure it was gray?"

The muscles in his thighs flexed and tightened as he drove. He smelled good, Annie thought suddenly, like fresh air and leather, a fading remnant of smoke from an open fire, and a warm, spicy sweet smell that she already recognized as being his own. It definitely wasn't fair. A man who looked as good as Taylor shouldn't be allowed to smell so good, too.

"Gray, four-door," Annie said. "Midsize. I think it might've been a Volvo." She twisted her neck to look up at him. His eyes were narrowed in concentration, his mouth an even grimmer line than usual. She pushed against him again. "Taylor, let me up!"

"Don't fight me," he snapped.

The muscles in his legs moved again, and Annie could feel the car slow. Pete moved his hand then, to downshift as he took the exit ramp off the highway.

She pulled herself up, sweeping her hair back from her face as she looked at him. He pulled into the lot of a 7-Eleven and parked, turning toward her.

"Are you okay?"

She nodded. There was real concern in his eyes. Pete took his job seriously—that much was clear.

"Did you get a good look at him?" he asked.

Annie nodded again. "I sure did," she said. "He could have been anywhere from twenty-five to sixty years old. His hair was brown and shaggy, he had a full beard and bushy eyebrows that grew together in the middle. He looked like he hadn't showered or shaved in about ten years, and he was skinny…. More than skinny—gaunt…you know, hollow cheeks. He had yellow eyes and black claws at the ends of his…paws."

"Paws," Taylor repeated expressionlessly.

"Did I mention the fangs?" Annie asked. "He had fangs. A complete set."

He sighed, looking away from her, out the front windshield. "Are you sure?" he finally said, turning back to look at her. But even as he asked, he knew from the set expression on her face that she meant exactly what she had said.

"I'm sure. I notice details, and I remember them," she said. "It's my job, it's what I do. And you know, pal, details like fangs and paws aren't easy to forget." She ticked off the other details on her fingers. "The outside of the car was dull gray, the inside was beige, vinyl seats. His rearview mirror had a crack on the upper-right corner, and the driver had fangs. His left lateral incisor was filed shorter than the other teeth. He had a small mole next to his left eyebrow. I didn't get a clear look at the right side of his face. Presumably it was covered with as much hair as the left side of his face."

Taylor's eyebrow had twitched a fraction of an inch upward. "Anything else?"

"His gun wasn't real."

His eyes narrowed very slightly. "That's not always easy to tell," he said. "Even for someone who's good with details."

"This detail was kind of hard to miss," Annie said. "The gun was orange."

She was grinning at him, her blue eyes sparkling with humor. "It was a water pistol, Taylor," she said. "The only danger I was in was from you—and the gearshift." She rubbed her side. "I think I've got one hell of a bruise. If I'd known you were going to go all macho on me, I would've told you about the gun a little bit differently."

She gave Pete a quick description of the bloodlike liquid the man had sprayed on the inside of his window. "It was probably just a coincidence," she said. "It's getting close to Halloween. It probably didn't have anything to do with me."

"I don't believe in coincidences," Taylor said.

"*I* don't believe in werewolves or ghosts or witches, Navaho or otherwise," Annie said. "I seriously doubt the spirit of Stands Against the Storm drives a gray Volvo. And no self-respecting Navaho witch is going to leave the Southwest, let alone cruise the highways of suburban New York City in wolf form on a Saturday afternoon. If this wasn't a coincidence, I'd say it's a sure bet that someone is trying really hard to make it look as if the Navaho are behind the death threats. But if that's the answer, it leaves an even bigger question. Why?"

JERRY TILLET WAS IN THE OFFICE, perched on the edge of Annie's desk, smiling at Cara.

His reddish hair had grown long, and he wore it pulled back into a ponytail at the nape of his neck. He had a thick beard and mustache, and he wore a battered Red Sox baseball cap on his head. His skin was sunburned on top of a deep tan, and his clothes looked as though they hadn't seen a washing machine in weeks.

"Is it safe to stand downwind of you, Professor?" Annie asked from the doorway. "That *is* you under all that hair, isn't it, Tillet?"

"Hey, Doc," Jerry said cheerfully. "Cara was telling me about the evil spirits. Bummer. So where's your little shadow?" His gaze flickered over Annie's shoulder. "Big shadow," he corrected himself.

Annie turned to see Pete standing behind her. She introduced the two men. "Peter Taylor, Jerry Tillet." Pete leaned past her to shake Jerry's hand, and she could feel the heat radiating from his body.

Why am I fighting this? she thought suddenly. *Why do I even bother when it would be so easy to give in?* But she knew the answer. She didn't know Pete at all. And if she slept with him just because her hormones were urging her to, and he turned out to be a real yuck or some kind of Attila the Hun, she'd feel mighty stupid. But still, there was something to be said for surrendering to the animal attraction.

Annie smiled, picturing the look on Cara's face if she suddenly said, "Excuse me, guys, but Taylor and I have to go upstairs and have sex now...."

Instead, Cara had her "I'm dealing with the village idiot" look on her face. "Well?" she asked Annie.

"Well, what?" Annie said. "Were you talking to me?"

"I asked if it was all right with you if Jerry and I left now. We were hoping to catch a double feature."

"Sure, I've just about had it myself," Annie said, straightening up, reaching her arms over her head, stretching out her back. She stopped, midmotion, aware of Taylor's dark eyes on her, aware that her sweatshirt was riding up, exposing several inches of bare stomach above the waistband of her jeans. With a quick tug, she pulled the sweatshirt back down.

"It's getting late," Pete said. "We have to go upstairs."

Annie froze. Then laughed nervously. Upstairs? There was no way he could have read her mind.... Was there? "Why?" she asked.

If he noticed any suspicion or hostility in her voice, he ignored it. "I need to check out the security system on your top floors. I need to know what has to be fixed or added to make this place secure," he said.

"I've got to lock this in the safe," Annie said, motioning to the box that she'd brought in from the car.

"Well, we're outa here," Cara said, grabbing Jerry's hand and pulling him toward the door. "See you on Monday, Annie."

Annie started to lift the heavy box, but Pete was there. "I'll get it," he said, picking it up.

She raised her eyebrows and he smiled. "I think I can probably risk carrying it all the way to the safe," he said.

Pete followed Annie down the hall and into the lab. "I've got the same alarm system upstairs as I do down here," she said, returning to their conversation. "You know, the kind that doesn't work real well? It also doesn't work real well upstairs, too."

Annie opened the door to the safe and Pete put the box on the shelf next to the crate containing Stands Against the Storm's death mask. She closed the door tightly, spinning the combination lock.

"You know how the alarm system works," she said. "So why do you need to look at it?"

"I need to do a window count," Pete said. "As long as Marshall's willing to foot the bill, you might as well let him upgrade your security."

"How? By putting bars on the windows?" she asked. "Then what? A barbed-wire fence and a pair of Dobermans? No thanks. I have no intention of turning my house into a high-security compound."

He shifted his weight, crossing his arms, still watching her steadily. *This,* Annie thought, *is what it feels like to be a specimen under a microscope.*

"Invisible bars," Pete answered. "Motion detectors to start. We can go from there."

"My neighbors are going to *love* this," Annie

muttered, following him up the stairs. "Every time a moth bumps against my window, the alarm's going to go off. I won't get any sleep—except when I'm in jail for disturbing the peace."

She trailed along after him as he went from room to room, checking the windows and recording information in his little pocket notebook. He finally paused in front of two closed doors on the second-floor landing.

"What's in here?"

"A linen closet," Annie said, opening the door to reveal her haphazardly stashed collection of sheets and towels.

He pointed at the second door. "And here?"

"Stairs to the attic."

Taylor opened the door, flicking on the light.

"There's nothing up there," Annie said.

He started up the dusty stairs. They creaked and moaned noisily under his weight.

Lit only by one bare bulb, the big attic was full of shadows—and junk. An old rocking horse sat in one corner with a broken television set. A collection of cross-country skis and poles and a child's wooden sled were in another. Boxes and boxes and boxes of books and clothing and stuff were everywhere, some of their contents spilling out onto the wooden floor.

"Nothing up here?" Pete said, a glint of amusement in his eyes as he watched Annie climb the last few stairs into the attic.

She smiled sheepishly. "Nothing important," she said.

But Pete's eyebrows had dipped slightly down in the closest thing she'd seen to a frown on his face as he crossed from one window to another.

"You don't have your alarm system connected to these windows," he said, a note of disbelief in his voice. "Not a single one."

"Well, it would've cost nearly double," Annie explained. She moved toward a window, looking down through the dusk at the ground three distant stories below. "There's no way someone would climb up here. I mean, they'd be crazy—"

"I've known some cat burglars who wouldn't hesitate to scale seventeen stories for an easy target," Pete said. "This would be a cakewalk."

"No way." Annie shook her head, glancing down again. The lawn was *so* far away. She couldn't imagine climbing up this high. The shingles on the roof were slippery and some were loose. One wrong step, one misjudged placement of a foot, and there'd be nothing but air. Air and then the bone-breaking earth.

Pete reached up to lean his arms against the rough wooden rafter, the muscles moving under his trim black turtleneck as he looked down at her. "I guess you're not a climber," he said with a small smile.

"A climber?" she echoed, trying not to melt under his warm gaze.

"People are either climbers or not," he explained. "The not-climbers are more comfortable on the ground. It's not that they're afraid of heights, they just have a healthy respect for gravity. Too healthy. As a result, they doubt the very existence of climbers."

"I'm definitely a not-climber," Annie admitted.

"Climbers were born knowing about toeholds, and wanting to touch the sky," Pete said. "And climbing up to the attic of a three-story house wouldn't even get them half the way there."

"Which are you?" Annie asked.

Before he had a chance to answer, she launched herself at him, screaming like a banshee. His hands automatically came down to catch her, but he lost his footing, and he and Annie tumbled to the dusty attic floor.

His body responded instantly, his arms going around her, his fingers threading into the fine, golden-brown hair that he'd so often imagined touching. Silk. It felt like silk. Softer.... Oh, man—

"Oh, man," Annie wailed, pushing herself away from him and scrambling to the stairs.

He heard her stumble in her haste, and then the solid slam of the door.

With a groan, Pete lay back on the floor, feeling as if he'd been run over by a truck. What the hell had just happened? She'd tackled him, out of the *blue,* for crying out loud....

He saw it then.

It was a small black shadow, flitting up near the eaves.

A bat.

Annie was afraid of bats.

She had leapt on top of him not from unrestrained attraction, but out of fear.

He tried to convince himself that the feelings flooding him were relief, nothing more. But he couldn't contain the laughter that bubbled up, laughter mostly aimed at his own overinflated ego.

He pulled himself up off the floor and opened one of the attic windows. Gently he herded the tiny bat in that direction, until it noticed the obvious path of escape and disappeared into the cool night air. Pete closed the window and looked around, dusting himself off.

ANNIE SAT AT THE KITCHEN TABLE, her hands wrapped around her mug of tea, as if for warmth. She glanced up as Pete came into the room, meeting his eyes only briefly before looking away, embarrassed.

"You okay?" he said.

"Yeah, I'm sorry," she said. "I'm, um…a little freaked-out by bats."

"A little," he agreed, amusement lighting his eyes.

She looked up at him again as he sat down across from her. A rueful smile slowly spread across her face. "You probably didn't know what hit you," she said.

"I *was* a little confused at first," he replied with an answering smile. "I got the bat out of there and found where he must've gotten in. I stuffed a rag in the hole. It's not a permanent fix, but it should keep him from coming right back inside."

"Thanks." She paused for a moment, then said, "Don't tell anyone. Please?"

"That you're afraid of bats?" Pete asked, surprise in his voice.

"Yeah. Cara doesn't even know."

"What difference does it make?" he asked curiously.

"I'm an archaeologist," Annie said. "Bats and I tend to hang out in the same places. I would be teased mercilessly if my colleagues knew I was afraid of them. And I'm really okay around bats if I'm expecting them to be there," she said. "It's when I'm not expecting them that I suddenly become nine years old again."

He was watching her with that funny little half smile on his handsome face, and Annie had an extremely vivid memory of the way his body had felt against hers. The man was all muscles, all hard, solid strength. But his hands had been so gentle as he touched her hair....

"Promise you won't tell," she said.

Her blue eyes were wide, watching him with such hopefulness, such trust and such innocence. She actually believed that if he told her that he wouldn't tell anyone, then he wouldn't. Pete had to look away, wishing he deserved that trust, knowing he didn't. Not by a long shot.

"I'd think at least you would've told Cara," he said. "You two seem pretty tight."

She shook her head.

"Why not?" he asked.

Her eyes narrowed slightly as she met his gaze. "Can you honestly tell me that *you* don't have some deep, dark secret that no one knows—not even your best friend?"

He laughed, but there was no humor in it. "I have way too many secrets," he said.

"Well, good. You tell me one of your secrets," Annie said, "and then we'll be even. You don't tell anyone that I'm a baby when I see a bat, and I won't tell anyone that...you secretly watch old Doris Day movies whenever they're on television."

Pete raised an eyebrow. "How did you guess?"

Annie laughed. "Do you really?"

"How many secrets do you want me to give away?" he countered.

He was flirting with her, Annie thought with a sudden flash of pleasure. "Just one," she said. "You know what I'd really like to know?"

"I can't begin to guess," he said.

"I want to know your real name."

Pete stopped breathing. She knew. How the hell could she know?

"You *do* have a Navaho name, don't you?" she asked.

He understood with a flash of relief. God, for a second there, he'd actually thought she knew he was undercover.... "Yeah," he somehow managed to say.

Annie looked across the table at him. He was watching her, his face suddenly guarded, expressionless. She wondered if perhaps she was prying too deeply. "I'm sorry. You don't have to tell me if you don't want to."

"Hastin Naat'aanni," he said. His voice was so soft, it was almost a whisper as he spoke the language of his grandfather. "That's what I was called."

Intrigued, Annie leaned forward. "What does it mean?"

He stood up. "It doesn't translate well," he said, obviously hedging.

"Roughly, then," she said. She stood up, too, testing her legs, checking to see that the wobble had truly gone away.

He turned to watch her closely, making sure she was okay. When had it stopped being annoying? Annie wondered. When had his presence changed from interfering to nice, to making her feel safe and protected?

"Roughly, it means 'Man Speaking Peace,'" he said. His lips curled up into a sardonic smile; then he turned and left the kitchen.

"That's a great name," Annie said, following him down the stairs. "Who gave it to you? How old were you? Why were you named that?"

At the bottom of the stairs he stopped and faced her, bringing them nose to nose.

"That's another secret entirely," he said.

They were standing close enough for him to kiss her. It would take very little effort on his part. She wanted him to kiss her, she realized suddenly. She actually *wanted* him to. Was she crazy?

But he didn't move.

"I'm going to use your phone," he said, "to call Steven Marshall. He'll authorize me to have your security system updated and rewired to include the third floor."

Annie felt the first sparks of anger. But that was

good—anger was better than whatever it was that she'd just been feeling. Wasn't it? "But I don't want my system updated," she said, turning and going back up the stairs. "I'm happy with everything exactly the way it is."

"Then you better get used to me camping out on the floor of your bedroom every night," Pete said. He followed her back into the kitchen. "Because until we get motion detectors and a laser security system installed, that's exactly where I'm going to be."

"Oh, come on, Taylor," Annie said. "You don't really think I'm in any kind of danger, do you?"

"I've been hired to protect you," he said evenly, crossing his arms and leaning against the door frame. His dark eyes watched her as she took a loaf of bread from the cabinet, and jars of peanut butter and jelly from the refrigerator. "What I think is irrelevant."

Annie pulled a clean plate out of the dishwasher and set it on the kitchen table, then selected a dinner knife from the utensil drawer. She folded one leg underneath her as she sat at the table, opening the bread bag and pulling out two slices of thick, dark whole wheat bread.

"I don't enjoy sharing my bedroom," she said, frowning down at the chunky peanut butter she spread on one of the slices of bread. "Particularly since I don't believe someone really wants to hurt me."

"Maybe not," Pete said. "But maybe you're wrong. If I were you, I wouldn't want to find out the hard way that I was wrong."

He was watching her as if he were memorizing the way she put jelly on bread. "You hungry?" she asked suddenly. "Want a sandwich?"

Pete shook his head, a small smile playing about the corners of his mouth. "No, thanks," he said. Then he added, "Is this your dinner?"

She shrugged, taking a bite. "Believe it or not, it's healthy," she said around the peanut butter in her mouth. "The peanut butter is natural—just a little salt added—and the jelly's that all-fruit stuff. I got the bread at the health food store. You sure you don't want some?"

"I'll send out for something, thanks," he said dryly.

"I still don't think anyone would be able to climb up to the third floor of this house," Annie argued after she swallowed a bite. "Even if someone managed to get up there, the neighbors would see them and call the police."

Pete stepped into the kitchen, sitting down across from her at the table. "But what if someone *could* get up there?" he said. "What if they could gain access to your house that way? Then what? Your artifacts are locked in the safe. They're secure. But the lock on your bedroom door wouldn't keep anyone out."

"I can take care of myself," Annie said. "I'm not defenseless, you know."

"So you could defend yourself," Pete said. One eyebrow went up a half a millimeter. "With that plastic gun you had in the lab—the kind that says Bang! on a little flag when you pull the trigger? Very effective."

Annie actually blushed, then couldn't keep a smile from spreading across her face. "I was improvising," she said. "Gimme a break. It was the middle of the night and the alarm system went off."

"Look, I'll make a deal with you," Pete said. "Lock me out of your house. Then give me five minutes to get back inside without triggering your alarm system. If I can do it, then you stop complaining about updating the system, and you let me sleep on the floor of your bedroom until I'm convinced the house is secure."

Annie had started to take another bite of her sandwich, but she pulled it out of her mouth. "There's no way you can get back inside in five minutes," she said. "No way." She bit down on the sandwich as if for emphasis.

"So is it a deal?"

"What do I get if you can't do it?"

His dark eyes rested warmly on hers. "You get whatever you want," he said. Even with his face expressionless, his words had a faintly suggestive quality.

I'm imagining it, Annie thought, turning away from him. *I'm reading things that aren't really there.*

Nodding, she stood up, gesturing toward the hallway. Sandwich in one hand, she followed Pete down to the front door. He opened it, and looked down at her before opening the storm door.

"Lock the door and turn on your security system," he said. "Then check the ground floor to make sure all the windows are locked."

"Can I turn on the outside lights?" Annie said, peeking out into the already dark evening.

Pete shrugged. "Whatever you like."

He pushed open the storm door.

"Hey, you better take your jacket," Annie said. "It's cold out there."

His eyes shone with that inner amusement she'd come to recognize. "I'm not going to be outside that long."

He vanished into the shadows.

Holding her peanut-butter-and-jelly sandwich in her mouth, Annie used both hands to quickly shut and lock the front door, activate the alarm system and turn on all the outside lights, including several spotlights that illuminated her stately Victorian house. She then went through the lab, and then the office, eating her sandwich and checking all the windows on the lower floor. They were all locked. There was no way he could get in that way.

Satisfied, she climbed the stairs. She would go into the kitchen, get the second half of her sandwich, then go down to the lab and— Oh, Christmas!

Pete Taylor was sitting at the kitchen table.

Annie felt her mouth drop open, and she looked at her watch. It hadn't even been three minutes, let alone five.

"How the hell did you do that?" she finally said.

"I climbed up to the attic," he said. "Came in the window."

"But—"

"I think I've proved my point," he said. "Now, can I use your phone?"

Annie was staring at him, her blue eyes troubled. "You just climbed up…that quickly?" she asked. "It was that easy?"

"Yeah," he said, all amusement gone from his eyes. "It was that easy."

She nodded, looking away and frowning thoughtfully. She met his eyes and nodded again. "Use the phone down in the office," she said.

Pete stood up.

"So you're a climber, huh?" she asked.

He nodded. "Yeah."

"You ever touch it? You know, the sky?"
He smiled then. "Not yet."

ANNIE LAY IN THE DARKNESS, listening for any sound at all from Pete Taylor.

Nothing.

No movement, no breathing, nothing.

But she knew he was there. He'd been there, lying on his bedroll, next to the wall by the bathroom when she'd turned out the light.

"Taylor—you awake?" she finally whispered.

"Yeah."

His voice was soft and resonant, thick, like the darkness that surrounded her.

"This is weird," Annie said. "Kind of like the first night of college, when my freshman roommate was still a stranger."

From where Pete lay on his bedroll, he could hear the rustling of her sheets as she sat up in bed.

"Except we didn't go to sleep," Annie's musical voice said, cutting through the darkness. "Instead, we stayed up, talking until dawn. It was my first all-nighter."

She was silent for a moment, then she asked, "You ever pull any all-nighters, Taylor?"

All the time, over in 'Nam. And twenty-four hours without sleep was a breeze. More often, it was seventy, eighty hours with nothing but caffeine and nicotine to keep him awake, to keep him alive— But Peter Taylor had supposedly gone to NYU, not Vietnam. "Yeah," Pete said softly. Still, it wasn't really lying, was it?

"I suppose in your business you still do it all the time," she said.

"Yeah," he agreed. That was closer to the truth.

"When's your birthday?" she asked.

"February 6th," he said.

"How old are you going to be?"

"Thirty-nine."

"What's your favorite color?"

Pete had to think about it. "Blue," he said finally. Yeah. Blue. The color of the sky, the color of the ocean. The color of Annie's eyes....

"Mine's red," she said. "Who's your favorite singer?"

He shook his head in the darkness. "I don't have one," he said. "I don't listen to music much these days."

"Why not?"

"I don't know," he said honestly. "I used to be into the Beatles...."

"I hate to break it to you," Annie said, "but they split up."

His laughter rolled through the darkness. "I said

I didn't listen to music. I didn't say I didn't know what was going on."

"When you were a little kid," Annie said, "what did you want to be when you grew up?"

Pete was quiet for a moment. "Honestly?"

"Of course."

"I wanted to be a priest."

Annie didn't laugh, the way most people would have. "What happened?" she asked.

He sat up, leaning back against the wall. She could barely see him in the darkness, but despite that, his quiet strength seemed to radiate out into the room.

"I found out about the restrictions that went with the job," he said, laughter in his voice. "So I changed my career goals—I decided I'd be president."

"Of the United States?"

"Yep."

She saw the white flash of his teeth as he smiled, and she lay back in her bed, afraid to look at him, afraid of the reaction her body had to him.

"How about you?" he asked. "You must've always wanted to be an archaeologist, right?"

"Well, no," Annie said, lacing her fingers behind her head as she stared up at the dark ceiling. "When I was eight, we came back to New York for a few months and I realized that most kids didn't live out of suitcases, in tents. I discovered that most kids didn't speak five different languages or have a monkey for a pet, and I developed a rather strong longing for what I now call 'TV normal.' It has nothing to do with reality, but, well, to make a long story short, I wanted desperately to grow up to be Mrs. Brady."

"You mean, the mother in 'The Brady Bunch'?"

"Bingo. I wanted suburbia, lots of kids..."

"A maid named Alice," Pete said.

Annie laughed. "A tall, handsome husband who kissed me on the forehead and called me 'dear' as he left for work," she said. "Fortunately for my parents, my fascination with a 'Brady Bunch' lifestyle lasted only a few months. I think after that I wanted to be an astronaut. Yeah, that was when we moved to Greece, and I caught reruns of 'Star Trek.' You know, I can say 'Beam me up, Scotty,' in seven different languages."

"Very impressive."

"Thank you. I've always been easily influenced by television and movies. I saw so little of them, and they seemed so magical. You know, I'm still affected by movies. I just saw *A Few Good Men,* and it made me want to go back to school and become a lawyer."

Pete laughed again. "That would be a major career switch," he said.

"Not as major as trying to be a suburban house-wife," Annie said.

They were both quiet for a moment; then Annie

said, "It's fantasy, you know? I mean, I love what I do. I really love it. It's not work to me. It's play. But still, I can't help but wonder what it would be like to do something different."

She was silent again for a moment. "Do you like your job, Taylor?" she asked.

Pete didn't answer. He couldn't answer. Yeah, Pete Taylor liked his job. He loved his job, since it meant lying there in the dark with Annie Morrow, talking to her, finding out that he liked her and that he wanted to keep finding out more about her.

But he wasn't Pete Taylor. He was Kendall Peterson. He was sent to spy on this woman, to uncover her secrets and betray her confidences. And Kendall Peterson had never hated his job more in his entire life.

CHAPTER SIX

THE MORNING PASSED QUICKLY. Annie stretched and, for the first time in hours, looked up from the test she was running. She caught Pete's eye and smiled at him. He didn't smile back, but that was okay—she hadn't expected him to. Instead, he pulled off the headphones of the Walkman she'd lent him, and pushed the button that stopped the tape he was listening to.

"Lunchtime," she said.

"Does this mean you're actually going to eat?" Pete asked, his eyebrows moving slightly upward. "Or is this going to be a replay of breakfast where you just wave a mug of tea in front of your face?"

Annie's smile turned into a grin. "I'm starving," she admitted. "I better get a chance to actually eat. Although, first I've got to hit the office, check the fax machine and return all the phone calls I didn't take this morning."

Pete trailed down the hallway after her.

"You must be going nuts," she said. "Sitting there watching me all morning. Not too stimulating, I'm afraid."

On the contrary, Pete thought. He'd had an entirely enjoyable morning just watching her and listening to her collection of cassette tapes. He'd heard everything from Bach to a band called the Spin Doctors, and he'd enjoyed it all. It had been a long time since he'd taken the time to listen to music. The headphones Annie had didn't cut out the room noise, so he felt secure knowing he could hear everything that was going on around him.

And watching Annie was never a chore. Even when she was sitting, she was in motion. A foot was always jiggling, a pencil tapping, fingers moving.... He'd particularly enjoyed memorizing every little worn spot in her faded jeans. There was a place on her left hip where the seam was starting to tear....

It was Sunday, and Cara was spending the day with Jerry, so the answering machine had been on all morning. Annie pushed the message button, then went to the fax machine. Something had come in. She tore the sheet of paper free and looked at it as the messages played.

There were three calls from people whose names she didn't recognize, then Nick's familiar English accent came on, reminding her of their date at the Museum of Modern Art bash. He wanted her to call him. No doubt he had some new find that needed to be authenticated with utmost haste and great urgency. And gratis, as a favor to an old friend, of course. He wasn't a client, but somehow he always brought her work. He would ask her to squeeze it in, offer to stay up late into the night with her as she ran the tests, ply her with wine and promises of dinner....

There were messages from the buyer and the seller of the copper bowl she was working on, and five other messages from other clients.

Annie dialed the first of the clients who had called, and after saying hello, spent the next ten minutes listening to questions he had about her latest report on a piece he was trying to sell.

So much for lunch.

Annie's stomach growled. "Can you hold on a sec?" she asked, and pushed the hold button.

Annie looked up at Pete. "Will you do me a big favor?" she asked. "Will you go up to the kitchen and get me the bread, the peanut butter, the jelly, a plate and a knife? I'm never going to get off this phone."

"I'll do even better than that," Pete said. "I'll make you a sandwich."

"You don't have to do that," she said, surprise in her voice.

"I know," he said and smiled. "And believe me, I wouldn't do it for just anyone."

But he'd do it for me, Annie thought, a shiver going down her spine as she looked into his dark eyes. The guy had a killer smile, on top of his being drop-dead handsome, and so far, she'd only found things to like about him. He couldn't possibly be perfect, could he? As unrealistic as it seemed, she found herself praying that he was. Peter Taylor, security consultant, a.k.a. bodyguard, had appeared in her life totally out of the blue. Was it possible to hope that he might be here to stay?

He backed out of the door, his eyes not leaving hers until the last possible moment. Annie found herself listening to his footsteps on the stairs as she reconnected the line to her client. She glanced at her watch. Quarter to one. She was actually looking forward to tonight—to locking herself in her bedroom with Pete Taylor. And talking, she reminded herself. Just talking.

Ten minutes later, Annie stared at the telephone. One down and five to go. She exhaled fully, and glanced up at the calendar on the wall. October. It was only October. Could she really keep up this pace until December?

A flash of movement at the window caught the edge of her vision, and she turned.

What the heck…?

Something was hanging from the tree right outside the window. Something red, and…

Very dead.

A carcass.

A very dead, very skinned carcass of an animal hung gruesomely from the tree, and she caught another streak of movement, as if someone were running away.

"Pete!" she shouted, rocketing out of her chair and scrambling toward the window. Whoever had been out there disappeared around the side of the house. She saw only the back of a black jacket. Or was it long black hair? "Taylor!"

She ran toward the front door, but Pete was already down the stairs, moving down the hall toward her with speed normally reserved for smaller, more compact men. He caught her in his arms to keep from plowing her down as he skidded to a stop on the slippery hardwood floor.

"What is it?" he said sharply. "Annie, what's wrong?"

"Someone was outside," she gasped. "Hurry! Maybe you can still catch him."

"Stay here," Pete ordered, then ran for the door. He drew his gun from his shoulder holster as he went out into the crisp afternoon air. Orange, yellow, brown and red leaves blanketed the wide lawn, and he could see the path the trespasser had made through them as he ran away from the house. That path led directly into one of the neighbors' yards, through a windbreak of tall bushes.

Pete raced up to the bushes, peering through them. The other yard was empty—no sign of anyone. He glanced back at the house. He didn't like leaving Annie alone, unprotected. What if this were only a diversion, designed to draw him away from the house, away from Annie?

She stepped out onto the front porch, and he felt a flash of annoyance. He trotted back toward her. "I thought I told you to stay inside," he said coldly. But his anger melted instantly as he saw the look on her face.

"I'm sorry," she said, hugging her arms across her body, trying to stay warm in the chill air. Her blue eyes looked even bigger than usual. "I, um, got spooked all alone in there."

Pete reholstered his gun. "Come on," he said, not unkindly. "It's cold out here. Let's get back inside."

But Annie was walking determinedly around to the other side of the house. "We have to cut it down," she said. "We can't leave it there."

Puzzled, Pete followed her, then stopped short at the sight of the animal hanging from the tree. He swore under his breath.

"I think it's a rabbit," Annie said, swallowing hard. "*Was* a rabbit, I mean. Do you have a knife?"

"Wait," Pete said. "We can't cut it down."

"Why not?"

"It's evidence," he said.

Annie stared at the skinned animal, blinking back the tears that suddenly appeared in her eyes. "It's hanging right outside my office window," she said, unable to keep her voice from shaking.

"I'll call the FBI," Pete said gently. "Hopefully they can send someone down to take care of it right away."

"And if they can't?"

"Annie, we've got to do this by the book."

"I don't know which is worse," she said. One tear escaped, rolling down her cheek before she brusquely wiped it away. "The fact that someone hung that thing there, or the fact that I can't cut it down when I want to."

"I'm sorry," Pete said, stepping toward her. He reached out toward her, well aware that this was exactly what he'd been so carefully avoiding—all physical contact. He wouldn't be able to hold her in his arms without wanting to kiss her. And if he kissed her, he'd be lost. He reached for her anyway, wanting only to stop her tears.

But she pushed past him, heading back into the house.

He followed her into the lab, where she ignored him completely, concentrating intently on the work at hand.

Pete went into the office and called the FBI, then brought Annie the sandwich he had made for her.

It lay on the counter, untouched, all afternoon.

ANNIE LAY SOAKING IN HER BATHTUB with her eyes closed. The water turned from hot to warm to tepid, and she was considering letting some of it out and running in some more hot when a knock sounded at the bathroom door.

"You all right in there?" Pete's husky voice asked.

She sighed. "Yeah. I'll be out in a minute."

"Take your time," he said, but he heard the sound of water spilling down the drain.

Five minutes later the bathroom door opened, and Annie came out, dressed in a pair of plaid pajamas. Her face was scrubbed, and she was brushing her hair. Her eyes found Pete, who was standing by the bedroom door.

"Can I lock this?" he asked.

She nodded, sitting cross-legged on her bed, still brushing her long, shiny hair. "How long till the motion detectors are installed?" she asked.

Pete knew that what she meant was, *How long till you're out of my room?* "With any luck, they'll be up in a couple of days," he said.

She nodded.

He used the bathroom quickly, washing up with the door open, so he could hear her if she needed him. He hung his towel on the rack next to hers. Annie's towel was damp from her bath, and smelled like her. The entire bathroom smelled like her—fresh and clean and sweet.

Pete turned out the bathroom light and went into the bedroom. He sat down on his sleeping bag, leaning back against the wall.

As he watched, Annie put her hairbrush on the small table next to her bed, then turned off the light.

Darkness.

It surrounded him completely, and he waited patiently for his eyes to adjust. He took advantage of the privacy the darkness provided and pulled off his T-shirt and slipped out of his jeans. He'd slept in his clothes the night before, and woke up much too hot. He lay back against his pillow, listening to the rustling of sheets as Annie moved about, trying to get comfortable.

There was silence then for several long minutes before he heard Annie ask, "Taylor, you still awake?"

He smiled into the darkness. "Yeah."

"I was wondering…"

"Mmm?"

"When do you get a day off?" she asked.

"I don't," he said. "Not until after the job's finished."

"But that's probably going to be at least six more weeks," Annie said. "Doesn't that get a little intense? You watch me all day, *and* all night. Aren't you going to burn out?"

"No."

It was said so absolutely, Annie had to believe him. "Is your job always like this?" she asked. "You know, round-the-clock? What about your social life?"

"I don't have a social life."

"By choice?" she asked.

He was quiet for a moment. "Yeah, I guess so," he said. "How about you? You work all the time, too."

"I have a social life," Annie said defensively. "I go…places, and do…things."

Who was she trying to convince? she wondered. Pete or herself?

She frowned up at the dark ceiling. When *was* the last time she'd had a date? It was when Nick had last been in town. He took her out to a little Italian restaurant in the city and tried to convince her to come back to his hotel room afterward. She'd had too much wine, she remembered, because she'd almost given in….

"Annie, I'm sorry about this afternoon," Pete said,

the faint Western drawl of his rich voice making all thoughts of Nick vanish from her mind. "I wish it could've been handled differently."

"It wasn't your fault," Annie said tiredly.

"Yeah, well, I still wish…" His voice trailed off. Man, he wished this whole investigation had been handled differently. He wished Annie hadn't turned out to be so friendly and funny and charmingly sweet. He wished he could allow himself to care what happened to her. *Too late,* a little voice spoke in his head. *Too late, you already do care…*

On the other side of the room, he heard Annie sit up. "What?" she asked, her voice little more than a whisper. "You wish what?"

Pete pushed himself up on his elbows, sensing her sitting there in the darkness, afraid she was going to get out of bed and move toward him. Disaster. That would be a disaster. If she as much as touched him, he would go up in flames. Spontaneous combustion. A life, a solid career reduced to little more than a sensational headline on the front of the *National Enquirer.*

He remembered running down the stairs that morning, adrenaline sweeping through his system after she'd shouted his name. He'd held her in his arms then. True, it had only been for a few short seconds, but he could take that memory, play it on slow motion and… Dangerous. Man, that was way too dangerous.

"What do you wish?" Annie asked again. He heard a noise, as if she were moving down to the foot of her bed, down where she could see him if she peered through the darkness.

"Too many things," Pete said. "Go to sleep, Annie."

The noise stopped.

Pete prayed, sending a few words up to the gods of his grandfather, as well. *Please don't make this temptation worse than it already is….*

There was silence for several long minutes.

Annie swore choicely, her voice breaking through the darkness. "I can't sleep. I'm exhausted, but my brain won't slow down. And I have to get up early tomorrow, and—"

"Are your eyes closed?" Pete asked.

"Well, not exactly—"

"Close your eyes," he said in his tone of voice that left no room for argument. "I'm going to teach you a relaxation technique, okay?"

"Okay," Annie said, doubt in her voice. "But I've tried this kind of thing before, and it doesn't work."

"This one does," Pete said. "Do you have a favorite place? Somewhere you can go and feel totally calm?"

Annie squinted up at the ceiling, thinking. "Monument Valley," she said decidedly. "I loved it there. Sunrises were *incredible.* Except… No, maybe the beach on Tahiti would win. *That* was fabulous." She sat up. "I *really* loved it there. Although, there was something about the pyramids in Egypt that made me feel like I was on another planet, which was surprisingly calming—"

"Annie."

"Yes?"

"Lie down."

She lay back against her pillow, pulling her sheet and the comforter up to her chin.

"I'm going to tell you about *my* favorite place, okay?" Pete's voice was soft but clear.

"Okay," Annie said.

"Close your eyes," Pete said, "*and* your mouth, or else it won't work."

She was obediently silent.

"My favorite place was a beach," Pete said. "It wasn't Tahiti, but it was the Pacific Ocean. Usually when I got there, I was tired and hot and dirty, so the first thing I'd do was take off my boots and walk straight into that clear blue water." He would come out from the jungles of Vietnam, and wash all the blood and death away from him in the ocean. "Picture yourself doing that. Picture yourself in the water, letting everything that happened today just get washed away. Out where you are, behind the break, the ocean's calm, with gentle swells that lift you up. You can look out toward the horizon, and it's all blue water, as far as you can see. It just goes on and on and on, almost forever."

Annie lay in the darkness with her eyes shut, letting Pete's soft voice wash over her. His twang was more pronounced as he himself relaxed and his voice grew lazy. She liked it. The drawl suited him far better than the clipped accentless voice he assumed when giving orders.

"You climb out of the water," he was saying. "And up onto the beach. The sand's fine and soft and hot under your feet. It feels real good. There's a blanket already spread out, and you lie down on it. It's warm and the sun feels great on your face. There's no one else on the entire beach—you've got the whole place to yourself—so you take off your wet clothes."

Pete paused a moment, unable to get the picture of Annie lying naked on the beach out of his mind. Damn, this was supposed to be relaxing....

"You lie back against that blanket, and feel that hot sun on your skin. The sky is the bluest you've ever seen it, and the sand is so white. You close your eyes, though, and listen to the sounds of the waves, and to the seabirds. It's like music, with its own special rhythm and rhyme. It's soothing, and soon you're so relaxed, you seem to be floating...."

He could hear Annie breathing, slow and steady as he let his voice trail off. She was asleep.

She trusted him. Another few nights like this, and he'd ask her about what she'd done in Athens—who she talked to, where she'd gone. He'd ask her if maybe she was in too deep....

Although he couldn't believe she was involved with any kind of conspiracy. He smiled to himself. She didn't seem to have the ability to lie. Another few nights and he'd know for sure....

Except the alarm system was scheduled to be updated starting tomorrow afternoon, and he'd soon be sleeping in the guest bedroom, away from her.

Pete lay awake, staring up into the darkness for a long time before he finally fell asleep.

PETE CALLED WHITLEY SCOTT IN the morning, while Annie was in the shower.

"Can you talk?" Scott asked.

"For maybe three minutes," Pete said. He stood in the office doorway, listening for Annie, and looking down the long hallway, watching the front door for Cara. "I need you to delay the installation of the motion detectors. Have the alarm installers call

Annie and tell her it'll be at least a week before they can get the system out here."

"Annie, huh?" Scott said meaningfully.

Pete ignored the comment. "Will you do it?"

"Sure."

"What have you found out?" Pete asked.

"You mean about the phone calls?" Scott asked.

"And the rock through the window, and the wolf man in the car, *and* the carcass hanging—"

"Right, right," Scott interrupted him. "Not much. It's not our main concern right now—"

"Push it up a little higher on the priority list," Pete said, his tone leaving no room for argument.

But Scott argued anyway. "Come on, Captain," he said. "You know those nutball groups. This could be any one of them. We don't have the manpower to waste an investigation on a threat that's not real—"

"I think it *is* real," Pete said tersely. "Get a team working on it immediately."

Silence. Whitley Scott didn't like being ordered around. But Pete waited him out, and Scott finally sighed with exasperation. "I'll see what I can do," he said grouchily. "So what's happening up there? Are you getting somewhere with Morrow?"

"She's starting to trust me," Pete said. "She's starting to think of me as a friend."

"A friend?" the head of the FBI division scoffed.

"What's this *friend* crap, Pete? Seduce her, for crying out loud. Women naturally trust the men they sleep with. She'll tell you all her secrets then."

"I've got to go," Pete said brusquely, even though he could still hear the water coursing through the house's old pipes, and there was still no sign of Cara. He hung up the phone, Scott's words echoing in his mind. *Seduce her.*

Why should Scott's nonchalant words make him so angry?

Because Annie was...well, *Annie.* She was special. Pete liked everything about her. He liked her a lot—way too much to take advantage of her that way.

He sat down heavily at Annie's desk, massaging the tense muscles in his neck and shoulders. The ironic thing was, if he really *were* Pete Taylor, if he really *were* plain and simply Annie's bodyguard, with no ulterior motives or hidden agendas, he would have been working hard to get into her bed long before this.

Life was too damn strange.

"Yo," Cara said, breaking into Annie's concentration. "You've got a phone call I figured you'd want to take. It's the burglar-alarm guy."

Annie looked up from her equipment, stretching

her stiff shoulders and back, and working out the kink in her neck with one hand. "Thanks," she said to her assistant. "I'll take it in here."

She crossed to the white lab phone that hung on the wall next to the door. It was late afternoon, and the light was already starting to fade. She picked up the phone and flicked on the bright overhead lights.

"Anne Morrow speaking," she said, glancing over at Pete. He sat leaning back in a chair, his feet up on a stool. His relaxed position was only a sham, she realized. He was watching her as intently as ever, no doubt noticing the way she couldn't keep her eyes from running the long, lean lengths of his jean-clad legs. Shoot, the man was just too good-looking. She turned her back, trying to focus on the voice speaking to her over the phone.

"We gotta little problem with scheduling," the man with the heavy New York accent said, after identifying himself as being the owner of the burglar alarm installation company Pete had called to put in the motion detectors. "The earliest I'm going to be able to send a crew out is next week. End of next week. Thursday, Friday at the earliest. Maybe not even till Monday."

"Oh, shoot." Annie chewed her lip. "You were supposed to be here today."

"Sorry, miss," the man said, not sounding

remotely remorseful. "It's that time of year. Halloween. You can try calling another alarm company, but
it's the same all over. Everyone's backlogged."

Annie stared out the window into the deepening
twilight. Another week and a half of Pete sleeping in
her room at night. Now, why didn't that news bother
her the way it would have a day or two ago?

"You still wanna keep your name on our list?"
the man asked.

"Yes," Annie said. "Yeah, thanks. Thanks for
calling."

Slowly she hung up the phone and told Pete about
the call. He took the news with his normal lack of expression. Was he disappointed? Pleased? She
couldn't begin to tell.

"Is this an official break?" Cara asked cheerfully,
coming back into the lab. "It's time. You've been
hard at it all afternoon. I, for one, have finished inputting all that data from the dread phony copper
bowl, so I'm ready to celebrate."

"You're always ready to celebrate." Annie smiled.

"Yes, but this time I have an excuse," Cara said.
"Jerry's coming over in a little while. What do you
say we all go out and have Chinese food?"

"I don't know," Annie said.

"Oh, come on," Cara urged. "You know how
weird you get when you don't leave the house for

days on end. A little fresh air and some moo goo gai pan'll be good for you."

Annie glanced at Pete. "Whaddaya say, Taylor? Do you want to go?"

"I go where you go," he said.

"I know that," she said impatiently. "I asked you if you *wanted* to go."

He pulled his worn-out cowboy boots off the stool and stood up. "I would love to," he said, a smile breaking across his face as he steadily met her eyes.

ANNIE WATCHED PETE AS JERRY talked about his latest exploits in South America, telling stories across a table that was littered with the remains of their dinner. As the busboys began to clear away the dishes, Pete looked over at Annie and smiled. She felt the now-familiar warm rush of attraction and had to look away.

This was not a date, she reminded herself for the hundredth time that evening. Pete was her bodyguard. He was there only to protect her, despite the fact that his eyes sometimes burned with an intensity that could take her breath away.

In the few short days that he'd been protecting her, he'd done nothing to make her think she meant anything to him besides a reason for employment. True, he was friendly, kind even, generally polite, but in short, he wasn't acting like a man who was going crazy, longing for her touch.

The way she was longing for him to touch her.

Damn, damn, damn, Annie thought. When had she crossed the line between *This is a guy I'd like to get to know,* and *This is a guy I must have?* When had it happened?

Last night, probably, when she'd drifted off to sleep listening to his soft, husky voice. Or it might've been earlier that day, when he'd offered to make lunch for her. Or maybe it was the night before, when they first lay awake, talking....

"You're awfully quiet tonight," Jerry said to Annie. "And you barely ate anything. What gives?"

Annie could tell from the way he and Cara were sitting that they were holding hands underneath the table. Cara looked so happy.

"She's had a bad week," Cara answered for her. "She lost a couple of days' work by going to England to pick up old Stands Against the Storm's death mask, and then when she came back, she got hassled by the feds while she was going through Customs. They detained her *six* hours."

"Why?" Jerry asked. "Whatd'ya do this time, Morrow?"

Annie glanced at Pete, who was watching her intently. "After I picked up the artifact from the

English Gallery, the place was bombed and robbed," she said.

"You're kidding," Jerry said with shock.

"I wouldn't kid about something like that," Annie said ruefully.

"God, you have the worst luck," Jerry said, shaking his head. "Maybe you should stay stateside for a while. I mean, another coincidence like that and—"

"No thank you," Annie said with a flash of anger in her eyes. "My job requires international travel. I'm not going to let myself get bullied into changing my life."

"Maybe you should've been more cooperative with the Athens thing," he said, frowning.

"How much more cooperative, Tillet?" Annie said tartly. "You mean, like giving them a signed confession? Because that's what they want." She turned to look at Pete. "We better get going. I've got more work to do tonight."

"Does she ever not work?" Jerry asked Pete. He turned to Annie. "You must be disgustingly rich. Maybe I should be hitting *you* up for funding for my latest project. See, I found a site in Mexico—"

"I know, I know!" Annie said, rolling her eyes. "I've heard it…what? Five thousand times this week already."

"You know that you're interested," Jerry said. "You could come along." He shot a sideways glance at Cara. "You, too," he added. He looked back at Annie. "When was the last time you participated in a dig?"

"It would be fun," Annie said, "but I *really* don't have the money."

The waiter brought the dinner check, and she reached for it, but Pete grabbed it first. "This one's courtesy of Mr. Marshall," he said with a smile.

"I'll drink to that." Jerry grinned.

Annie watched Pete bring the check to the cashier. She stood up, pulling on her jacket. Pete's leather jacket was on the back of his chair, and she picked it up. God, it was heavy. "See you guys tomorrow," she said, giving Cara an overobvious "have fun" wink.

Pete met her at the door and took his jacket. "Thanks," he said.

"What are you carrying in your pockets?" Annie said, leaving the warmth of the restaurant and going out onto the sidewalk. "Your jacket weighs a ton."

Zipping her own jacket up, she shivered slightly in the cold autumn night.

"It's armor," Pete said. "In case I have to throw myself in front of any speeding bullets."

Annie laughed.

"I'm serious," he said. "It's bulletproof."

He was watching her in the dim light from the street lamp on the corner. His dark eyes were soft and warm, luminescent. If any other man had looked at her like that, she would have bet her life savings that he was going to kiss her. But not Pete Taylor. He broke the eye contact, looked down at the ground and took two solid steps backward, away from her.

Hiding her exasperation, Annie turned, and they walked to his car in silence.

CHAPTER SEVEN

ANNIE THREW HER JACKET OVER the back of her chair in the office and pressed the playback button on her answering machine.

The first voice on the tape was Nick. He didn't even bother to identify himself, assuming that she'd recognize his voice. Which, of course, she did.

"Sweet Annie," he said in his proper English accent. "I'm beginning to consider taking your answering machine to the party at the museum instead of you. I've spoken to it more often in the past few weeks. Where are you? MacLeish says you're busy, but you've never been too busy for me before. What's going on? Call me."

Pete had assumed his regular position, leaning in the doorway.

"That was Nick York," she told him.

"I know," he said. "Why don't you call him back?"

Annie sighed, temporarily stopping the tape. "Because he's going to ask me to authenticate some very tiny, but *very* important, archaeological find for him. It'll be really easy, he'll tell me, it'll only take a few hours of my time, I can surely squeeze him in. Except something will go amazingly wrong— there'll be some glitch in the test, and I'll end up working until dawn four nights in a row." She sighed again. "Somehow Nick always talks me into doing things. This time I really *don't* have the time, so it's easier to avoid him." She met Pete's eyes and smiled ruefully. "I know it's the coward's way out. I also know that he's going to catch up with me sooner or later. At the fund-raiser at the Museum of Modern Art, at the very least."

Pete kept his face expressionless, afraid that the flash of jealousy he'd felt at the sound of York's voice would still somehow show. Jealousy? Man, what the hell was he doing feeling *jealous?* He had no right. No right at all. So just stop it, he ordered himself.

He cleared his throat. "What other messages are on there?" he asked, motioning toward the answering machine with his head.

Annie started the tape rolling again.

Another message was from the Westchester Archaeological Society, asking if Dr. Morrow had any free time in the next few months to come and give a lecture at one of the group's monthly meetings.

"Free time," Annie laughed. "If they only knew...."

There were four hang-ups in a row, then a voice spoke.

"I am calling on behalf of Stands Against the Storm." Annie looked sharply up at Pete. He hadn't moved a muscle, but he was instantly a picture of intensity, his dark eyes burning into hers as they both listened. The voice belonged to a man and was accentless and soft.

"You must surrender the death mask," he said, almost mildly. "Return it to the Navaho people. It is for your own good that I tell you this. The evil spirit within the mask will awaken if you disturb it. Do not touch it, do not hold it—or be ready to face the spirit's wrath. Your life as you know it will crumble. Await further instructions."

There was a click, and the answering machine beeped twice, signaling that there were no more messages, and shut off.

Annie sat so still at her desk that Pete could hear the wall clock ticking as its second hand jerked around the dial. But as if her energy couldn't be contained, she stood up suddenly, pushing past him out of the room and down the hallway. He followed her into the lab, where she switched on the bright overhead lights and crossed directly to the big safe.

It only took several quick spins to the combination lock, and the heavy door swung open. Without a word, Annie took out the heavy crate from England and carried it to the wide lab counter. She set it down and got a hammer from one of the cabinet drawers.

Pete didn't ask what she was doing—he already knew.

"You know," Annie said evenly, "this thing is such a pain in the butt, and I haven't even taken a good look at it yet."

She used the forked end of the hammer to pry the top of the crate up and off.

The crate was filled with large foam peanuts. Annie dug through them, finding the top of the heavy artifact about six inches down. She pulled it out, careful to keep the foam chips in the box.

The death mask had been wrapped in layers of bubble pack. She peeled them back to find the artifact surrounded by a soft cloth. Carefully she unwrapped it, setting it on the counter on top of that same piece of fabric.

It was amazing. The gleaming, golden face of Stands Against the Storm sat in front of her, every wrinkle, every sagging muscle in the old man's face recorded forever by the casting that had been done shortly after his death. His eyes were closed, and he looked so tired, so sad. Annie wondered what his eyes had been like, wondered if he'd had eyes like Pete's—dark and burning with intensity and life.

Annie glanced up at Pete. "Curses, shmurses," she said, and picked the death mask up, holding the cool metal in her hands. Nothing happened. She wasn't immediately struck by lightning or attacked by a flock of screaming evil spirits. And as far as her life crumbling…well, it couldn't really get *that* much worse. Could it?

She carried the death mask to the other side of the lab, to a big magnifying glass that was clamped to the counter with an accordion-like arm. She turned on another, even brighter, light and held the artifact under the glass, looking at it closely.

Pete pulled up a stool and watched.

Annie examined the casting marks, moving slowly across the piece for several long minutes. Finally she looked up at Pete.

"Is it real?" he asked.

She didn't answer at first. Instead, she brought the artifact up to her mouth and licked it. She grinned at the way his eyebrows moved upward. "Well, it's real gold, at the very least," she said.

"You can tell that by tasting it?"

Annie nodded. "Yes."

"That doesn't seem too scientific," he said. "All these high-tech instruments in this lab, and you end up using your tongue."

"That was just a preliminary test," she said. "I'll

get a full metal content when I have more time. But I think the final outcome is going to have to be decided by carbon dating."

"Why?" asked Pete, watching her.

She had put the death mask down on the counter, and now she gathered her long hair away from her face, pulling it easily into a ponytail and using a rubber band to hold it back. She was wearing her worn-out jeans and a red sweater that was textured, designed to be touched. Pete hooked his thumbs through his belt loops and tried to concentrate on what she was saying.

"Well, it certainly passes a quick inspection," Annie said. "The casting marks all look comparable to what was being done in England in the nineteenth century. But without written records—you know, receipts or bills of sale, something to document it— the only way to be sure it wasn't cast last month in Liverpool is to carbon-date it."

Pete leaned in for a closer look. "So, how long will that test take?"

She turned and found herself nearly nose to nose with him. Up close, his eyes were beautiful. They were exquisitely shaped and surrounded by thick, black lashes. But his expression was so closed, so guarded, he might have been a statue. He didn't seem to notice that he had long since invaded her personal space, that he was sitting at a distance more appropriate for an embrace than a conversation.

She swallowed, moistening her dry lips with the tip of her tongue. "Even if I start the tests now, it will probably be weeks before I get the results. I have to contract out for carbon dating."

There was a flash of relief in his dark eyes, and Annie's heart leapt. He was glad. He wanted to stick around for a while. More than ever, she wanted him to kiss her. *Kiss me,* she thought, staring into his eyes, hoping he could read her mind.

But he didn't move.

She was going to have to do it, she realized. She was going to have to kiss him. She looked away, gathering her courage. The worst he could do was laugh at her, right? So she should just do it—

Pete straightened up, pushing his stool back, out of range.

Damn, Annie thought. The moment had passed. What was wrong with her? she wondered. Wasn't she making her interest in him obvious enough? Or maybe it was Pete, she thought glumly. Maybe he had a reason to fight the attraction that sparked between them every time they were together in a room. Maybe he was in love with someone else. Shoot, maybe he was married....

She sat at the lab counter for a long time, pretending to study the death mask, but in truth thinking long and hard about Peter Taylor.

ANNIE TURNED OFF THE LIGHT on her bedside table, determined to follow the resolution she had made while she was brushing her teeth in the bathroom just a few moments ago. She was not going to chase this man. She had let him know—subtly, of course, but Pete Taylor was a smart man—that she was interested in him. It had been up to him to do something about it. Or not.

Obviously, he'd chosen "or not."

Well, okay. That was fine. She was a grown-up; she could deal with that.

But it wouldn't do her any good to lie in the dark, talking to him until the early hours of the morning. It wouldn't do her any good at all to share more secrets with him. And it certainly wouldn't do her any good to fall in love with him.

She lay in the dark, in silence, hoping that it wasn't already too late.

Minutes passed. Long, endless minutes, during which she tried to organize and prioritize the work she had to do tomorrow. Then she tried to think of all the songs she knew that started with the word *I*. "I Think I Love You," "I Wanna Hold Your Hand," "I Had the Craziest Dream," "I Do," "I'm Dreaming of a White Christmas"—no, that was the first line, not the name of the song.

She gave up. "Taylor, are you awake?"

"Yeah."

On the other side of the room, Pete closed his eyes briefly. Annie had been quiet for so long, he had been afraid that she had broken her pattern and was already asleep.

"Do you think that guy on the phone meant he's going to call again and tell me to bring the death mask someplace, when he said, 'Await further instructions'?"

Pete knew exactly which guy she was talking about. "Probably," he said. "But first I think he and his buddies are going to try to scare you badly enough so you won't want to get the police involved."

"The police are already involved," Annie said. "What do these guys think I'm going to do? Simply hand them a piece of gold that's worth tens of thousands of dollars? And that's ignoring any possible historical value. Even if I do hand it over, then what? I call up Ben Sullivan and say, 'Oops. Lost your artifact. Sorry'?"

"*I* know you're not about to do that," Pete said. "But these people don't know you. They don't realize you don't scare easily."

"Maybe you don't know me, either, Taylor."

Annie's voice was soft. "Sometimes I think I'm scared of everything."

"It's one thing to be scared," he said, "and another thing entirely to let it affect you."

"Like my fear of bats," Annie said wryly.

"Obviously you've dealt with that pretty damn well," he said, "since I'm the only one who knows about it."

"Aren't you afraid of anything, Taylor?" Annie asked.

Pete stared at the outline of the windows for a long time before he answered. "Yeah," he finally said. "I get afraid when the line between right and wrong isn't clear. Lately it seems it never is. It's been scaring the hell out of me."

There was silence for a moment, then he laughed, but there was no humor in it. "I'm also afraid I haven't lived up to the name my grandfather gave me."

Pete hadn't wanted to go to Vietnam and had seriously considered losing himself up in the Rocky Mountains, much in the way his ancestors had when they'd received orders from the federal government that they hadn't liked.

But he obeyed the draft, and he went to Vietnam. At first he wondered what the hell someone named Man Speaking Peace was doing stalking through a

foreign jungle with an automatic weapon in his hands
and camouflage gear on his back. But it didn't take
him long to realize that he was good at staying alive,
and especially good at keeping the men around him
alive, too. And somehow, when the real war was over
and the American troops were shipping out of
Saigon, he'd remained behind, part of the exclusive
force assigned to locate and rescue the massive
numbers of POWs and MIAs still in the jungles.

Ever since the summer that he was drafted, when
he was barely eighteen years old, not even old
enough to drink in Colorado, he'd always carried at
least one gun. He felt it now, a hard lump, tucked
under his bedroll where he could reach it easily if he
needed it.

"A man of peace needs no weapon," he could
remember his grandfather telling him. "Only a conscience, a will and a voice loud enough to carry."

"Man Speaking Peace." Annie's voice cut into his
thoughts. "Why were you named that?"

He was silent for so long, she thought maybe he
wasn't going to answer.

"I haven't thought about any of this in a really long
time," Pete finally said. "I'm not sure I want to...."

"I'm sorry," Annie said. "I was just— I shouldn't
have—"

"I was thirteen years old," he said, interrupting her.

"It was the summer that my aunt died—my mother's sister. It really messed my cousins up. They came to stay with us at the ranch. There were five of them—Jack was the oldest, he was twelve. Then there was Wil, Thomas, Eddie and Chris, who was just a baby really. He couldn't have been more than five. He missed his mother something fierce. They all did, but Chris was the only one who would cry. He would cry, and Tom would taunt him, saying boys didn't cry, only babies cried. Then Jack would beat the hell out of Tom, and soon they'd all be fighting.

"Well, I spent all of July being a mediator, keeping the peace between those five boys. I was older than them, and they looked up to me. But more often than not, as soon as my back was turned, *wham,* someone would end up with a fist in his eye.

"After a few weeks, I began to realize that there was a pattern to when little Chris would cry about his mother. He usually cried first thing in the morning, and at a certain time in the afternoon—about one o'clock, I think it was—because that was the time his mom had set aside a half an hour every day to read to him and play with him—with *just* him, giving him her full attention, while the other boys were off at school.

"So I started distracting him. I'd be the one to wake him up in the morning, and I'd keep him so busy, he'd never really notice the emptiness. And I did the same thing in the afternoon, and his bouts of crying happened less and less often."

Annie listened, realizing she was almost holding her breath. Pete had never spoken at such length in the entire time she'd known him, and certainly never about himself, about his childhood.

"Unfortunately, the same couldn't be said about the fighting," he said, with a low laugh. "Even when Chris's crying stopped, the older boys found other reasons to set themselves off. I couldn't figure out what had gotten into them. They'd never fought before—not like this."

He paused. *Don't stop,* Annie thought. She could picture him as a thirteen-year-old boy, tall and serious, with those same intense, dark eyes. "So what happened?" she asked softly.

"I went and talked to my grandfather," Pete said. "I asked him why my cousins were fighting. He told me it was their way of grieving for their mother. Well, I thought about that for a couple of days. But after I watched Wil give Jack a broken nose, and after Jack damn near broke Tom's arm, I decided that those boys needed to find a different way to deal with their mother's death.

"I took the whole pack of them out on a hike, up into the mountains, to a place I knew about where you could see down into the whole valley," Pete said quietly. "It was like heaven up there. You could look out across my father's ranch, at the fields laid out like squares on a patchwork quilt. Everything was alive and growing. There were so many different shades of green, and the sky was so blue, it hurt to look at it.

"We sat down on some rocks, and the boys were quiet for once, just taking it all in," he said. "I sat there, thinking about my aunt Peg, their mother. I thought about her, and it didn't take me long to start to cry. So I sat there, with tears running down my face, and one by one those boys noticed I was crying. They were shocked, really shocked, because, as Tom was so fond of pointing out, boys weren't supposed to cry.

"Wil asked me why I was crying, and I told him it was because I missed his mother. I told them that sometimes even men had to cry, and if it was okay for a man to cry, then it was surely okay for a boy to cry. And they believed me, you know, because I was older than them. Soon Chris started in—it never took much to set him off—but then Tom broke down, and Wil and Eddie, and finally even Jack was crying. We all just sat there and cried for about an hour. Then I told them that this place that we had climbed to was my special place, but that they could use it whenever they needed it.

"We went back down that mountain, and from that day on almost all the fighting stopped," Pete said. "It was at the end of that summer my grandfather gave me the name Hastin Naat'aanni, Man Speaking Peace. It was the name of a great Navaho leader, back more than a hundred years ago."

He had been so proud, so young and full of hopes and dreams. Pete didn't have to wonder what had happened, what had changed him. He knew damn well. Vietnam.

"That's a great story," Annie said, her voice soft in the darkness. "Thanks for telling me. Your grandfather sounds like he was really cool."

"Yeah," Pete said, closing his eyes, remembering. "He was a full Navaho. He must've been in his sixties back then, but he still had long, black hair that he kept out of his face with a headband. He was a silversmith and he traveled all the time, selling his jewelry at fairs and rodeos. When he was visiting, he'd set up a workshop in the barn. He didn't want me to go."

"Go where?"

To Vietnam. His eyes snapped open. Oh, man, what was he doing? Had he actually forgotten who he was, why he was here? Peter Taylor hadn't gone to Vietnam. "To New York University," he said, glad he had a ready answer.

"Why *did* you go?" she asked, her voice slipping

through the dark of the room as if it were something he could reach out and touch.

"I had to," he said simply.

"You didn't *have* to," she said. "Nobody *has* to do something if he doesn't want to."

"Not true," he said. "There are some things that you have no choice about."

He had to get back on track, Pete thought. They had to stop talking about him, and focus the conversation on her. He had to get her talking about Athens, about England and about the people she had met with there. But how?

"Annie."

She closed her eyes, loving the way he said her name, and knowing that she shouldn't. "Mmm-hmm?"

"If you ever find yourself in any kind of trouble," he said slowly, searching for the right words to say, "I hope that you'll come to me and let me help you."

The room was suddenly silent. The little sounds Annie made—all the restless movement, the whisper of sheets, even the sound of her breathing—all stopped. Fifteen seconds, twenty seconds, the silence stretched on and on….

"Taylor, I can't figure out what you're trying to say," Annie finally said. "Why don't you do me a favor and just say it?"

Pete laughed, unable to hold it in. Man, this woman was too much…. "Okay," he said. "I guess what I'm trying to say is, if you're somehow involved with this art robbery thing, and you're in too deep, I wish you would tell me, because I can help you."

There were another few seconds of silence. Then Annie said, "Thanks, Taylor, that's really sweet. Good night."

CHAPTER EIGHT

WAFFLES. ANNIE WOKE UP WANTING waffles. It didn't happen too often—only about twice a year—but when the urge came upon her, she'd get the waffle iron down from the top shelf of the kitchen cabinet, pull out the one-hundred-percent pure maple syrup and actually spend more than her usual five minutes in the kitchen.

She climbed out of bed, pulled her bathrobe on over her pajamas, found her slippers and shuffled into the kitchen.

A short time later, the batter was nearly entirely blended, and the waffle iron was heating and Annie was rummaging through the refrigerator, looking for the maple syrup. She spotted the glass bottle way, way in the back. Almost diving in headfirst, she triumphantly pulled it out, only to discover it was nearly empty.

"Oh, shoot," she said crossly. She turned the waffle iron down to the very lowest setting, and went back into her bedroom.

Pete was in the bathroom. Annie could hear the sound of the shower running, so she quickly pulled on her jeans and a sweatshirt and slipped her feet into her sneakers. She ran her brush quickly through her hair, and pulled it back into a ponytail, then grabbed her purse and her car keys.

She was nearly out the front door when she realized she should probably leave a note for Pete. She quickly scrawled one on the back of an envelope, and left it at the bottom of the stairs.

Her car started grouchily in the cold morning air, and Annie found herself wishing that she'd taken the time to grab her jacket from where she had left it in the office. It was only a few minutes' ride to the grocery store, though, so she didn't go back for it.

She parked in a space close to the store, and ran to get inside quickly. The automatic doors opened with a mechanical swish, then closed behind her. She didn't bother to get a shopping cart or even a basket, going straight to the aisle that held the boxed pancake mixes and the syrup. There were shelves and shelves of the cheap, imitation syrup, but only one brand of the real stuff. It was from Vermont, no less. She took the glass bottle to the express line and was standing there, cheerfully reading the headlines on the sensational gossip newspapers, when she was roughly grabbed.

Startled, she let out a yelp before she realized who had grabbed her.

Pete.

He was barefoot, wearing only his jeans and an unbuttoned shirt. His hair was wet and he brushed a drop of water from his nose as he glared angrily at her.

"What the hell did you think you were doing?" he said, his voice getting steadily louder until the very last word was practically roared.

The cashier looked at him curiously, and rang up Annie's maple syrup.

"I had to get this," Annie said, wide-eyed, motioning to the syrup. "You were in the shower, so—"

He was holding her tightly, his fingers encircling her upper arm. "So you should've waited until I got out, dammit," he spat out.

He was furious, and he wasn't trying to hide it. She could see the muscles in his jaw working, the force of his anger in his eyes. She had never seen such emotion on his usually carefully controlled face.

"Four dollars and seventy-nine cents," the cashier said, snapping her gum and watching them with unconcealed interest.

Before Annie could take her wallet from her purse, Pete threw a five dollar bill down on the counter and snatched up the bottle of maple syrup. He pulled her toward the door with him. "You are to go *no*where without me," he said, his voice harsh. The mechanical door didn't open fast enough for him, and he slammed it with the palm of his hand, pushing it, accentuating his words. "*No*where."

As they stepped out into the parking lot, out into the cold, crisp air, Annie pulled free of him, taking the maple syrup possessively and stashing it in her purse. "Oh, come on, Taylor," she said, getting angry herself. What gave him the right to drag her out of the store and shout at her in front of the entire town? What gave him the right to tell her what to do, anyway?

"No. *You* come on, Annie. You're a smart lady." Pete made a tremendous effort to lower his voice, and his words were clipped, spoken through tightly clenched teeth with a quietness that sounded far more dangerous than his outburst. "Nowhere means *no*where. I don't want you stepping outside of the *house* without me, do you understand?"

When he couldn't find her in the house, he had been so scared, he could barely breathe. There was some kind of electric frying pan in the kitchen, and the power had been left on. There was a mixing bowl filled with something on the counter, eggs and flour all over the place. The first thing he thought was that somehow she'd been snatched right out from underneath his nose. Her car keys and purse were missing, but her jacket was right where she'd thrown it last night. He had been damn close to calling the FBI when he found her little scribbled note at the foot of the stairs.

And the fear that had tightened his chest had turned instantly to anger. White-hot, burning, seething anger.

But fear gripped him again as he raced to the grocery store without even taking time to pull on his boots. What if someone had been watching, waiting for the moment when she was alone, unprotected...?

"Aren't you getting a little carried away, Taylor?" Annie said, her own eyes flashing with anger now, her breath making a white mist in the cold air. "I only went to the grocery store, for crying out loud."

She turned on her heel and started toward her car. But Pete caught her arm, spinning her around, hard, to face him.

"What, you think you can't get killed in a grocery store?" he said roughly. "Think again, Annie. I've seen more victims of assassins' bullets than I care to remember—every one of them killed because they were careless, because they didn't think they needed protection while they ran to the bank or the pharmacy. *Or* the grocery store."

She tried to pull free, but his hands were on her shoulders, and he wouldn't let go.

"You can *not* go out by yourself," he said, his eyes burning with intensity as he tried to make her understand how important this was. "Annie, there's someone out there who says that he wants you *dead*." His voice broke with emotion. "Damn it—"

She was staring up at him, her lips slightly parted. Her long hair had come free of its restraint, and it hung down around her face, moving slightly in the chill wind. Pete didn't notice the cold air blowing against the bare muscles of his chest. He was unaware of the cold, sharp pebbles of the parking lot underneath his bootless feet. All he could see, all he could feel, was Annie. He was drowning. Drowning in the shimmering blue ocean of her eyes...

He wasn't sure how it happened, but suddenly she wasn't trying to pull away from him anymore. Suddenly she was in his arms and he was kissing her.

He wasn't supposed to be doing this.

Her lips opened under his, and he plundered the sweetness of her mouth desperately. He wanted more than just a taste, he wanted to consume her, totally, absolutely, utterly.

Her mouth was softer and sweeter than he'd ever dreamed, so soft, yet meeting the fierceness of his kisses with an equally wild hunger. She clung to him, one hand in his hair, pulling his head down toward her, the other up underneath his shirt, exploring his muscular back, driving him insane.

He shouldn't be doing this.

He groaned, pulling her even closer to him, pressing her hips in tightly against him, kissing her harder, deeper, longer. He kissed her with all the frustration, all the pent-up passion of the past few weeks. Man, he'd wanted to kiss this woman since he first set eyes on her from behind the one-way mirror in the airport interrogation room.

He shouldn't be doing this.

She moved, rubbing against his arousal, and he heard himself make a sound—a low, animal-like growl in the back of his throat. Oh, man, he wanted her more than he'd ever wanted anything in his life. He wanted to bury himself deep in her heat, deep inside of her. He wanted to make love to her and never stop, never stop, never…

Stop.

He shouldn't be doing this.

It wasn't right.

He couldn't do this.

Kendall Peterson, a.k.a. Pete Taylor, was a strong man, but he didn't know how strong he was until he pulled away from that kiss.

Annie stared up at him, her eyes molten with desire, her cheeks flushed and her lips swollen from the force of his mouth on hers. He watched her chest rise and fall rapidly with each breath she took, saw the pebbled outline of her taut nipples even underneath the thick material of her sweatshirt.

"Pete," she breathed, reaching for him.

Somehow he kept her at arm's length. "Get in your car," he said hoarsely. "I'll follow you home."

FOR THE HUNDREDTH TIME THAT afternoon, Annie found herself staring sightlessly at her lab equipment, unable to concentrate. She looked across the room to where Pete was sitting and pretending to read a newspaper. He had to be pretending—he hadn't turned the page in over an hour.

As she watched him, he glanced up, meeting her eyes. His expression was so guarded, he might have been carved from stone. In a flash, she remembered the way his face had looked after he had kissed her. She'd read so many things in his eyes. She'd seen desire, but no, it was more than mere desire. It was hunger—a burning, scorching need. But she'd also seen confusion and uncertainty. And fear.

Annie sighed, glancing over to the other side of the room, where Cara was working. Cara had been in the office when they'd come back from the grocery store.

Pete had just kissed Annie like no other man in her

life had ever kissed her, and she had a million things to say to him, only they had no chance to talk, no privacy to continue what they'd started. And she got the feeling that he was relieved about that.

That feeling turned to certainty as the day wore on and Pete made a point to keep Cara around, like a chaperon at a high school dance. And those rare times when Cara was out of the room, he managed to be on the telephone.

Annie restarted the test she was running, a test to check the purity of a bronze knife blade, and sighed again. He'd kissed her, and suddenly it all seemed so clear to her, so obvious. Sure, they were friends. It was true that she liked him on that level. But there was no way she would've reacted the way she had to a kiss from a mere friend. That kiss had been more disturbingly intimate, more earth-shatteringly intoxicating than anything she had ever felt before.

No, there was more than mere friendship here.

Truth was, she was falling in love with this man.

And he was scared to death of her.

ANNIE LOOKED AT CARA ACROSS the office. "Well, shoot," she finally said with a smile. "It's about time."

Cara nervously fiddled with the toys on her desk. "It still seems so sudden to me," she said. "I mean, marriage…"

"MacLeish, you've known the man for three years." Annie shook her head.

"But as friends," Cara said. "We were just friends."

"I can't think of a better way to start," Annie said quietly. "Have you set a wedding date?"

Cara grinned. "Jerry wants us to fly to Las Vegas this weekend."

"Good old Jerry," Annie said, rolling her eyes. "Always the romantic."

They both were quiet for a moment, then Annie asked, "So, are you trying to work up the courage to give me notice?"

Cara looked up, shocked. "No!" she said. "I mean, I don't know.... You know, Jerry's trying to get funding to go to Mexico in February...."

"You're irreplaceable, MacLeish," Annie told her. "But don't worry, somehow I'll muddle through."

"I'll definitely stay until the end of December," Cara said. "Remember, we were going to take January off anyway...."

Annie turned away, not wanting her friend to see the sadness that she knew must be on her face. January was looking to be a very cold, very lonely month, with both MacLeish and Taylor leaving for good.... She managed to smile at Cara as she left the room, though. "Congratulate Tillet for me, will you?"

CHAPTER NINE

FROM THE LAB, ANNIE HEARD THE sound of the door closing as Cara left for the evening. She heard Pete slide the bolt home and turn on the alarm system.

This was it. They were finally alone in the house, just the two of them.

She heard the sound of Pete's cowboy boots on the hardwood floor of the entryway, and her heart went into her throat. Turning, she saw him standing in the doorway. His face was carefully expressionless, but there was a tenseness about the way he was standing, an infinitesimal tightness in his shoulders. He was as nervous as she, Annie realized.

"I'm sending out for a pizza," he said.

It was the first full sentence he'd spoken to her since they'd gotten home from the grocery store, since that kiss.

"Want to split it?" he asked. "There's a place in town that delivers. Tony's. Unless you know some-place better...."

He was trying to pretend nothing had happened, Annie thought. He was standing there talking about the best place in town to get a pizza, when they should have been addressing the fact that that morning he had taken her into his arms and nearly kissed the living daylights out of her.

His casualness didn't come as a surprise—not after the way he'd avoided her all day. He was telling her, not in so many words of course, but he *was* telling her that he regretted the kiss, that it had been a mistake.

Disappointment shot through her, and she turned away, not wanting him to see it in her eyes.

"You know, if you're not done working, I can wait to call," Pete offered. "'Course, it'll be about forty-five minutes before the pizza's delivered even if I call now."

Her composure regained, Annie looked at him. From the tips of his boots to the top of his short, dark hair, the man was extremely easy on the eyes. Faded blue jeans cut loose, but not loose enough to hide the taut muscles of his legs—long, strong legs—stretched way up over narrow hips. His plain brown leather belt with the shining buckle encircled his trim waist. He was wearing a heavy white canvas shirt, the kind with snap fasteners instead of buttons, open at the throat, sleeves rolled up to just below his elbows.

He drove his hands deep into the pockets of his jeans, and the tanned, sinewy muscles of his forearms strained the fabric of his shirt. His shoulders were broad, his chest powerful.

And that was just his body.

Inside that perfectly shaped head, behind those intense dark eyes, underneath that thick, black hair, beneath the movie-star features, was a mind and a soul that Annie couldn't help but like, couldn't help but fall in love with.

But he didn't want her. Not the way she wanted him. If he did, he wouldn't be acting so business-as-usual, would he?

"Pizza sounds great, Taylor," she said, keeping her tone light. "Forty-five minutes'll give me just enough time to finish up in here."

He turned so that his face was in the shadows. "I'll call from the office," he said, and disappeared.

It was clear, Annie thought later as they ate their pizza, that to Pete, the morning's kiss had been an aberration, a slipup, a mistake. Their conversation wasn't as stilted or awkward as Annie had feared it would be, but Pete's face never lost its carefully guarded expression. And his eyes never even once lit with the heat she'd seen that morning—not even when they accidentally collided in the small kitchen as they prepared a salad to go with the pizza. He'd reached out to steady her, and she'd looked up into his face. But his eyes were distant, emotionless.

After dinner, Annie spent several restless hours in her office, putting little more than a small dent in the paperwork that sat on her desk. As she sat there, buried in files, Pete's eyes seemed to haunt her. Even though he wasn't in the room, she could still see his eyes, so detached, almost cold.

Oh, Christmas, she thought suddenly, sitting up straight in her chair. *What if it was me? What if I threw myself at him this morning?*

How exactly had it happened? Who kissed who first? She closed her eyes, trying to think back.

Pete had been so angry, holding her arms tightly enough to bruise her. She'd been trying to pull away from him, hadn't she? But he just held on to her; he wouldn't let go. She remembered staring up at him, intrigued by the sparks of anger that seemed to fly from his eyes, startled by the raw emotion displayed on his face. She remembered seeing the fire in his eyes change to a heat of an entirely different kind. And then she remembered him bending to kiss her.

He kissed her. Yes, she thought with relief, he definitely kissed her. Thank goodness she could remember. It wasn't that she necessarily minded making a fool of herself. But she hated the thought of not being aware she'd made a fool of herself. *That* was too much to take. But it was okay. She *hadn't*—

"You working or sleeping?" Pete's husky voice cut into her thoughts and her eyes flew open. He was leaning in the doorway, with his arms crossed in front of him, watching her.

Annie grinned wryly. "Would you believe neither?" she said.

"It's nearly midnight," he said quietly, his eyes following her movements as she shut off the computer and restacked the files, putting them into her in basket. As she pushed her shining hair back behind one ear. As she unconsciously moistened her lips with the tip of her tongue…

Oh, damn, thought Pete. He'd spent the entire day and evening trying to fool himself into believing he was unaffected by that kiss. He'd tried to ignore the fact that when he kissed her, she'd kissed him, too. She wanted him. Even now, even though she was trying to hide it, he could see it in her eyes.

All he had to do was say the word, and he could have her.

But while making love to her would certainly solve tonight's immediate and pressing problem, it would generate a vast array of other, even more difficult future problems. If he slept with her without telling her who he really was, she would hate him.

On the other hand, if he told her who he was *before* he slept with her, she wouldn't sleep with him, *and* she would still probably hate him.

But maybe not as much.

Pete followed Annie up the stairs and checked the windows in the bedroom while she went into the bathroom and got ready for bed.

Maybe if she didn't hate him quite so much, he'd still have a chance....

To what?

To have a future with her?

Ruthlessly, he crushed that thought, pushing it away, out of sight.

Pete refocused his attention on the sound of water running in the bathroom. Annie was brushing her teeth. She'd be out any minute now.

He locked the door to the bedroom and sat down heavily on his bedroll.

Tomorrow would be easier, he thought. All he had to do was get through tonight. He closed his eyes, hoping, praying to whatever gods were listening, that Annie wouldn't try to talk about that kiss.

He'd been waiting for her to say something all through dinner. He'd never even tasted the pizza, he'd been wound so tight. He'd half expected her to reach out for him, to touch him, to try to finish what they'd begun.

Expected? Or hoped?

No, he couldn't hope for it. As much as he wanted to kiss her again, he couldn't even allow that much to happen.

Because if she touched him, she'd know. And how the hell was he going to explain why he wouldn't make love to her when he wanted her so badly, it was making him shake?

The bathroom door opened and Annie came out.

She was wearing her oversize plaid flannel pajamas, and she was brushing her hair.

Pete couldn't watch. He lay back against his pillow and closed his eyes.

It didn't help.

Annie set the brush on her bedside table, the same way she did every night, and turned off the light. She pulled the covers up over her and curled onto her side.

"Good night, Taylor," she whispered, but Pete didn't answer.

For once she could hear his breathing. It was slow and steady, as if he already were asleep.

She sighed, flipping onto her back, trying to get comfortable. She stared up at the dark ceiling, willing herself to relax.

Picture yourself on a tropical beach, she told herself, closing her eyes. Remembering the way Pete had talked her through it just a few nights ago, Annie pictured herself wading out into the warm Pacific Ocean. She imagined the clear water washing all her problems away. She imagined herself coming out of the water, taking off her silly plaid pajamas as she walked up to a beach blanket that had been spread out upon the sand. She imagined Peter Taylor lying on it, as naked as she was. He smiled up at her, reaching for her hand and pulling her down next to him, covering her mouth with his own—

Annie's eyes opened. What the heck was she doing? This was supposed to be a relaxation technique, not self-torture. How could she possibly rub salt into her own wounds by fantasizing about a man whom she *knew* wasn't interested in her?

But…

Annie squinted up through the darkness at the ceiling. Wait a minute.

She didn't really *know* he wasn't interested in her. She was only assuming it. He never actually *said* that he only wanted to be friends. He never actually *said* that he didn't want their relationship to progress any further.

Shoot, she was supposed to be some kind of brilliant scientist, and here she was *assuming* a whole hell of a lot of unproven facts….

"Taylor, you awake?"

The sound of Annie's voice came slicing through

the darkness. Pete almost jumped. Almost. Instead he continued to breathe slowly and deeply, pretending to be asleep.

Coward, he silently accused himself.

"Taylor?" she said again. Then, "Pete?"

The sound of her voice saying his first name nearly did him in. But somehow he didn't move, and he didn't answer.

Come on, Annie, he thought. *Roll on over and go to sleep.*

The sheets rustled, but she wasn't pulling them up. She was pushing them back. He heard the sound of her bare feet on the hardwood floor. Oh, damn, she was out of bed. She was walking toward him—

"Pete, wake up," she said, her voice next to him in the darkness.

He opened his eyes to see her crouched down beside him. He could just barely make out her features in the dim light from the windows.

"Go back to bed," he said. But he didn't sound very convincing, even to his own ears.

Annie sat down, cross-legged, next to him. It was obvious that she wasn't planning on going anywhere. At least not real soon. "We have to talk," she said.

Pete pushed himself up so that he was sitting, his bare back against the coolness of the wall, putting several more inches between them. Man, she was still

sitting much too close. He could smell her gentle fragrance, see the pulse beating at the delicate juncture
of her neck and collarbone. His gaze was drawn to
the deep-V neckline of her pajama top. He made
himself look away.

"Annie, go back to bed," he said, louder this time.
His eyes met hers and locked. "Please," he added, but
it was little more than a whisper.

He turned his head away, but not before Annie saw
it. It was only a flash, only a glimmer in his dark eyes,
but it was there. The same deep hunger she'd seen
that morning before he'd kissed her....

"Pete, why did you kiss me?" she asked, her
voice husky.

"I shouldn't have," he said. "I was out of line." He
braced himself to look up at her, steeling himself to
remain expressionless. "I'm sorry."

"But I'm not," she said. She frowned very slightly.
"You didn't answer my question. See, I just can't
seem to figure out why you'd go and kiss me, and
then act like I've got the plague. What's the problem?
Are you married?"

"No."

"Involved?"

He was involved more than he wanted to be, and
it was getting worse every second. "No. Annie,
please—"

"So why did you kiss me, Taylor?"

"Let's just drop this—"

"I don't want to *drop* this," she said fiercely. He was saying one thing with his words, but his eyes were telling her something entirely different. "If there's a problem, tell me what it is. If there's not a problem—" She waited until he looked up at her. "Kiss me again."

Pete drew in a long, shaky breath. "You don't know me—who I really am," he said, caught in the depths of her eyes.

"I know enough," she said. Her hair was shining in the pale light from the windows, her eyes colorless and mysterious. She reached up to touch the side of his face, but he caught her wrist.

"You wouldn't like me," he rasped.

"Isn't that for me to decide?" Annie asked.

It would have been so easy to kiss her. She was leaning toward him, inviting him....

"I can't get involved with you," he said harshly, releasing her wrist as if it burned him. "It's not possible. It's not smart—"

He saw the flash of hurt in her eyes, and it did him in. "Annie, believe me, I have no choice," he said, his voice gentler. "It's damn near killing me, but I care too much about you to start a relationship that I know won't go anywhere." He reached out, turning her chin so that she looked up at him. "You'll see, it's better if we just stay friends."

This time Annie moved toward him first, thinking that if he still told her he only wanted to be friends after she kissed him, then she'd believe him. So she kissed him.

He groaned, his voice a note of despair, as his lips and then his tongue met hers in a long, deep kiss that sent fire racing through his body.

His arms went around her, pulling her toward him, closer, closer, until she was on his lap, pressed against him, and still that wasn't close enough.

He kissed her, again and again, almost frantically now as his need for her increased with each pounding beat of his heart. She received him feverishly, her hands sweeping down his back, over his chest and arms, as if she couldn't get enough of touching him.

And still he kissed her.

So much for his words. So much for his good intentions.

She was straddling him now, and his hands explored the strong muscles of her thighs. Moving upward, he found the soft flannel edge of her pajama shirt and swept one hand underneath it. Annie shuddered with pleasure as his roughly callused hand caressed her back. His fingers moved down, slipping under the elastic waistband of her pajama pants, stroking the soft, smooth skin of her buttocks.

Slowly, so slowly, he tightened his grip on her, pulling her hips forward until she was positioned directly on top of him. It was exactly what he knew he shouldn't do, but he couldn't seem to stop. It was an invitation, a silent question. Did she want more?

She gave him her answer by pressing herself down against the hardness in his jeans, by moving against him.

Yes, she wanted him.

And despite his resolve, despite knowing that he shouldn't, he was going to take her. He knew now that all along he'd been fooling himself. He had no choice—that much had been true. He was aching for her, dying for her. He reached for her, and she was there, her sweet mouth against his.

You're weak, a small voice in his head accused. But he had to protest. The odds weren't exactly in his favor. It was two against one—his body and her body against his resolve to stay away from her. He didn't stand a chance.

But it wasn't right. She didn't know the truth about him.

He kissed her, determined to ignore the tiny disapproving voice that chastised him. *Don't think,* he told himself. *Don't think....*

Annie pulled her pajama top over her head, and Pete stopped thinking.

In one movement, he flipped them both over, so that he was on top of her. Her blue eyes sparkled as she smiled up at him, and he kissed her again. He started at her mouth and moved down her long, slender neck. He traveled slowly across her collar-bone and kissed his way down to her breasts, taking first one and then the other firm nipple into his mouth, caressing it with his tongue until she cried out.

He lifted his head then, gazing down at her. The sparkle in her eyes had been replaced by liquid fire. Man, he'd fantasized about her looking at him like that. He'd fantasized about having sex with her. What he *hadn't* fantasized was that sex with Annie would be the best he'd ever had in his life. But it was. He'd never felt like this before. Never. And he still had his pants on....

She smiled at him again and lifted her mouth to be kissed. He met her lips slowly, a gentle, lingering kiss that grew into an earth-shattering touching of souls.

Suddenly Pete knew what was different. Shaken, he pulled back. He rolled off her and scrambled to his feet.

Annie sat up. "Pete?"

He'd done something really stupid. Outrageously stupid. He ran his fingers through his hair. When had it happened? How could he have let it happen?

"Pete?" Annie said again. She got to her feet and took a tentative step toward him. "Are you all right?"

He'd gone and fallen in love with her.

That's what was so different. Sex with Annie wasn't simply sex, it was making love. Oh, man, he *loved* her....

She took another step toward him, concern on her beautiful face.

He had to get out of here. He had to think. He had to figure out what the hell he was going to do.

"I'm sorry," he whispered to Annie. "I'm—"

He spun on his heels, nearly leaping for the door to the hallway, leaving Annie alone in her bedroom for the first time in a week.

PETE LEANED HIS HEAD BACK against the wall and stared at the closed door that led to Annie's bedroom. This was crazy. This was ridiculous. He had never even believed in love before. He thought it didn't exist. But all the symptoms were undeniably there. He was in love with Annie, no doubt about it. It felt so much like what was described in all those silly songs he'd scoffed at for so many years, it was almost laughable. Except he didn't feel very much like laughing right now.

For the first time since he was a kid, he knew exactly what he wanted. He wanted Annie. He wanted her to fall in love with him. He wanted a chance at a future together. He wanted...forever.

Forever. Now *there* was a good joke. What were the chances that she'd want to spend forever with him after she found out he was a government agent sent to gather evidence against her?

Pete ran his fingers through his hair for the hundredth time and looked at his watch. Three-fifteen. Man, was this night never going to end?

He swore under his breath, knowing that he was in too deep. He was emotionally involved. He should be on the phone with Whitley Scott right now, making arrangements to be taken off this case.

But if he were removed from the case, who knew who they'd assign to take his place? What if the replacement agent wasn't able to protect her? There was no way he was going to trust her life to someone else. No way.

He closed his eyes for a moment. Damn, he ached all over.

He put his head in his hands, remembering the look on Annie's face as he bolted for the door. Talk about coitus interruptus, he thought with a strangled groan. She must think he was nuts, the way he jumped up like that, right in the middle of such serious foreplay.

He groaned again. She must not be very happy with him right now. He doubted if Miss Manners had a book on sexual etiquette, but he was willing to bet if she did, she would frown heavily upon a gentleman heating a lady up and then leaving her out in the cold.

But if Pete had made love to Annie, if they'd gone all the way, he'd have blown his chance at a future with her. When she found out he was CIA, she would assume he'd been assigned to seduce the art robbery information out of her. Which he had. Which was why he couldn't... This was *way* too complicated.

ANNIE WOKE UP TO THE CLOCK RADIO, and lay in bed for at least half an hour, listening to the country station and wishing that Pete was lying next to her.

But Pete didn't want her.

A tear slipped out and slid down her cheek, and she wiped it quickly away.

Why hadn't she listened to him? It was the same question that had kept her tossing and turning all night long, and the only answer she could come up with was that she was a fool. He had told her in no uncertain terms that he only wanted to be friends. But no, she had to go and throw herself at him. She had to go and try to show him how wrong he was. But she was the one who had been wrong.

It wasn't fair, but love never was. There was never a guarantee that two people would feel the same way about each other. In fact, it seemed like happy, mutual love was the exception rather than the rule. Why else would there be so many songs about unrequited love? Four out of seven of the country songs she'd heard that morning had that age old "you-don't-love-me-as-much-as-I-love-you" theme.

Another tear escaped, and Annie brushed it away. What was it Cara always said? Look on the bright side.

She stared up at the ceiling, trying to find the bright side as another song started. Look on the bright side, she thought. At least this had happened before she let herself fall in love with him.

But deep down inside, she knew that was a lie.

THAT NIGHT, PETE LAY ON HIS bedroll in the dark, waiting for Annie to ask him if he was awake.

The day had seemed endless, with Annie avoiding him when she could and being distantly polite when she couldn't.

He'd apologized, and she'd shrugged it off, telling him to forget it, it was her fault.

Pete frowned. She'd seemed so flip, so casual. Was it possible she didn't care? Was it possible that all she'd wanted was a quick roll in the hay?

No. He'd seen the hurt in her eyes, hurt that she couldn't hide. He closed his eyes, flooded by a wave of shame and remorse. His only comfort was knowing that he would be feeling equal amounts of shame and remorse if he *had* made love to her. Not to mention an additional dose of guilt.

Come on, Annie, he thought, lying there on the floor of her room. *Talk to me.*

But she didn't say a word.

CHAPTER TEN

CARA LOOKED AT ANNIE SPECULATIVELY. "Why?"

"Does it really matter why?" Annie asked.

"You're asking me to spend all my waking hours over the next three days virtually locked in the lab," Cara said, crossing her arms. "Is it so strange for me to want to know why?"

With a sigh, Annie got up and closed the office door. "If we work overtime, we can get a sample of Marshall's death mask ready to go to the carbon-dating lab by the end of the week. Then it'll only be another week, maybe two before we get the results. *Then* both the death mask *and* the people making those threats will be out of my hair."

"Pete Taylor will be out of your hair, too," Cara commented.

"Yes," Annie agreed. "Taylor, too."

Cara leaned back in her desk chair, eyes narrowing. "I thought you were starting to really like this guy."

"Yeah," Annie said, looking away. "I was."

"So why do you suddenly want to get rid of him?" Cara asked, lazily reaching out to bob the spring-attached head of her Homer Simpson doll. "What happened?"

"Nothing," Annie said.

"What, did he put the moves on you?" Cara asked, grinning. "Did he come on too strong, too fast?"

Annie put her head down on her desk.

"Give the guy a break," Cara said. "You should see the way he looks at you. It's like he's been struck by lightning—"

"He's just embarrassed," Annie said, looking up at Cara, her own cheeks flushing slightly from the memory. "I...well, I sort of... I tried to seduce him. But he just wants to be friends."

"You're kidding," Cara said, looking very shocked. "You mean you...? And he *didn't...?*"

Annie buried her face in her hands. "You got it."

"But I've seen him look at you like he's totally in love with you," Cara protested.

"Well, you're wrong," Annie said sadly. "He's not."

THE FRONT DOORBELL RANG, AND Pete put down his book. He went out into the foyer, checking the gun in his shoulder holster before opening the door.

Three men stood on the front porch. A van was in the driveway behind them; a colorful sign on the side read Mt. Kisco Security Systems.

"Dr. Morrow?" the older of the three men said.

"No," Pete said.

"We're here to install a burglar alarm," the man said, glancing at his clipboard, checking the address.

"Wait here," Pete said, and closed and locked the door, leaving them outside.

He swore silently to himself as he walked down the hall to Annie's office. This was really going to mess things up. With the system upgraded, he'd have no reason to sleep in Annie's room. And if he didn't sleep in her room, they'd never get back to the same friendly, easygoing relationship they'd had before.

He knocked on the office door.

"Come in," Annie's musical voice called.

He opened the door.

She was sitting at her desk, wearing a long-sleeved, flower-print T-shirt and her faded jeans. Her long hair was pulled back into a ponytail, making her look more like a college coed than a Ph.D. As she looked up at him, there was apprehension on her face.

Pete swore to himself again, but for an entirely different reason. "There are some guys at the door," he managed to say expressionlessly. "From Mt. Kisco Security. Did you call them?"

She stood up. "Yeah," she said. "I thought it would be a good idea to get the new system installed as soon as possible." Her cheeks flushed slightly, but she met his eyes solidly. "I thought it would make it easier…for both of us."

"What kind of system are they going to put in?" Pete asked, following her down the hallway.

He wasn't happy about this. Annie wasn't sure how she knew since his face betrayed nothing. But she did know. "The same kind you wanted that other company to install," she answered. "I wrote down the model number and the manufacturer's name. This company had the equipment in stock, and the manpower to do it today…."

"All right." Pete nodded and turned to open the door.

Later that afternoon, he called Scott to inform him of the setback to the investigation. Scott told Pete to get what he needed, and then get out. When he hung up the phone, Pete cursed softly.

THE DAYS SPED PAST WITH ANNIE and Cara spending nearly three straight days and nights in the lab. Cara often didn't leave before midnight, and Annie frequently worked until two or two-thirty in the morning.

With the new alarm system installed, Pete slept in

the guest bedroom. He moved the bed so that he could clearly see the new secondary burglar alarm control panel that had been installed next to Annie's bedroom door. If he woke up in the night, he could look over across the hall and be reassured. A red light meant the system was on-line and working. Green would mean it had been shut off.

Regardless of the new security system, Pete insisted that both bedroom doors be left open. But despite the fact that Annie was just across the hall, it seemed as if she were miles away.

He was no closer to finding out about her involvement in the art robberies than he'd been before. And he was slowly going crazy, wanting to hold her, wanting to make love to her....

Pete was plagued by the notion that if he *had* made love to her that night, she probably would have opened up to him by now and told him if she was involved in anything illegal. And if he had made love to her, he wouldn't have to face that flash of hurt confusion that even now still sometimes crossed her face. And, if he had made love to her that night, he probably would have made love to her the next night, and the next, and the night after....

Instead, he sat with her as she ate her lunch and dinner, telling her stories about his grandfather, about his childhood. They were pieces of himself he hadn't shared with anyone, secrets he'd kept locked away since Vietnam. In Vietnam, he hadn't talked about himself; he never got personal, he hadn't made friends. In Vietnam, if you made friends, you had to watch those friends die.

And after the war, when he'd joined the agency, he was always on assignment, always undercover. His past was fictional, part of an assigned bio.

Pete Taylor hadn't grown up on a ranch in Colorado. But Kendall Peterson had, and despite knowing better, despite being unable to tell her his real name, Pete wanted Annie to know who he was, who he *really* was.

And he wanted to make her smile again.

ON THURSDAY, THE DOORBELL RANG, and Annie peeked through the window to see a stranger on the front porch. She pushed the button on the intercom that had been installed with the new security system and buzzed Pete, who was up in the kitchen.

"Yeah," he said, his voice sounding surprisingly clear over the cheap speaker. "What's up?"

"There's an unidentified male Caucasian outside the door," she reported. "He's approximately forty-five years old, wearing a dark business suit and a black overcoat. He hasn't smiled yet, but he doesn't quite seem the fanged wolfman type...."

The doorbell rang again.

"Just the facts, ma'am," Pete said, coming down the stairs and smiling at her. "No speculation, please."

Annie's heart flipped until she remembered that his smile was only a smile. He wanted to be friends, nothing more. "He *does* look like a thug," she said. "And *that's* a fact."

Pete's tweed jacket had been casually draped over the end of the banister, and he picked it up and slipped it on over his T-shirt, hiding the brown leather straps of his shoulder holster.

"Stay back, okay?" Pete said, and Annie nodded. He pushed the override button that would allow them to open the front door without shutting down the entire system. The light on the control panel still glowed red, but now there was an additional orange light signaling that the front door could be opened without triggering the alarm.

He opened the door. "Can I help you?" he asked the man politely, but with no nonsense in his tone. He adjusted the lapels of his jacket, pulling it back slightly on the left side so that his gun was briefly, but quite clearly revealed. It was no accident, Annie knew.

If the man standing on the porch was at all disturbed by the sight of the gun, he didn't show it. "You must be the butler," he said dryly.

"Something like that," Pete said.

The man held out a business card. "I'm looking for Dr. Anne Morrow," he said. "She at home?"

Pete took the card. He glanced down at it, then handed it back, behind the door, to Annie. "Joseph James," it said. "Antiquities Broker." There was a New York City address and telephone number.

"What's this in reference to?" Pete asked.

"I'm afraid I can discuss that only with Dr. Morrow," James replied smoothly.

Pete's gaze flicked back to James's face. The man's nose was flat, as if it had been broken many times. There were several small scars up by his eyebrows, and a longer one on the left side of his jaw. Antiquities broker and knee breaker, he thought.

"So. May I come in?" James asked.

"No," Pete said pleasantly. "We're not inviting anyone inside these days." He leaned closer and added almost conspiratorially, "We're having a little problem with evil spirits."

"Lookit, I have a business matter to discuss with Dr. Morrow," James said. "So if you don't mind...?"

Pete looked back at Annie, who told him with a shrug that she didn't recognize the name on the card.

"If you want to talk to her, I'm going to have to search you first," Pete explained in that same pleasant tone.

James stared at him. "You're kidding, right?"

Pete stepped out onto the porch, pulling the door most of the way shut behind him. "Hands on the top of your head, legs spread," he said. "Please."

"Lookit," James said. "I'm carrying. But I've got a license, it's legal."

"Hands on your head, legs spread," Pete said again.

James crossed his arms, his patience obviously flagging. "I know you're just doing your job, buddy, but why don't you let it go. I didn't come out here to shoot Dr. Morrow. I came to talk."

"Hands on your—"

"Will you give me a break?" he said. Annoyed, James moved past Pete, reaching for the door.

It happened so fast, Annie realized that if she had blinked she would have missed it. One second James was heading toward the door, and the next, Pete had him backed up against the porch's sturdy wooden pillar, his gun dangerously close to the broker's face, his other arm pressed up under the man's chin. Annie rubbed her neck, remembering how unpleasant that felt.

"Taylor, is everything okay?" she called out, stepping into the doorway.

"Hey, lady," James squeaked. "Call off Fido, will you?"

Pete released James, but still held his gun trained unwaveringly at the center of the man's chest. "Please keep your hands on your head," he said calmly.

"You wanted to talk to me, Mr. James?" Annie asked.

James rested his hands reluctantly on the top of his thinning hair. "This wasn't exactly what I had in mind," he said crossly.

"I'm sorry," Annie apologized. "There've been a number of threats to my life recently. Taylor likes to err on the side of caution."

"Does he do this to all your customers?" James asked. "It must be great for business."

"Please get to the point," Pete said. "Dr. Morrow is very busy."

James gave Pete a black look, then turned toward Annie. "In that case, I'll be as brief as I possibly can. I have a client, Dr. Morrow, who is interested in purchasing the gold death mask owned by one Benjamin Sullivan that is currently in your possession. This client will pay four million, sight unseen, uncertified."

Annie's mouth fell open. "You can't be serious."

"I'm quite serious," James said. "My client is willing to give you a broker's fee of ten percent if you submit this offer to Mr. Sullivan and convince him to sell."

With great difficulty, Annie closed her mouth. "But I haven't authenticated it yet," she said. "It may not be genuine."

"My client wants this artifact, authentic or not," James said. "In fact, my client has a personal relationship with another authenticator, and would prefer that authenticator check the piece out instead of you."

Annie nodded slowly. "What's so special about this death mask?" she asked.

James smiled. Annie was reminded of a shark. "My client is…shall we say, eccentric? I'm afraid I'm not at liberty to discuss his motives any further."

"Ten percent of four million, huh?" Annie asked. "I'm assuming the transaction will be legal, with contracts and taxes paid…."

"Of course," James said, sounding affronted.

"Why can't you broker this yourself?" she asked, direct as usual.

James shrugged. "I've tried. Mr. Sullivan won't take my calls."

"What makes you think he'll take mine?"

"My *client* thinks he'll take your call," James said. "I think it's a gamble, just like anything else. Except this is one sweet gamble for you. You stand to lose nothing, or gain four hundred G's."

Annie thought about that for several long

moments. "All right," she finally said. "I'll talk to Sullivan, and get back to you."

Annie and Pete watched in silence as Joseph James got into his Cadillac and pulled out of the driveway.

"Four hundred thousand dollars," Annie said wistfully as Pete closed and locked the door, and turned off the override to the alarm. The control panel glowed with a single red light.

"That's a lot of peanut butter and jelly," he said.

She smiled. "I could finance one hell of a field project with that much money," she said, warming to the subject. "I could back Tillet's dig in Mexico. I could cohead the excavation, get my hands dirty for a year or so, learn something new…. Do you know how long it's been since I've been camping?"

Pete shook his head, smiling at her excitement. "No."

"*Too* long," she said with a grin and disappeared into the office.

BENJAMIN SULLIVAN WAS BACK in town, and he greeted Annie warmly when he picked up the phone. "You know," he said, in his upper-crust Bostonian accent, "I had dinner with your parents two evenings ago."

"How are they?" Annie asked. "*Where* are they?"

"Fine and Paris." Sullivan chuckled. "I was on a stopover, they were on their way to Rome. Their book is coming along quite nicely. They've finished a first draft."

"Now *that's* good news," Annie said. She took a deep breath and plunged right in. "Mr. Sullivan—"

"Please, call me Ben," he interrupted. "Mr. Sullivan makes me feel so old, and I'm only in my seventies."

"Okay, Ben." Annie briefly outlined the offer for the death mask.

Ben didn't answer right away. "Well," he finally said. "This is a bit unfortunate, isn't it? The contract with Mr. Marshall has been signed. Even though it's only for a tenth of what the other collector is offering." He sighed. "I suppose we might be able to try to wriggle out of the deal," he said, "but that's just not for me. I guess being honest costs a bit of money, but in the long run, it's worth it. At least I hope it is." The old man laughed, then went on. "Strange, though, that this offer didn't come until now—I had put the word out that the piece was for sale some time ago." He paused for a moment. "No matter. I can't do it."

"I see," Annie said.

Ben chuckled. "You sound disappointed, Annie. What was your take going to be? Ten percent?"

Annie laughed. "Yeah. The money could have come in handy. I have a friend who's looking for funding for a project in Mexico, and ten percent of four million would've been perfect."

"Anyone I know?" Ben asked, interest evident in his voice.

"Do you know Jerry Tillet?" Annie said.

"Haven't met him," Ben said. "But I've heard only good things. Mayan specialist, if I remember correctly."

"That's him. He's found a site that he believes was a major trading center. The dig's scheduled to start in February, if he can find the backing."

"Sounds exciting," Ben said. "I'll have my accountant look into it, see what I can do to help out."

Annie laughed. "Oh, that's terrific."

"I've got to get back to work," he said. "I'm sorry I can't accept Mr. James's client's offer."

"Let me know if you change your mind," Annie said and hung up the phone.

She looked up to find Pete standing in the doorway, watching her. She made a face at him. "Sullivan won't sell," she explained, "but he's thinking about backing Tillet's project, so it wasn't an entire washout."

She shuffled the papers around on her desk, searching for Joseph James's business card. She quickly dialed his number and left a brief message on his answering machine, then tossed the business card into the top drawer of her desk.

Pete came into the office and sat down across from her. Annie looked up to find his dark eyes on her. She couldn't look away, trapped by his gaze. He was looking at her as if he wanted…what? She knew he didn't want her, so what did that heat in his eyes mean? Damn, damn, *damn*—she couldn't figure this guy out for the life of her.

The phone rang, loud and shrill.

Annie jumped. "Excuse me," she said to Pete, then picked up the receiver.

Pete watched her glance up at him, then swivel her chair so that she turned slightly away. "I haven't been avoiding you," he heard her say. She was talking to Nick York. It had to be him. Pete resisted the urge to clench his teeth.

"All right," Annie said, laughter in her voice. "Yeah, you're right. Okay! I give in. I *have* been avoiding you." She paused, then laughed. "Yeah, but if you bring anything with you, it had better be flowers, not some archaeological find you want me to test." She laughed again. "Don't count on it, pal."

Pete stood up, unwilling to listen to Annie being flirted with over the telephone. Particularly not by someone who was probably far better suited for her than he was….

Annie watched Pete leave the room. Before he closed the door, he glanced back at her, briefly meeting her eyes.

It was that look again, Annie realized. He wanted something, and he wanted it badly. Too bad it wasn't her.

CHAPTER ELEVEN

FRIDAY MORNING DAWNED BRIGHT and clear—a perfect autumn day. Despite working late the night before, Annie woke up early and pulled on her rattiest pair of jeans, an old sleeveless T-shirt and a sweater whose collar was starting to come undone. She rummaged in her closet, searching for a moment before she located several pairs of work gloves.

Whistling, she crossed the hall to Pete's room.

The door was open as usual, but he was still in bed. His hair was getting longer, and it was rumpled. He needed a shave, and his night's growth of beard made him look dangerous, particularly with his shirt off and so much hard muscle showing.

Annie steeled herself against the attraction that threatened to overpower her whenever they were together. She tossed the larger pair of gloves onto his chest.

Pete stared down at them for a moment, then up

at Annie, one eyebrow quirked. "If you're challeng-
ing me to a duel," he said, "you missed."

Annie grinned. "It's leaf-raking day," she said.

Pete rolled over to look at his alarm clock. "Didn't
we just go to sleep?" he asked.

Annie crossed to the window and pulled up the
shade. Sunlight flooded the room. "How can you
sleep on a day like today?"

Pete squinted from the brightness. "Leaf-raking
day, huh?"

"Hurry up and get dressed," Annie said. "I want
to go outside. If we work fast, we can get most of the
lawn done before Cara even gets here."

She turned to leave, but Pete's voice stopped her.
"Annie."

He was pulling on his jeans, and her eyes were
drawn to his hands as he fastened the button and
pulled up the zipper. *Oh, Christmas, stare, why don't
you,* she chastised herself, feeling her cheeks flush.

"I'm not sure if this is such a good idea," Pete said,
gracefully ignoring her discomfort. "You're much
safer inside the house. Out in the yard, you're a
target. It's harder for me to protect you."

"You know, Taylor," Annie said, "a perfect day like
this doesn't come along all that often. I'm sorry, but
I can't let it pass me by. I'll wait for you downstairs."

When Cara's car finally pulled into the driveway,

Annie and Pete hadn't finished raking half of the big yard. The day was unusually warm, and Annie had long since stripped off her sweater. Even with only her old T-shirt on, she had sweat running down her back and trickling between her breasts.

"Darn," Annie said. "Guess I miscalculated how long this would take."

Pete leaned on his rake and looked at her. It was that look again, Annie thought, nervously tucking a loose strand of hair behind her ear. Why did he watch her that way? With his shirt off, and his upper body glistening with perspiration, she couldn't bear to look at him. Instead, she turned and watched Cara climb out of her car.

"If you promise to keep the alarm on after you go inside," Pete said, "I'll finish up."

"Oh," Annie said, glancing back at him. "No…"

"I don't mind," he insisted. "In fact, it feels good to be out here. But you've got to promise to let the answering machine pick up all the phone calls. And if anything strange happens—anything at all—you call me. Immediately. Is that clear?"

She smiled. "Yeah."

He reached out, and for one heart-stopping moment, Annie thought he was going to touch her, to pull her in close to him. But he only plucked a leaf from her hair and tossed it to the ground. She turned quickly then, and nearly ran back to the house, hoping that he hadn't seen the hope that she knew had briefly flared in her eyes.

She tried to comfort herself by counting the days until the carbon-dating test results on Stands Against the Storm's death mask would come in. Eight more days at the most, maybe even less. Eight more days, and then he would be gone.

Now, why didn't that make her feel any better?

ANNIE TOOK A GALLON OF ICE TEA and a pile of peanut-butter-and-jelly sandwiches out to Pete at lunchtime. She sat and ate with him, then closed her eyes and let the sun warm her face.

She'd showered and changed earlier that morning, and she now wore a bright yellow T-shirt with her jeans. Her hair was down loose around her shoulders, shining as it moved slightly in the gentle breeze.

Pete lay on his back in the grass, pretending to watch the clouds, but in truth watching Annie. Just when he thought he'd memorized every angle and plane of her face, he'd see her in a different light. With her eyes closed, her face held as if in worship up toward the sun, she looked angelic and serene— two characteristics Pete didn't normally associate with Annie Morrow.

He ached from wanting her. But every time Annie

called him Taylor, he was slapped in the face with the magnitude of the lies he had told her—was continuing to tell her.

And the worst part of the situation was that he no longer doubted her innocence. Annie Morrow was not involved in an art conspiracy. Pete would bet his life on that. He'd been with her every moment for weeks now, and she'd neither received nor made one single suspicious phone call. No one had tried to contact her any other way. She left her mail opened and out on her desk—there was nothing she was trying to hide.

Except her feelings for him.

Pete knew that it was only a matter of time before he gave in to his own feelings, his own needs. Man, when she looked at him, when he saw that longing in her eyes—

Annie opened her eyes slowly and caught him staring at her.

Embarrassed, she looked away. When she glanced back at him, he'd sat up and was scraping some dirt off the well-worn toes of his cowboy boots.

"I have a date tonight," she said.

His dark eyes flashed toward her, and for an instant, Annie thought she saw surprise on Pete's face. But it was quickly covered up, if it was ever even there.

"Tonight's the fund-raiser at the Museum of Modern Art in the city," Annie said. "All kinds of backers and grants people and just plain rich folk are going to be there." She smiled wryly. "Along with every museum and university and private researcher vying for any extra cash that might be lying around. It'll be a real schmoozefest."

"Who's the lucky guy?" Pete asked.

Annie looked at him blankly.

"Your date," he said. "Who is he?"

"Nick York," Annie said.

Pete nodded slowly.

Annie fought a wave of disappointment. But what did she expect? she scolded herself. Did she really expect Pete to be jealous? In all likelihood, he was probably relieved. If she was with Nick, she wouldn't be at home, mooning over Pete like a star-struck teenybopper.

"I'd better get back to work," she said, standing up and brushing off the seat of her jeans. She started toward the house.

"Annie."

She stopped, turning slowly back around.

Pete was standing there, looking like an ad for Levi's, with his snug jeans riding low on his hips, and his tan muscles gleaming in the sunshine.

"Thanks for the lunch," he said.

His eyes seemed to drill into her, burning with that same, unmistakable intensity. It was that look again.

Annie shook her head, letting all the air out of her lungs with an exasperated laugh. "Taylor, what do you want from me?"

He blinked. "What?"

"Why do you look at me that way?"

Pete looked down at the ground. "What way?" he asked, knowing damn well exactly what she was talking about.

"Oh, forget it," she muttered and stalked back to the house.

"Keep the alarm system on," he called after her, and without turning around, she held up one hand, signaling that she'd heard him.

He watched as she went inside, then picked up the rake and went back to work.

What did he want from her?

He should have told her. What would she have said, he wondered, if he'd told her the truth?

AT ONE-THIRTY IN THE AFTERNOON, the phone rang. Annie was in the office, and she answered it without thinking, remembering only after she said hello that Pete had told her not to answer the phone.

"Sweet Annie!" came a familiar voice. It was Nick York. "What are you wearing?"

"Jeans," Annie said. "Why?"

"No, not right now, you darling idiot." Nick laughed. "Tonight. What are you wearing tonight?"

Outside the office window, Pete carried a bundle of leaves toward the compost pile. Annie followed him with her eyes, trying not to crane her neck too obviously as he passed out of view. "I don't know," she said. "I haven't thought about it yet."

"Go all out tonight, will you, love?" Nick said. "Wear something tiny, with lots of leg and cleavage. Maybe something blue, to match your eyes. I want 'em drooling."

"And *I* want to preserve my reputation as a legitimate scientist," Annie protested.

"You're the best in your field," Nick murmured. "Everyone knows that. Promise me you'll wear high heels?"

"I promise I'll wear blue," Annie said. "Tiny or high heels I can't guarantee."

"Fair enough," Nick said cheerfully, "though if you love me, even just the teeniest little bit, you'll wear high heels tonight. I'll pick you up at seven."

Annie hung up the phone, mentally reviewing the clothes that hung in her closet. Blue, she thought. What did she have that was blue? She had a new pair of blue jeans. She snickered, imagining the look on Nick's face if he came to pick her up and she was wearing jeans—and her navy-blue high-top sneakers. *That* would be perfect.

But how often did she get a chance to dress up? She wore jeans all the time.

Outside the window, Pete was almost finished raking the leaves. Annie imagined coming down the stairs, wearing something tiny, with high heels showing off her long legs. She imagined breezing past Pete to kiss Nick fondly on the cheek. She and Nick would get into his sports car and drive off, leaving Pete openmouthed and jealous.

Well, probably not openmouthed, Annie thought. She sighed. And probably not jealous. Pete wouldn't even notice.

She stood up. Pete might not notice what she was wearing, but Nick sure as heck would. And maybe that would give her bruised ego a well-needed boost.

Annie took the stairs up to her apartment two at a time. Somewhere, in the back of her closet, was the perfect little dress for this particular occasion.

The door to her bedroom was closed, and Annie hesitated, her hand on the doorknob. That was funny, she thought. She hadn't closed the door. It had been open a few hours ago when she brought the plates back from lunch....

Maybe Cara had been up here.

She retraced her steps back down the stairs, and

went into the lab where Cara was painstakingly cleaning the rust from an ancient iron pot.

"MacLeish, have you been upstairs?" Annie asked.

Cara looked up, thinking for a moment. "Nope," she said. "Not today."

"How about Jerry?" Annie prodded. "When he was here at lunchtime, did he go up?"

"No," Cara said, putting down her brush. "Why? Is something wrong?"

But Annie had already gone into the foyer. She overrode the alarm system, allowing the front door to be opened, and went outside.

Pete was by the toolshed, folding the tarp. He still wasn't wearing his shirt, and he still was gorgeous. He looked up as she approached. "What's the matter?" he asked, dropping the tarp immediately and crossing toward her.

He'd picked up on her tension, Annie realized. His dark eyes raked her face, narrowing slightly, trying to read her mind.

She swallowed, and smiled weakly. "This is probably silly," she said, "but my bedroom door is closed, and I'm sure I left it open. Cara didn't close it, Jerry wasn't even upstairs when he was here, and..." She shrugged. "It was probably just the wind."

Pete looked up at the house, his sharp eyes quickly locating Annie's bedroom. "Your windows are closed," he said. He gave her a quick, fierce smile. "I'm proud of you. You didn't open the door. You came and told me. That was the right thing to do."

He took her by the arm and hustled her around the side of the house to the front door. He had already pulled his gun from its holster in his back pocket, Annie realized, and held it in front of them as they went inside.

Pete looked up the long staircase, then back at Annie. If an intruder was in the house, it didn't necessarily mean he was behind that closed door. She would be safer if she was near him.

"Stay right behind me," he said quietly.

Annie nodded, and Pete started up the stairs. He glanced at her over his shoulder. "Closer," he whispered, reaching back with his left hand to pull her in toward him, almost pressing her against his back.

She put her hand out to keep her nose from bumping into his solid shoulder blades. Her fingers touched the heat of his back and the hard smoothness of skin stretched tightly over his well-defined muscles. She resisted the urge to press her lips against him, to taste the saltiness of his skin with her tongue.

Pete positioned them against the wall next to her door, out of any possible line of fire. Slowly he reached out and turned the doorknob. He gave a push, and the door swung open.

The bedroom was dark inside, all the curtains drawn. There was no sound, no movement.

"I left the shades up after my shower," Annie breathed, her mouth close to Pete's ear.

He nodded once. "Stay back," he whispered, checking his gun, making sure the safety was off.

She caught his arm. "Be careful, Pete," she said softly.

His eyes moved down to her mouth, and for a heart-quickening instant, Annie thought he was going to kiss her. Instead he smiled, touching her cheek briefly with his work-roughened fingers.

Without warning, he leapt in front of the open door. His arms were outstretched, his left hand supporting the gun he held in his right. Startled by his sudden movement, a cloud of bats erupted from Annie's room.

Bats!

Pete swore, ducking as the bats fluttered and screeched around him.

Annie was flat against the wall, panic in her eyes. He grabbed her and pulled her down to the floor, covering her with his body. With one hand he reached out and caught the bottom edge of the door, yanking it shut.

"Cara, close the door to the lab!" he shouted.

He heard the thump of the downstairs door slamming closed, then Cara's voice raised in a plaintive wail, "Oh, yuck, are those *bats* out there?"

There were hundreds of them. They fluttered and swooped, dazed and confused by the bright sunlight.

Pete pulled Annie toward the stairs, half carrying, half dragging her down with him. He had to get her out of there, more than just her fear motivating him. Bats carried rabies. He couldn't let her get bitten, but there were so many of them, and they were *every*where....

He pulled her toward the front door, pulling it open. As if sensing the freedom, a bevy of the bats rushed toward the open door.

Annie ducked, desperately trying to get out of their way. But she wasn't quick enough. Its radar off kilter, one of the bats swooped too low.

Annie felt the tug as the bat became entangled in her hair. Panic engulfed her, and she swatted at it, breaking free from Pete and running for the open air of the front yard. The bat struggled, equally frightened, but only became more firmly ensnarled.

"Pete!" Annie screamed, and he was instantly at her side. His strong fingers plucked the bat from her hair, throwing it onto the ground. Rabies, he thought. What if the bat had rabies? He crushed it with the heel of his boot.

Annie's knees buckled. But Pete's arms were

around her, holding her. Gently he lowered them both down, so that he was sitting on the ground with Annie on his lap. He could feel her trembling as she clung tightly to his neck.

He held her close for several long minutes, until he felt her heartbeat start to slow. Then gently he tried to pry her fingers loose. But she wouldn't let go of him. "Come on, sweetheart," he murmured. "I've got to make sure it didn't bite you."

Annie released him and sat quietly with her eyes closed, letting Pete run his fingers through her hair, meticulously checking every square millimeter of her scalp and neck.

By the time he was done, the paramedics Cara had called had arrived, followed closely by the police and a fire truck. The FBI even pulled up, glaringly obvious in their big, unmarked car and dark suits. Last but not least to make the scene was a pest control van. As the paramedics checked Annie, a man and a woman dressed in sturdy protective gear went into the house and rounded up the rest of the bats. Pete pulled on the T-shirt he had discarded on the lawn while he was working.

The police bagged the dead bat that had been in Annie's hair, to send it to the county lab to test for rabies. As far as anyone could tell, Annie hadn't been bitten. But if the bat turned out to be rabid, the police officer told her, she'd probably still want to look into having a series of rabies shots—better safe than sorry.

It was after five by the time the pest control folks finished locating and removing all the stray bats. By then the burglar alarm company van had appeared in the driveway. The same man who had installed the system was in the foyer, deep in argument with Pete, insisting that if the motion detectors had been operational and on-line, there was simply no way an intruder could have gotten into the house without triggering the alarm.

"Maybe the bats made their way into the house through a hole in the roof," Annie heard the alarm specialist suggest as she approached the two men.

"Did they also close my bedroom door and pull down the shades?" she asked tartly.

Pete glanced at her. Her face was still a shade or two too pale, but she'd bounced almost all the way back, and the fire had returned to her eyes.

"The system was on all day," Pete added, crossing his arms as he brought his attention back to the man. "Occasionally we bypassed the front door, but I was in sight of that door each time, and believe me, no one unauthorized entered or exited that way."

The alarm specialist shrugged. "I'll check the system again," he said, returning to the control panel.

Pete turned to Annie. "I'm so sorry about this," he said, emotion in his voice.

"I have to wash my hair," she said, then shuddered. "Lord, I hate bats."

Pete's face darkened. "*I* hate knowing that someone was in here with you while I was out in the yard." He rubbed his forehead, then ran his hand through his hair as if he had a headache. "If they'd wanted to kill you," he said, his voice harsh, "they could've. And I wouldn't have been able to do a damned thing. Annie, I wouldn't have even *known*."

She put her hand on his arm. "It didn't happen," she said. "It's all right."

"It's *not* all right," Pete said. He looked down at her hand, her fingers pale and smooth against his tanned skin. He took a step back, and her hand fell away from him. "We can't stay here tonight. It's not safe."

"It was a prank," she protested. "They only wanted to scare me." She smiled ruefully. "They succeeded."

"If they got in once, they can get in again," Pete said.

"You said yourself that if they wanted to kill me, they could've," Annie said. "Obviously, they don't want to."

"Yet." Pete shook his head. "I'm authorizing a further upgrade of your security system. Until it's installed, we're not going to stay here. We're going to a hotel. I've already talked to the FBI team about additional protection."

Annie crossed her arms. "What about the artifacts? I've got over two million dollars' worth of antiquities in my safe. I'm not just going to leave them here."

"I'll post a guard," Pete said. "Round-the-clock, outside the house. I've also made arrangements to have all your locks changed."

Annie stared at him. "Did it occur to you to ask me if I *wanted* my locks changed?" she asked, annoyance in her voice. This was just too much....

"I assumed you'd want to stay alive," Pete said.

Annie glanced at her watch. It was nearly six o'clock. She had only an hour to get all these people out of her house, shower and change. "Where's Cara?" she said suddenly, noticing that the front lab was empty.

"She's in the office, being questioned by the FBI," Pete said.

"Questioned?"

"She's a suspect, Annie," he said. "She and Tillet are the only ones who have keys to this house besides you and me. If Tillet's as desperate for money as he says he is—"

Annie's eyes were shooting fire. She took an

angry step toward him. "You go in there," she said, "and you tell them that Cara is *not* a suspect."

Pete held up his hands as if to placate her. It didn't work. "Annie, you've got to admit, Cara had access to your bedroom all day. There's no proof that she's not somehow involved—"

"I don't need proof," Annie said hotly. "Now, are you going to tell them to stop harassing her, or am I?"

Before Pete had a chance to reply, the office door opened, and Cara came out, looking dazed.

"Are you okay?" Annie asked, her eyes filled with concern for her friend.

Cara's lower lip trembled. "Annie, *you* don't think I had anything to do with putting those bats in your room, do you?"

"I know you didn't, MacLeish," Annie said, forcing herself to make light. "I just can't picture you handling two hundred bats."

"Yuck," Cara said, smiling shakily.

"I'm giving you two weeks' paid vacation," Annie said.

Cara frowned. "You can't afford that right now—"

"Courtesy of Mr. Marshall," Annie said with a grin. Her smile faded. "MacLeish, I'm not going to let you get blamed for everything that goes wrong around here. Do us both a favor. Leave tonight and don't come back for two weeks."

"I'll feel like I'm deserting you," Cara protested.

"You're not," Annie said. "I'll see you at the museum tonight, all right?"

"What?" Pete asked.

"Oh, no, look at the time," Cara said. "I should've been home an hour ago. Jerry wanted to get there early...." She hugged Annie. "See you later."

Pete's jaw tightened as he watched Cara let herself out of the house. He turned to Annie. "You're not going to that fund-raiser."

Annie raised her chin. "Oh, yes, I am."

Pete ran both hands down his face, and took a deep breath, trying to calm himself. "Annie." He shook his head. "We're both exhausted. This isn't the best time to go out into a crowd. It's too dangerous."

Maybe if he had talked to her before changing the locks, maybe if he had stood up for Cara, maybe then she would have agreed with him. She *was* exhausted. But she was angry—angry that things had gotten out of control, angry that her life seemed to be no longer her own, angry at Pete...

"I've got a date," Annie said coolly. "I've got to go get ready."

She started up the stairs. When she reached the top, she turned and looked back at Pete. He was standing where she had left him, looking up at her. His jeans were dirty, his T-shirt was stained with sweat and grass and he hadn't shaved or showered all day. "Please tell the FBI agents to leave," she said. "I don't want them here when Nick shows up."

ANNIE WAS PUTTING ON HER stockings when she heard a soft knock at her bedroom door. She slipped into her bathrobe and opened the door. Pete stood in the hall.

"York's here," he said expressionlessly. "He's waiting in the living room."

Annie nodded, unable to meet his eyes. "Thanks."

She started to close the door, but he stopped it with his hand. "I'm going to take a shower," Pete said. "Don't leave without me."

Annie crossed her arms. "Taylor, I'm going on a date. Somehow I don't think Nick's going to appreciate it if you tag along."

Pete smiled, and Annie had to look away. "Understandable," he said, watching her study the floorboards. "But I'm going to protect you. From Nick York, at the very least."

Annie looked up sharply. "What if I don't *want* to be protected from Nick?"

Pete didn't say anything; he just looked at her. "Don't forget to pack a change of clothes," he finally said. "We might as well spend the night at a hotel in the city."

Annie felt a stab of annoyance. "What if I decide to go home with Nick?" she said, then instantly regretted saying it.

Pete looked stunned. He covered it almost immediately, but he couldn't hide the hurt that lingered in his eyes. "I'm sorry," he said. He shook his head. "I…didn't know you and York were…"

"No," Annie said quickly. "We're…*not*. I don't know why I said that. It was stupid. I—" She looked away from him, embarrassed. "I was just trying to make you jealous," she admitted in a low voice. "I'm sorry."

"It worked," he said.

She met his eyes, and shook her head. "I still don't know what you want from me, Pete. It would've been really nice if things had worked out between us, but, look, they didn't, and tonight I'm going out with Nick. If you've got to come along, be inconspicuous, okay? Do you have something to wear? This is a formal event…."

"I can handle it," Pete said, releasing the door.

Great, thought Annie, closing the door tightly. *But can I?*

CHAPTER TWELVE

IT WAS TWENTY AFTER SEVEN BEFORE Annie, walking carefully in her high heels, went into her living room.

Nick, resplendent in his tux and black tie, got to his feet. The gleam in his blue eyes was almost as bright as the light reflecting off his golden hair as he came toward her, arms outstretched. He kissed her, first on one cheek, and then on the other, before he nuzzled her neck.

"Perfect," he said, his quick grin showing off a white flash of teeth. "I couldn't have dreamed up a better dress. You look good enough to devour, sweet Annie. All of New York City will be salivating. I love it when you wear your hair up, darling—you look like a little girl playing dress-up."

Pete stood quietly in the doorway, looking at Annie. York was right, he realized. With her hair elegantly swept up off her neck, with those wispy bangs in the front, with her wide blue eyes and generous mouth, Annie actually looked younger than when she wore her hair down. But her dress revealed a body that was all grown-up. It was blue velvet with an off-the-shoulder neckline that plunged down between her breasts. Short stand-away sleeves further framed her long neck and smooth shoulders. The bodice of the dress was tightly fitted, sweeping down into a short skirt that hugged her every curve. Sheer stockings covered elegantly shaped legs that went on and on and on, tucked into a pair of black-velvet high-heeled pumps. Her only jewelry was a pair of dangling coin-silver earrings. They were Navaho, Pete noticed.

"Hel-lo." Nick had spotted him. "Who's this?"

Annie's eyes widened at the sight of Pete. His tuxedo was perfectly tailored, fitting his trim body exactly. With his hair slicked back and his cheeks freshly shaven, the only similarity between him and the dangerous-looking man who'd so recently raked her yard without a shirt was his dark, glittering eyes.

Pete couldn't help himself. Involuntarily, his gaze swept down and then back up her body, lingering on her long legs and the soft, exposed tops of her breasts and throat. His eyes met hers, and he knew from the look on her face that he wasn't able to hide his desire, his need from her any longer. Hell, he'd given himself away. Turning, he tore his gaze away from her, staring blindly down at the Persian rug that covered the floor.

Annie had to work to catch her breath, wondering if she'd only imagined the raw desire she'd seen in Pete's eyes. But no, she knew what she had seen. She just couldn't begin to explain it.

"Nick, this is Pete Taylor," Annie said, trying to cover her sudden breathlessness. "He let you in, remember? Pete, Dr. Nicholas York."

The two men shook hands. Annie could see Pete quietly sizing Nick up. Nick was a little less subtle, giving Pete an obvious once-over.

"I thought you were the gardener," Nick said. "Apparently I was mistaken." He turned to Annie. "Darling, you didn't tell me you'd gotten a new research assistant."

"Taylor's my bodyguard," Annie explained.

"A bodyguard," Nick said, turning to look at Pete again. "You're kidding."

"Annie's been getting death threats," Pete said, his gentle Western drawl a sharp contrast to Nick's clipped English accent. His eyes met Annie's again for only the briefest of instances before he looked away.

"*Annie* has, has she?" Nick said, exaggerating Pete's use of her first name. He looked at Annie. "You know, that's the problem with you Americans. You're so focused on equality, you let the servants call you by your first names." He turned back to Pete.

"Take the night off, old boy. I can protect her just as well as you can. Better, no doubt—my IQ's probably twice as high as yours."

"Don't be a jerk, Nick," Annie said sharply.

Nick put his arms around her waist, pulling her in close to him. "I had a *very* romantic evening planned," he whispered. "I intended to seduce you in the back of the limo on the way into the city."

Pete clenched his teeth. It wasn't hard to squelch the urge to grab Nick York by the front of his white tuxedo shirt and rearrange his perfect, golden-tanned features, but the fact that Pete had had the urge in the first place was alarming. Pete had no claim on Annie. He'd had his chance, but he'd declined, he'd passed, and now, God help him, he had no right to do or say anything at all.

"A *limo?*" Annie said, pulling away from Nick.

Nick grinned. "I'm in desperate need of funding," he said. "Down to my last nickels and dimes. But there's going to be quite a bit of money floating around tonight. And I figured, people like to back a winner, right? And winners arrive in limos. Speaking of arriving, we should get going. We don't want to miss the buffet—it may be my one square meal all week."

"I'll be right there. I just want to check to make sure everything's locked up." Annie headed down to the lab with Pete and Nick trailing after her.

As Nick went toward the front door, Annie went into the office and turned off the lights. She then checked the lab. The instruments were put away, the sinks were clean, the counters were cleared off. Everything was in order, the safe was securely locked. She turned back to the door, coming face-to-face with Pete.

Their eyes met and again she saw heat. This time he didn't look away.

"You look beautiful," he said softly.

Annie stared up at him, hypnotized by the look in his eyes. "Thank you," she murmured.

Pete couldn't stop himself. He took a step toward her, and another step. As he watched, she nervously moistened her lips, and he felt desire slice through him, hot and sharp and very painful.

God help him, he had to kiss her—

Nick's voice floated in from outside. "Darling, I hate to be a nag, but we really must be on our way."

Pete turned abruptly away, nearly consumed by a wave of anger and frustration. He wasn't sure who he was angrier at—York, for interrupting them, or himself for nearly giving in to his weakness.

Annie turned off the lights in the lab, then hurried past Pete, heading out the door.

"Ready then, are we?" Nick smiled, taking her arm and leading her toward the waiting limo.

Pete carried out Annie's overnight bag and his backpack and put them in the trunk. He was about to join Annie in the main body of the car when Nick stopped him.

"Servants go up front," Nick said, his eyes cool. "You can sit with the driver."

Pete kept his expression carefully neutral. "Not this time," he said and climbed into the back. He sat down across from Annie, sinking into the soft leather seat.

As Nick climbed in beside Annie and the limo rolled slowly out of the driveway, Pete stared out the window, steeling himself for the long night ahead. He could feel Annie's eyes watching him. Her confusion was nearly palpable, and he knew he shouldn't look into her eyes again—it would only make things worse.

But he couldn't help himself. He looked up. He'd meant only to glance in Annie's direction, but her gaze caught and held him.

As he stared into the bottomless blue depths of her eyes, he knew for damn certain he was out of control.

INSIDE THE MUSEUM OF MODERN ART, the party was in full swing. An orchestra played music in the main lobby, and people were dancing. A buffet table had been set up, and it was loaded with wonderfully aromatic food.

Pete left Annie's jacket and their two bags at the coat check, keeping a careful eye on her the entire time.

Nick had whisked her out onto the dance floor where they moved gracefully to an old song. "Stardust," Pete thought. It was called "Stardust." He moved to the edge of the crowd, where he could see Annie and Nick clearly.

Annie stood out in the crowd. With her gleaming hair, her long, graceful neck, those creamy white shoulders contrasted by the deep blue of the dress... She looked as if she belonged here, amid the glitter of New York society. And Nick York looked as if he belonged at her side.

Pete watched York bend down and say something in Annie's ear. She smiled distractedly. She was looking around, searching the crowd.... Her eyes landed on Pete, and he realized with a sudden breathlessness that she'd been looking for him.

Even across the room, the charge that their locked gaze generated seemed to spark and crackle with heat. But then York spun Annie around, turning her so that her back was to Pete.

Pete took a deep breath and glanced around the room, looking for any sign of trouble, anything out of the ordinary. It wouldn't be too difficult in a crowd like this for an assassin to get up close and do some real damage with a knife. One quick thrust, and the victim wouldn't even fall, held up by the crush of people. Man, what he wouldn't give to be next to Annie, to be able to shield her with his own body. What he wouldn't give to be able to dance with her, to hold her in his arms....

The orchestra ended the song, and the dancers applauded. Pete watched York lean close to Annie's ear again and gesture toward the food.

ANNIE LET NICK LEAD HER BY THE hand to the buffet table. She glanced back through the crowd to where she'd last seen Pete, but he was gone.

He'd been standing there through the entire dance, watching her, looking at her the way he had back at the house, and for most of the limo ride. What was going on? By running out of her room that night, Pete couldn't have told her any more clearly that he didn't want her. So why was he suddenly looking at her as if he did? Was this some kind of macho possessive thing? Annie wondered, frowning slightly. Maybe even though Pete didn't want her, he simply didn't want Nick to have her, either. Or maybe he just liked the idea of jerking her around. Maybe he liked having her panting after him. Maybe—

Pete was standing by the buffet table, looking at her as if *she* were the main course. His dark eyes swept her face, lingering on her mouth a heartbeat or two longer than necessary. Silently, he offered her a plate, but she shook her head.

"No, thank you," she said. "I'm not very hungry."

Through the throng of party-goers, she spotted Jerry Tillet. "Excuse me," she murmured to Nick, and slipped her hand out from his arm. As she approached Tillet, she saw that he was talking earnestly to a tall, broad-shouldered man who was wearing a cowboy hat. It wasn't until she was closer that she realized it was none other than Steven Marshall—the buyer of Stands Against the Storm's death mask, and Pete's employer. She greeted both men with a smile.

"Dr. Tillet, I didn't realize you knew Mr. Marshall," she said.

Despite his smile, Jerry looked uncomfortable. "Yeah, well," he said, "in this business, everyone knows everyone else. You know how it is...."

Marshall shook Annie's hand, then brought it up to his lips. "How's it goin', darlin'?" he asked. "Everything okay?"

Annie extracted her fingers from his grip. "To be perfectly honest, things are getting a little out of hand."

Marshall's light brown eyes sparkled in amusement. "Dr. Tillet told me about the bats," he said. "That musta really shook things up."

A waiter with a tray of champagne glasses passed, and Marshall deftly removed two, handing one to Annie with a flourish. She took a sip, glancing around the room—and directly into Pete's eyes. He stood about fifteen feet away, leaning against the wall, watching her. Deliberately, she turned her back to him.

"I bumped the death mask up on my list," Annie told Marshall. "I should be getting carbon-dating results back any day now."

Marshall's smile broadened. "Well, all right," he said. "Your rainy day makes my garden grow. But that's the way life is, isn't it?"

"Yeah, that's life," Annie agreed.

Tillet looked positively antsy, and Annie realized she'd broken into the conversation before he'd had a chance to hit Marshall up for funding. "Has Dr. Tillet told you about his latest Mayan project?" she asked him. "It's fascinating."

With a grateful smile, Tillet launched into his well-rehearsed patter. Annie had heard it too many times before, so she let her attention wander, sipping her champagne and looking around the room.

Pete Taylor had moved, planting himself once again directly in her line of sight.

Annie tried to stare him down, but the heat in his eyes only intensified. *It's a mind game,* she told herself. *He's just toying with me.* She held on to her anger, trying not to give in to the molten feeling of desire that was forming in the pit of her stomach.

She turned away abruptly, heading back to the buffet table in search of Nick and safety. She had to laugh at the thought of that. Nick would be highly offended to find out she considered him safe.

But he was deep in conversation with three wealthy-looking women, no doubt trying to charm them into making a sizable donation to the Nick York fund.

Annie frowned down at the table that held the food, wishing that she had stayed home, thinking sourly about the way her colleagues had to scrape and grovel for money to support their scientific research. Ever since government funding had virtually disappeared, brilliant scientists were forced to spend nearly all their free time begging and scratching for money to keep their projects alive. And not just their free time, Annie realized, but also much of the valuable time they should have been spending doing research.

Still frowning, she stabbed a black olive with a toothpick, popped it into her mouth and turned away from the table.

"Don't tell me that's all you're going to eat."

Startled, Annie looked up, directly into Pete's

obsidian eyes. He was standing much too close, only inches from her.

She backed away. "You're not being very inconspicuous," she accused him.

He moved closer. "Do you want me to get you a plate?" he asked. "There are some tables free, if you want to sit down."

Annie was staring up at him, an odd mixture of disbelief and longing on her face. Still, he moved toward her, stopping when there was only a hint of space between them. If she took a deep breath, he realized, her breasts would brush his chest.

"Pete, why are you doing this?" she asked softly.

It was a good question. Why *was* he doing this? He knew damn well that if he made love to her tonight, the way he wanted to, he would be risking everything. For one brief moment, he thought crazily, fleetingly, of taking Annie and running away. They could leave the country, leave behind the art conspiracy charges, leave behind Captain Kendall Peterson. He could spend the rest of his life as Pete Taylor. Annie would never have to know; he would never have to tell her who he really was, tell her that he'd lied to her.

"What do you want from me?" she whispered.

"Dance with me, Annie," he said, his voice husky.

Annie felt her throat tighten, and she steeled

herself, ordering herself not to cry. "Don't do this," she said, her voice shaking slightly despite her attempts to keep it steady. "Don't play with my feelings, Taylor. You know full well that I..." She closed her eyes, and took a deep breath. "...want you. There. I admitted it. You win. Now leave me alone."

She turned, nearly diving for the other side of the room. She could feel the sting of unshed tears on the backs of her eyelids, but she forced herself to smile brightly at the faces she recognized in the crowd. How she wanted to go home. But home was off-limits, unsafe until a new, more elaborate security system could be installed.

She caught sight of the bar, stretching across one entire end of the gaudily decorated lobby, and headed for it. She'd get a tall, cool glass of seltzer, then hunt for Cara. They could hang out in the ladies' room together, away from Pete Taylor....

"Dr. Morrow! What a pleasant surprise!"

Annie turned to find a small man with brown wavy hair standing before her. He wore a thick gold chain around his wrist and a white carnation in the lapel of his tux. It was Alistair Golden, her chief competitor.

"Dr. Golden," she said, taking the hand he had extended.

"How's work?" he asked, his startling green eyes probing.

Talking to this man was a lot like being interrogated, Annie thought. It wasn't his words, but rather the penetrating way he had of staring. He reminded her of a frog eyeing a fly it was going to eat for dinner. And she was the fly.

"Fine," she lied. "And how are things with you?"

"Fine," he said, and she wondered if he was lying, too. "I heard you're having some security problems lately. Something about…evil spirits?"

"News does travel," Annie murmured, looking longingly at the bar.

The man's gaze focused over Annie's right shoulder, and she turned to find Pete standing there.

"I don't believe we've met," Dr. Golden said.

"Dr. Alistair Golden, Pete Taylor," Annie said briefly. The two men shook hands.

"Taylor works for me," she said, intentionally labeling him as mere hired help. "He's a security guard." She didn't call him a bodyguard, not wanting to make their relationship even that personal. "Excuse me," she added, taking the opportunity to escape both from Golden's inquisitive eyes and Pete's presence.

She was still twenty feet from the bar when a hand caught her arm. She froze, knowing without turning around that it was Pete.

"Annie, we have to talk," he said, his soft drawl somehow cutting through the noise of a thousand people talking and laughing, through the sound of a twenty-piece orchestra playing an old romantic song.

She turned, then. "No, we don't," she said. "Give me a break, Taylor. Please? I don't feel like talking."

"Then dance with me."

Her eyes flashed with anger. "Read my lips, pal. No. Get it? *No*—"

She turned away, but he caught her wrist and pulled her back. "Then *listen* to me," he said. "You don't have to talk, you don't have to say anything."

"I don't want to listen—"

"Annie, have mercy on me—"

"Sweet Annie!" Nick York bounded up, startling them both. "They're playing our song!"

Nick pulled her out onto the dance floor and wrapped his arms around her. Annie looked over his shoulder. She could see Pete shake his head slightly with frustration. When he looked up and met her eyes, Annie caught her breath, recognizing that same look, the one that had been confusing her for weeks now.

Why now, out of the blue like this, did Pete suddenly want to dance with her? It didn't make sense. *None* of this made any sense at all.

A wave of fatigue washed over her and she

stumbled. Only Nick's arms around her kept her from falling.

"Nick, I'm exhausted," she said, looking up into her friend's eyes. "I'd like to leave."

"Shall I call you a cab?" he asked, then, realizing how callous he sounded, added, "I can't leave now, Annie." His eyes were serious and he actually had the decency to look ashamed. "I'm sorry, darling, but I've got a few leads on some backers and—"

"It's all right," she said. And it was. She hadn't really expected Nick to leave this party three hours early. She'd hoped, but not expected. "I'll get a cab my—"

"Oh, Lord, there's Mr. and Mrs. Hampton-Hayes," Nick said. "And they're heading for the door. Annie, they're richer than God and I've *got* to talk to them. Call me, darling."

He was gone, leaving her standing alone in the midst of all the dancers. Good old Nick. If there was one thing you could count on, it was that you couldn't count on him.

"I was going to ask if I could cut in, but it looks like your partner already cut out."

Pete.

Annie turned to find him standing behind her, and before she could say anything, before she could move, he'd taken her into his arms.

It was heaven.

He held her so close, she could feel his heart beating. His arms were strong, yet he held her gently, one hand at her waist, the other holding her hand.

Annie closed her eyes, leaning against him. This had to be a dream. Certainly she'd dreamed about Pete holding her like this often enough. In a heartbeat, all her resistance had vanished. She pulled her hand free and slipped it up around his neck, pulling him even closer, running her fingers through the softness of his hair.

His arms tightened around her waist, and she looked up to see desire growing in his eyes. He slid one hand up to the deep-V back of her dress, letting his fingers trail lightly across her bare skin, up to her smooth shoulders, and back down again.

Pete felt, more than heard, the small sound she made as he touched her, and it was almost too much for him to take.

"Annie," he breathed. "Annie…"

He'd lost his mind—there was no doubt about it. He'd told her that they had to talk, but really, what was he going to say to her? He couldn't tell her he was CIA; he couldn't do that.

He could tell her that he loved her.

He could pray that she loved him, too—enough to forgive him for all the lies, all the half-truths, all the deception.

His thighs pressed against her as they rocked back and forth, pretending to dance, and Annie looked up at him again, losing herself in the bottomless depths of his eyes.

Why didn't he kiss her?

She couldn't stand it another second. Standing on her toes, she pulled his head toward her and brushed his lips with hers. "Kiss me, Taylor," she said, her lips parted invitingly.

He gave a sound that was half like a laugh, half like a groan. "I can't."

She pulled back, as far as she could with his arms still around her. "Why not?"

Pete could see frustration in her eyes, frustration and questions and a shadow of hurt. She didn't understand. She thought he didn't want to kiss her. Man, if she only knew…

He reached up and touched the side of her face, gently tracing her lips with his thumb. "Annie, I want to," he said softly. "But I'm supposed to be protecting you. How can I watch for trouble if I'm kissing you?"

He could feel her trembling in his arms. "Kiss me with your eyes open."

"Not a chance." Pete shook his head. "When I kiss you, I'm going to do it right."

Their eyes locked and for several long seconds,

Annie couldn't breathe. *Why now?* The question kept popping into her head. He'd run away from her the night she'd offered herself to him. He could have had her, but he'd turned her down. So why did he want her now?

Don't think, she ordered herself. *Don't wonder, don't ask questions, don't ruin this. And maybe whatever "this" is could last forever....*

She nervously wet her lips. "If you won't kiss me with your eyes open, then we should go someplace you feel is safe enough to close your eyes."

His fingers were at the nape of her neck, gently stroking her soft skin. "That sounds like a great idea to me," he said.

He took Annie's hand and led her off the dance floor, knowing full well that leaving the lights and the crowd was a mistake. Tonight they would share a hotel room, and unless he got a sudden burst of self-control, he'd share her bed.

Pete looked at the woman following him, looked at her soft, smooth skin, her beautiful face, her blue eyes, so wide and trusting— He swore, silently, harshly, knowing his self-control was long gone, and praying she'd forgive him when she found out the truth.

CHAPTER THIRTEEN

THE CITY STREETS WERE CROWDED EVEN though the night air was cold.

Pete had his backpack and Annie's overnight bag slung over his right shoulder. His other arm was wrapped tightly around her shoulders. She looked up at him and tried to smile. Pete realized she was as nervous as he was.

"Where are we going?" she asked.

"I know a place over on the west side," he said, looking casually over his shoulder. But his eyes were sharp, his swift gaze missing no detail of the people and cars around them.

"Are we going to walk? Usually I don't mind walking. It's just these shoes aren't exactly cut out for— Hey!"

In a flash, Pete scooped her up in his arms.

"I was thinking more along the lines of a cab," she said, looping her arms around his neck. "But this is nice." She closed her eyes, leaning her head against his shoulder. "Yeah, I could get real used to this."

"We're going to get a cab," Pete said, carrying her across the street. "I didn't want to find one too close to the museum. We'll be harder to trace this way."

He gently set Annie down on the sidewalk, but she kept her arms around his neck. "I feel very safe," she said. "Are you sure you can't kiss me yet?"

"Definitely not yet." He glanced down at her, a smile softening the lines of his face. "I feel like we're targets at a shooting range. If I kiss you now, it would have to be over quick," he said, looking boldly into her sweet blue eyes. "And, Annie, when I finally do kiss you, it's going to last a long, long time."

Annie smiled. "I like the sound of that, Taylor."

Taylor. Right. Pete had to look away. Would she still smile at him that way after he told her who he really was, and why he'd been sent to play the part of her bodyguard? *Please,* he prayed to his vast collection of deities. *Please let her forgive me....*

When he glanced back, she was still smiling at him. "Think maybe it'll be safe enough in the cab for you to kiss me?" she asked softly.

Pete's arms went around her, and he pulled her in tightly. "It better be," he murmured into her soft hair.

He reluctantly detached Annie's hands from his neck and stepped toward the curb. Down the block, the light turned green, and a wall of headlights approached. They were too far away for Pete to distinguish the cabs from the regular vehicles, but there was one car traveling faster than the others. It moved to the right lane, as if the driver had spotted them. Pete lifted his hand, signaling that they needed a cab.

He saw that there was no taxi roof light at the same instant that he realized the car was speeding up, not slowing down. Something was wrong. Something was really wrong....

He turned, and fear hit him like a solid punch to the gut. Annie wasn't next to him! God, where was she?

Searching wildly, he spotted her several yards away, leaning against an open-air telephone booth. She stood on one foot, serenely unaware of any danger. Her shoe was in her hand as she gracefully bent her leg to examine a rubbed spot on her heel.

Pete dropped her overnight bag, and went for Annie at a dead run, catching her around the waist as the speeding car jumped the curb and came onto the sidewalk. Around him, everything switched into slow motion. Out of the corner of his eye, he could see the startled look on Annie's face, and her shoe pinwheeling from her hand. There was a storefront ahead of him, with a door set back from the sidewalk. If he could make it there, they'd be safe. But the distance he'd have to cross, the actual sidewalk itself, seemed to stretch, to lengthen into an impossibly unattainable goal.

As the car came closer, he could see the face of the driver. The man's teeth were bared in a grimace of concentrated rage; his eyes were wild. Pete's training kicked in, and he glanced down at the car's license plate, instantly committing the three numbers and three letters to memory. Memory, yeah, right. As if he'd even have a memory after this was over....

Pete had been faced with his own probable death before, but it had never angered him the way this did. No way was he going to let Annie die. And no way was *he* going to end up dead, either. Not now. Now when he'd finally found the best reason he'd ever had for staying alive.

With herculean effort he pushed his straining muscles harder, and threw both Annie and himself into the storefront. The car missed them by mere inches, but hit the phone booth, knocking it down and dragging it several hundred feet before driving away, tires squealing.

Pete turned instinctively into the fall, to cradle and protect Annie. With a tearing sound, the left sleeve was torn off of his tuxedo jacket as he skidded on the rough concrete. His shoulder was badly scraped, but he felt nothing but relief as he pulled Annie onto his lap.

He ran his hands quickly down her arms and legs to reassure himself that she was still in one piece. Her right knee was scraped, the stocking destroyed, but other than that she was all right.

"Pete, you're bleeding," she said, her voice remarkably clear.

As he looked up, he realized she was checking him over as carefully as he had checked her. His elbow was a mess, along with his left knee, and blood stained the fine fabric of his tux. He couldn't see his shoulder—didn't want to see it.

"Still feel safe?" he asked her hoarsely.

To his surprise, she smiled. It was shaky, but it was definitely a smile. "If you're with me," she said, "then I'm safe."

Man, she was giving him an awful lot to live up to. Painfully, he stood up, pulling Annie to her feet. There was a crowd gathering, and he wanted to get away from all the curious eyes.

"We've got to get out of here before he comes back," he said. His pack was still on his back, but he'd dropped Annie's bag on the sidewalk. Miraculously, it hadn't been stolen; it still lay where it had fallen. Wincing, he bent to pick it up. There was a distinct tire track on the soft leather.

Someone in the crowd handed Annie her missing shoe.

She thanked them politely, calmly, as if this sort of thing happened every day.

Several cars had stopped at the accident scene, one of them a cab. Its off-duty light was lit, but Pete pulled several twenty-dollar bills from his wallet, and the driver was happy to get back to work.

"Where you heading?" the cabbie asked as they got in.

"Madison Square Garden," Pete said. "And I'll give you another fifty bucks if you keep the off-duty light on."

"But that's illegal—"

"A hundred."

"You're the boss."

As the cab pulled away from the curb, Pete pulled Annie down with him so that they were both lying on the seat, hidden from view. Her face was illuminated in spurts by the streetlights they passed under, and she stared up at him, her eyes wide.

"You okay?" he asked.

She nodded, looking into his eyes as if he were a lifeline. "That was no accident," she said. "Someone tried to kill us, didn't they?"

"Yeah."

Annie nodded again, still looking into his eyes. "Are *you* okay?" she asked him.

"I'm fine."

"Really?"

The cab's suspension system squeaked as it hit a pothole. Annie's hair had all but fallen down around her shoulders, and he pushed a lock off her face. "Ask me that same question in a minute," he murmured. "Something tells me I'm going to be even better than fine."

He kissed her gently, just a slight brushing of his lips against hers. She smiled, then lifted her mouth to his for more. He kissed her again, a long, slow, sweet kiss that made his heart pound and sent his blood racing through his veins.

"Madison Square Garden," the cabbie announced. "Uh, you folks want me to go around the block a few more times?"

Annie grinned. "What does he think we're doing back here?" she whispered into Pete's ear.

"Probably exactly what we *are* doing," he whispered back, kissing her neck. "Yeah, keep going," he said in a louder voice to the driver. He lifted himself up slightly, so he could peek out the back window.

After the cab made three right turns with no cars following them, Pete had the driver pull over, and he and Annie climbed out.

The cab had no sooner pulled away from the curb when Pete flagged down another taxi. They quickly climbed in.

"La Guardia Airport," Pete directed the driver.

An hour and a half later, they ended up in an expensive hotel overlooking Central Park. The room was large and elegant, decorated in hushed shades of rose and burgundy, with a beautiful floral-printed wallpaper that reminded Annie of an English garden. A table and chairs sat in the corner by the window, a couch and several overstuffed chairs were positioned around a cold fireplace and a big bed was against the wall. One bed. Annie pulled her eyes away from it and looked at Pete.

"You know, when you told that cabdriver to take us to the airport," she said, "for a while there, I thought you wanted to catch the next flight out of town."

Pete slipped the chain on the door and fastened a deadbolt. "Would you have gone?" he asked.

"Yes," she said without hesitating even a second. "If that's what you wanted."

She trusted him. It was clear from her eyes and her voice. Perfect, Pete thought grimly. She trusted him absolutely, yet he'd told her nothing but lies and half-truths. She would have every right to be furious with him when she found out the real story, every right never to trust him again.

Annie watched as he pulled the desk chair over and wedged it tightly underneath the doorknob. He seemed more silent and expressionless than ever, as if he were hiding something. Were they really safe here? Maybe they *should* have taken a flight out of New York, away from the city....

"Does that work?" she asked, gesturing to the chair.

"It's not going to stop anybody who's determined to get in here," Pete said. "But it makes me feel better."

"Are we safe?" she asked.

His eyes met hers, and electricity seemed to crackle between them.

Safe.

If they were safe, Pete could relax. He could close his eyes and kiss her. And if he could close his eyes and kiss her...

"Yeah," he said. "For now."

His gaze was so intense, Annie had to look away. Her overnight bag was on the floor, and she looked at it, seeing for the first time the tire mark that marred its leather surface. Her eyes were very wide and very blue as she looked back up at Pete. "I nearly got you killed. Didn't I?"

Pete shook his head. "*You* didn't try to run me over," he said, painfully shrugging out of what was left of his tuxedo jacket, depositing onto the table a small gun that he'd somehow concealed up his sleeve.

"Don't go doing the guilt thing on me, Annie. I knew exactly what I was getting myself into when I took this job."

He pulled another gun out from where it had been tucked into the back of his pants.

"Did you really?"

He turned to glance at her, and froze. Annie had taken off her evening jacket, too, and she stood in front of him, her sexy blue dress wrinkled, her stockings torn, her makeup smudged, her hair disheveled and down around her smooth shoulders. She was gorgeous, perfectly, mind-numbingly gorgeous. Desire slammed into him, running him down and crushing him so that he could barely breathe.

"No," he managed to say, his voice sounding raw. "I didn't have a clue."

He couldn't hide how badly he wanted her—he knew it was written clearly across his face. He turned away abruptly, unfastening his shoulder holster and putting that gun with the others. He knew he should wash the scrape on Annie's knee, and maybe take a look at his shoulder in the bathroom mirror....

Annie walked slowly toward him, hoping for another glimpse of that exhilarating fire she'd seen burning in his eyes. "Do me a favor, Taylor," she said, her voice even lower and huskier than usual. "Unzip me?"

She turned, sweeping her hair in front of one shoulder, exposing her slender neck and smooth back, waiting. For several long seconds, she was afraid he wasn't going to do it. Then his big, gentle fingers found the tiny zipper pull and tugged it slowly down. Annie heard Pete take a deep breath.

"You should take a shower," he said on the exhale.

Pete briefly closed his eyes, willing her to walk away from him. But she didn't. When he looked again, she was still standing in front of him. And he couldn't resist.

Annie sighed with pleasure as she felt Pete touch her shoulders, his callused fingers stroking her soft skin.

"Annie," he breathed close to her ear. "*I* should take a shower—a cold one."

"I have a better idea," she said, turning to face him. The heat in her eyes left him no doubt as to what she had in mind.

He knew that he should stop touching her, he should stop tracing the line of her delicate collarbone, he should keep his fingers out of her silky hair....

She took a step toward him, closing the shrinking gap between them, and suddenly his arms were around her and he was kissing her.

This was not like the sweet kisses they'd shared in the back seat of the taxi. This was an explosion, a scorching, turbulent eruption of emotion and desire held far too long in check. He molded her body against his as their mouths met hungrily, frantically. He welcomed her tongue into his mouth, pulling her inside him, as if he wanted to devour her whole. She moaned, a soft, sensual sound that nearly brought him to his knees, and he swept his tongue past her lips, piercing her, possessing her, claiming her as his own.

Annie heard herself moan again, as Pete's hands moved down to her buttocks, pressing her tightly to the ironlike hardness of his arousal. Feeling herself flood with even more heat, Annie wrapped one leg up around him, fitting herself against him. She could feel his hand slide up the silky nylon that covered her thigh, slipping underneath her dress.

Suddenly, violently, Pete pulled away from her. He crossed to the other side of the room, as if to put as much distance between them as possible. Not again, Annie thought with frustration, watching him lean against the far wall, pressing his palms to his forehead. She took a deep breath, trying to calm her ragged breathing. At least he didn't run away, she told herself. This was definitely a step in the right direction....

"Annie, I'm dying to make love to you," he said. "But we have to talk first. You need to understand that there are things I can't tell you—"

Annie slipped out of her dress, kicking her shoes into the corner of the room. She wore a black bustier that ended in a point just above the black silk of her panties. Pete watched, almost hypnotized, as she peeled off her tattered stockings and tossed them into the wastebasket.

She walked toward him then, saying, "We were attacked by a flock of bats *and* nearly run over by some maniac, all in the space of a few hours. Maybe this is just a day's work for you, pal, but I've had it. I don't want to talk. I don't want to deal with any problems. And I don't want to have to wonder if I'm going to get killed before I get a chance to make love to you."

"Annie—"

She pressed her fingers to his lips. "Tell me tomorrow," she said, her blue eyes beseeching him. "Please?"

The last time Pete had seen her dressed in only her underwear, she'd stood this close to him, but she'd been on the other side of a thick pane of glass. This time, with no barrier between them, he couldn't help himself, and he reached out for her.

She went into his arms willingly, thankfully, kissing him as his hands swept over her body, stroking, touching, exploring. Her fingers fumbled as she unbuttoned his shirt, but finally it was open, and she ran the palms of her hands up and down the hard, smooth muscles of his chest. "Make love to me, Pete," she whispered.

In one sudden movement, he scooped her into his arms and carried her to the big bed. Still holding her with one arm, he grabbed the covers and wrenched them back. He sank down onto the clean white sheets, pressing himself on top of her, kissing her eyes, her mouth, her neck, sliding lower and lower until his mouth found her breast. Her nipples were already hard with desire, and he took one into his mouth, sucking and pulling through the delicate lace of her bra. His hands found a hook and eye at her back and he undid it, but it was just one of a whole long row of fasteners. Growling with frustration, he rolled her onto her stomach. With his fingers and eyes working together, the bra was easy to remove, and he quickly tossed it onto the floor.

He sat back to pull his shirt off, uncaring of the pain in his scraped shoulder and elbow, knowing only that he had to feel his body against hers with no barriers in between. He watched Annie sit up, her breasts round and full, her nipples invitingly taut.

He knew that it was a mistake to make love to her like this, before she knew the truth about him. But he also knew that mistake or not, it was too late to turn back—his need for her possessed him. The only way he'd be able to turn away from her now was if she begged him to stop. Pete groaned as her slender fingers unfastened the button at the waist of his pants. No, she definitely didn't want to stop.

He took her hand, pulling it down and pressing it against the hard bulge in his pants. Their gazes locked, and they both smiled, quick, fiery grins of recognition at the need for haste that they saw in each other's eyes. Pete pushed off his shoes as Annie tugged at his pants. He lifted his hips and yanked both his pants and his shorts down, then groaned with pleasure as her hand closed around his shaft. He rolled on top of her, pinning her with his body as he kissed her almost feverishly.

His hand slipped underneath the thin black silk of her panties, finding the heat between her legs, finding her moist and ready for him. He slid his fingers into her tightness, and she moaned, lifting her hips and pressing against him.

"Pete," she whispered huskily, looking up at him with passion in her eyes. "Please…"

Her soft words ignited him, and the black panties joined her bra on the floor. He scrambled for his pants, searching the pockets for the condom he'd put in his wallet weeks ago, back when Annie was only a suspect to be investigated. He'd put that condom there in anticipation of good sex—nothing more than physical pleasure with a beautiful adversary. But it was more than sexual desire that made his hands shake as he put it on now. It was knowing that he wanted Annie in ways that he'd never wanted anyone before. It was love, pure and simple, and oh, so complicated. Too complicated for words....

Pete turned back to Annie and kissed her as if the world were coming to an end. His body covered hers, and she put her arms around his sleek, strong back, pulling him even closer to her, opening herself to receive him. But he paused, his muscles tight in his arms and chest as he looked down at her.

"I love you," he breathed. "Annie, I love you so much—"

Beads of sweat stood out on his forehead and he was breathing hard, as if holding back was a test of endurance. But while his eyes blazed with the intensity of his desire, they also held another flame, the softer, smoldering fire of love that promised to burn forever.

Annie felt her eyes fill with tears. He loved her....

"Promise me you'll never forget that," he said, his voice husky with emotion.

"How could I ever forget?" she asked, pulling his head down, meeting his mouth with her lips. She kissed him, drinking in his sweetness, pulling him toward her, wanting more, more. She lifted her hips up, pressing against his hardness, wanting him, needing him, now and for all time.

He entered her with one smooth thrust and they both cried out, their voices intertwined in the hushed stillness of the room.

Harmony. There was perfect harmony in the way their bodies moved together, harmony in the emotions that seemed to charge the very air around them, harmony in the love Pete felt for her, a love he knew she felt, too, just from looking into her beautiful eyes. It was like the sonorous consonance of nature, the perfectness of marriage between a Colorado mountain peak and the blue sky above it. Two bodies, two hearts, two souls joined in the ultimate collaboration. They were one, part of each other forever.

Annie exploded, swirling in a barrage of colors and sounds and sensations that focused on the man in her arms, this man she held so tightly, this man who had stolen her heart. Through the waves of her pleasure, she heard him call out her name, felt the shudder of his own tremendous release.

She held on to him tightly, feeling the pounding of both their hearts begin to slow. Spent, he lay on top of her, and still she clasped him to her, holding his body against hers, wanting to freeze time, keep them in this special place forever.

Pete's breathing became slow and steady, deep and relaxed.

"Taylor, are you awake?" Annie whispered.

He lifted his head to find himself staring directly into Annie's blue eyes. "Yeah," he said, then smiled, a slow, satisfied smile that made Annie's heart turn a quick somersault.

"I love you, too, you know," she said, and Pete closed his eyes briefly, feeling the warmth of her words surround his heart. She loved him.

"Pete, why did you leave my room that night?" she asked softly. "You know, I wanted you to stay."

"I couldn't," he said, tracing her eyebrows with one finger. "I wanted to, but I couldn't."

"Why not?"

He shook his head, uncertain of the best way to explain. "I wanted—I *still* want—more than just a sexual relationship," he finally said. "I want more than just a night or two or even two months of nights. I want forever, Annie. I want you to marry me—"

"Yes," she said, interrupting him.

Pete laughed. "But I wasn't— That wasn't—" He took a deep breath and started over. "There are things you need to know about me before I can even ask you to marry me."

He was looking at her with such love in his eyes, such emotion on his face. Annie shook her head. "I love you, Pete," she said simply. "And there's nothing you can tell me that will make me stop loving you."

He rolled onto his back, pulling her with him and holding her close. "I hope so," he said. "I hope so."

CHAPTER FOURTEEN

MORNING DAWNED COLD AND GRAY, but Annie was warm and secure, wrapped in Pete's arms in the hotel bed. She slept soundly, her long hair fanned out against the pillow, her legs comfortably intertwined with Pete's.

Pete watched her as she slept. He'd watched her sleep before, but this was the first time he'd watched her as he held her in his arms.

She loved him.

She'd told him that over and over last night, with more than just words.

Pete studied the freckles on her nose and the way her eyelashes lay against her cheek, hoping against hope that she loved him enough to handle the truth, to understand why he'd intentionally misled her.

What he couldn't figure out was how the hell he was going to find the right time, the right moment to tell her who he really was. He had to wait until the investigation was over, of course. But that wouldn't be long—not after Whitley Scott received Pete's report, which stated that, in his opinion, Annie Morrow was not involved in any kind of conspiracy.

How long would it take to get the report filed and the investigation dropped? A week, maybe two. By then they'd have this death mask mess cleared up, too. They'd track down whoever it was who had tried to kill them—

He'd come so close to losing her last night. Pete stared at the ceiling, holding Annie tighter. He couldn't bear the thought of losing her.

But when he imagined himself telling Annie he was CIA, it was so easy to picture her anger, to picture her storming out the door.

But she loves you, he reminded himself. Or did she? She loved Peter Taylor. Maybe she wouldn't feel the same about Kendall Peterson.

He closed his eyes, willing himself to stop thinking, letting sleep wash over him.

"ANNIE." PETE'S LAZY DRAWL whispered in her ear. "Wake up."

She awoke to the sensation of his roughly callused hands sweeping across her body. His thumb gently flicked her nipples to life, as his other hand moved lower, starting that now familiar surge of fire through her body. He pulled her hips toward him, entering her slowly.

She opened her eyes to find him watching her, his eyelids half-closed, a small smile on his handsome face. He moved languorously, unhurriedly, deliciously.

"Morning," he said.

"Well, this sure beats an alarm clock," Annie said with a smile. She stretched, lifting her hips and joining his rhythmic movements. "I could get used to this."

"You and me both," Pete said, rolling onto his back, pulling her on top of him. She leaned forward to kiss him, and the telephone rang.

Annie froze. "Nobody knows we're here," she said. "Do they?"

She moved to get off him, but he held her in place, reaching with his right hand to answer the phone. "Yeah," he said into the receiver, tucking it between his ear and shoulder. He looked up into Annie's eyes and pushed himself more deeply inside of her. She swallowed a sound of pleasure that almost escaped, and glared at Pete in mock outrage. He grinned at her. *Oh, yeah?* thought Annie. *Well, two can play this game.*

She began to move on top of him. His eyelids slid halfway down again and he smiled, his dark eyes molten with desire.

"Yeah, that's fine," he said into the telephone. His gaze strayed downward, caressing Annie's body. "Really fine," he said to her.

But she wanted to see him squirm. She leaned forward, leaving a trail of light, feathery kisses up his neck to a little extrasensitive spot she'd found right underneath his ear—

"Uh!" Pete said, then covered it with a cough. He wiggled away, pushing her back up, keeping her at arm's length. "No, no, I'm all right," he said into the telephone, flashing Annie a look of surrender. "Okay, but we need an hour." There was a pause, then he said, "Tough. Go eat a doughnut. I'll see you in an hour."

He hung up the phone, then pulled Annie down, kissing her hard on the mouth.

They made love slowly, tenderly, in the morning light.

"Who was on the phone?" she asked later, lying back, satisfied, in his arms.

He kissed the top of her head. "A guy named Scott, from the bureau."

Annie sat up, turning to look at him. "Bureau? As in Federal Bureau of Investigations? As in the FBI?"

Pete nodded. "Yeah. I called them last night while you were in the shower. I thought they might like to know the plate number of the car that tried to flatten us. At the same time, I figured we could use 'em for a safe ride up to Westchester this morning. That was what they were calling me about. They've got a car ready, down on parking level one."

"You actually got a look at the license plate of that car last night?" Annie said, her eyes wide. "*And* you remembered it? I'm impressed."

"Just doing my job, ma'am," Pete said a little too modestly. He swung Annie up, pushing her out of the bed. "In about twenty-five minutes, there's going to be a swarm of FBI agents knocking at the door, ready to escort us down to the car. I recommend taking a shower now, because when we get back to your house, we're going to have to give them a detailed account of the hit and run attempt. It could take some time."

"Don't I know," Annie muttered under her breath.

She took a quick shower, then eased her blue jeans on over the scrape on her knee. She sat on the bedroom floor and rummaged in her overnight bag, pulling out a well-worn T-shirt and a pair of socks and her sneakers, and quickly got dressed.

There was a pile of weaponry on the table—Pete's guns. Bemused, she counted three different guns. Why so many? she wondered. In case he dropped one?

A loud hammering at the door made her jump. Startled, she scrambled to her feet, backing toward the bathroom door.

Pete was still in the shower; she could hear it running. But the water shut off as the pounding was repeated.

The door to the bathroom was ajar, and Annie pushed it open. "Pete?"

Steam swirled in the small room, fogging the mirrors, curling around Pete as he stood naked on the bath mat, drying his lean, athletic body. He looked up at her, reading her face swiftly and accurately as usual. "What's wrong?"

"Someone's at the door."

He swore under his breath, giving himself a few more swipes with his towel before he wrapped it around his waist. Annie followed him out into the bedroom, and Pete motioned for her to move to one side as he grabbed one of his guns and approached the door. Obediently hanging back, Annie watched as he looked out into the hallway through the door's peephole. The tension in his shoulders and neck visibly decreased, and he pulled the chair away from under the doorknob and opened the door a crack.

"You're early," Annie heard him say.

"Brought ya breakfast," she heard a man's voice say. "A bag of doughnuts and coffee. Figured you could probably use the extra energy more than I could."

"Give me ten minutes," Pete said, "and we'll be ready to go."

"Take all the minutes you need," the man said. "No one's going anywhere for a long time."

The tightness returned to Pete's shoulders. "What's going on?"

"You'd better open the door, Captain," another, different voice said.

Captain, thought Annie. *Now why the heck would they call Pete that?*

He shot a quick look over his shoulder at her, then moved closer to the door, saying something in a low voice.

"To hell with your cover, Captain Peterson," the first man said. He pushed his way through the door, into the room, his eyes falling on Annie. "This entire investigation's over," he said, waving a folded document in the air. "I'm holding a warrant for the arrest of Dr. Anne Morrow."

Annie stared. "What?" she said. She looked at Pete. "Pete, what's going on? Who is this man?"

"It's simple, lady." The man smiled at her from behind a thick pair of glasses. "I'm Whitley Scott, with the FBI. You're already familiar with Captain Peterson, here. He's CIA."

Pete had taken the paper from Scott's hand and was reading it, his eyes quickly skimming down the pages. He looked up to meet Annie's shocked gaze.

"No," Annie breathed. But she knew it was true. She could see the guilt in Pete's dark eyes.

"And you," Scott continued, "are busted. We're

charging you with five different felonies, including robbery, conspiracy, felony murder." He turned to Pete. "You wanna Miranda her?"

"Oh, God," Annie said. Pete was CIA....

"No," Pete said, his voice low.

"Collins," Scott addressed one of the other men who had come into the room with him. "Read her her rights and frisk her."

"No," Pete said, his voice sharp. "She's clean."

"You know it's gotta be done," Scott said.

"You have the right to remain silent," Collins began to drone.

"I'll frisk her," Pete said.

"Anything you say can and will be used against you in a court of law."

"Nice room," said Scott. He looked at the unmade bed, at the condom wrappers that still lay scattered on the floor. He smirked. "Must've been one hell of a night, eh, Peterson?"

"Oh, *God*," Annie said. Pete was *CIA*....

Pete took her arm, and she looked up at him, startled by his touch. "You son of a bitch," she said, pulling away from him.

"You have the right to an attorney," Collins said.

"Annie, I don't know what this is all about," Pete said, talking low and fast, "but I'm going to find out. Right now you need to stay calm."

"If you cannot afford an attorney," Collins said, "one will be appointed for you at no cost."

On the other side of the room, Scott opened the curtains and the gray light of a rainy October morning did little to illuminate the room. "Nice view of the park," he said.

"This has to be done," Pete told Annie, "and I'll do it as quickly as I can, but you've got to help me."

"Do you understand these rights as I have read them to you?" Collins said.

"Spread your legs apart and put your hands on your head," Pete said.

Woodenly, Annie obeyed him.

"Dr. Morrow," Collins said. "Do you understand these rights?"

"Yes," Annie whispered. She closed her eyes as Pete's hands moved methodically and impersonally over her body. Oh, *God…*

"She's clean," she heard him say, his voice tight, clipped.

Everything he had told her was a lie. His name was Peterson, not Pete Taylor. He wasn't a bodyguard. He probably wasn't even half-Navaho, probably had never even been to Colorado. He'd only been using her to get information.

He didn't love her.

It was all a lie. He didn't love her….

"I'm going to be sick," Annie said, lunging for the bathroom.

Collins and the other FBI agent moved to follow, but Pete blocked the door. "I'll handle it," he said.

He went into the bathroom, closing and locking the door behind him.

Annie knelt on the floor in front of the commode. Her face was pale. Taking a washcloth from the towel rack, Pete ran it under cool water and handed it to her.

"Pete, how could you?" she asked, reproach in her eyes. "How could you use me this way?"

His clothes lay in a pile near the shower. He pulled his shorts on under his towel, then used the towel to dry his hair. "There's something really wrong here," he said, almost to himself.

"Captain Peterson," she said, looking at him with new horror in her eyes as he pulled on his jeans. "You're that horrible man who was behind the mirror window at the airport, aren't you? And I *slept* with you. You *bastard*—"

"Annie, I meant it when I said that I loved you," he said. "You've got to believe that. And you've got to trust me until I figure out what's going on."

She laughed, a dull, hollow sound. "You're kidding, right?"

He grabbed her by the shoulders, pulling her up to her feet. "You made me a promise," he said, shaking her slightly. "You promised not to forget that I love you, so don't forget, damn it."

She pulled away from him. "I made that promise to Pete Taylor, and you're obviously not him." Her eyes filled with tears, and she fought them back. "You can go to hell, Captain Peterson."

She turned and walked out of the bathroom, closing the door tightly behind her.

CHAPTER FIFTEEN

THE INTERROGATION ROOM HELD ONE table and some stiff-backed wooden chairs. The walls were a dull, ugly shade of beige, and the floor was cheap, industrial linoleum tile. *This is what hell looks like,* Annie thought, fatigue washing over her as she looked around the table at the myriad of FBI agents that sat looking back at her. She was even willing to bet that Satan wore a dark suit exactly like the ones these men had on.

She clasped her hands tightly in front of her on the table. "If you can't get more specific with your charges," she said tightly, "then you better release me."

Scott leaned back in his chair. "So you're saying that you've never been in possession of these artifacts, and you don't know how they got into your house."

Annie glanced down at the pictures for the hundredth time in the past few hours. They were antiquities—some she recognized, most she didn't. But none had ever been near her house, much less in her possession. "I told you I don't know how any of this happened," she said, not for the first time.

Scott nodded, obviously not believing her.

She leaned forward. "Tell me, Scott," she said. "Why in God's name would I become involved in some idiotic art robbery? Why would I bomb museums? I've got an impeccable reputation, I make a decent living, I'm respected by my peers—why would I risk all that?"

"You tell me."

The door opened and Pete came in. Captain Peterson, Annie corrected herself, trying to numb the pain that seeing him brought. He was wearing a conservative dark suit exactly like all the other agents, and Annie almost didn't recognize him. Almost. He looked around the room, and one eyebrow went down very slightly in his version of a frown. Annie's stomach hurt. She could read his face so well, even now. How was it that she hadn't picked up on his lies?

"Where's your lawyer?" he asked Annie.

Scott answered for her. "She's waived her right." He grinned. "She says she's not guilty, so she doesn't need an attorney."

"Get her one," Peterson said coldly.

"She doesn't want one," Scott said. "I can't force one down her damned throat."

Annie was looking at Pete as if he were something that had crawled out from under a rock. "I don't want him in here," she said to Scott. "Make him leave."

Scott shrugged, obviously enjoying her discomfort. "Can't do that," he said. "Captain Peterson's as much in charge here as I am."

Pete set a file down in front of Scott and sat down across from her. Annie turned away, not looking at him.

"All right," Scott said to Annie, opening the file and shuffling through the papers. "You want to get specific?" He pulled out a piece of paper, and began to read it.

"'Two packages were observed on a counter in the laboratory of the suspect's house. They were open, and contained articles numbered one through eight. The articles, in plain view of the investigating officers, matched the description of those articles missing from the English Gallery. The packages were seized in accordance with the warrant blah blah blah.'" He pushed the report across the table to her. "Read it and weep," he said.

The room was spinning. Annie leafed through the pages of the report, describing the room-by-room search, the description of the artifacts...

"What gave you the right to search my home?" she asked quietly.

"The warrant was obtained as a result of evidence gathered over the course of this investigation, and a tip—"

"Who?" Annie demanded. "Who gave you this *tip?*"

"This information came to us anonymously," Scott said.

"Oh, terrific!" Annie threw up her hands. "Obviously a reliable source—"

"It certainly turned out to be, didn't it?" Scott said, leaning across the table. "Especially when we found materials to construct explosives in a desk drawer in your office."

"What?" Annie gasped. Her eyes moved involuntarily to Pete's face. He was expressionless, his dark eyes watching her steadily. "This is some kind of setup," she said. The enormity of the situation crashed down around her, and she realized for the first time that she was in serious trouble. The stolen artifacts, the explosives... "I want a lawyer."

She looked back at the report in front of her. "Two packages were observed on a counter in the laboratory of the suspect's house."

On a counter in the laboratory of the suspect's house.

In the laboratory!

Yes!

Pete had been in the lab with her before they left for New York City. He'd seen that the counters were clean, everything put away. He had locked the place up as they left the house, and had been with her ever since. He could confirm her story. He would tell them she had nothing to do with this!

Yes!

"Pete," she said, excitement vibrating through her voice. She handed him the report. "You were with me when I went into the lab to turn off the lights before we went out last night, remember? The lab was all cleaned up—the counters were clear. You were right there in the doorway."

Pete glanced up from the report. His eyes were expressionless, his face guarded.

"Remember?"

He had to remember. Of course he'd remember.

"Nick was waiting for us outside. You told me I looked beautiful." Suddenly she looked down at her hands, and blushed at the memory. But she had to go on; she desperately needed him to stand with her now, no matter how humiliating. "You were looking at me—" she swallowed and looked up at him "—like you wanted to kiss me."

Pete met her gaze for only a second before

looking back at the report, his eyes narrowing as if in concentration.

"Remember?"

He handed the paper back to Scott, glancing briefly at Annie, his eyes cold, detached. "No."

She stared at him, shock draining the blood from her face, leaving her pale. Oh, God, he was part of it, part of the setup....

Pete stood up, careful not to meet her eyes. "I'll go make arrangements for a lawyer," he said, leaving the room.

Annie stared down at the table, forcing herself not to cry as what was left of her heart shattered into a billion tiny pieces.

ANNIE WALKED UP THE DRIVEWAY to her house. Her thin formal jacket was wrapped tightly around her, but it did little to keep out the rain on the long, cold walk from the train station. There were no lights burning in her windows, nothing to welcome her home.

Home. Lord, she couldn't believe she was actually here. Once her attorney had arrived, the endless interrogation had stopped and bail was set. She'd been ready to call her parents to ask for help in posting the quarter-million-dollar bail when she found out that bail had already been paid by an anonymous source.

Her father, she thought gratefully. Somehow he had found out she was in trouble even before her call, and he'd come to her rescue.

The trial date was set for three months from now, and her license was revoked until that time. She couldn't work, couldn't even finish the work she'd started.

With a disparaging laugh, she remembered the phone call that had told her not to touch the golden death mask, warning her that Stands Against the Storm's evil spirit would harm her if she did. As a result, her life would crumble.

You win, Stands Against the Storm, she thought. Her life had indeed crumbled.

Keying her authorization code into the outside alarm control panel, she waited for the light to go from red to green. Unlocking the front door, she sighed. First thing in the morning, she'd have to pack up everything in her safe, ship it back to all the owners....

She turned the alarm back on and climbed the stairs in the dark and went into her bedroom. Was it only last night that she'd been so happy? Dancing with Pete, making love to him— How could she have been so stupid? He must be laughing at her now.

She dumped her bag on the floor. Shivering, she went into the bathroom, turned on the light and quickly stripped off her wet clothes.

Steam from her hot shower soon fogged the mirror, and she washed herself, washed off the very last trace of Pete's scent. Closing her eyes, she let the water run over her face, disguising the tears that she couldn't hold back any longer.

"ANNIE, WAKE UP."

She opened her eyes to find Peterson sitting on her bed, looking down at her. She didn't move, she just stared.

"Are you awake?" he asked. The morning light coming in behind the curtains dimly lit his face. He looked tired, his eyes red and bleary, as if he hadn't slept. He had changed out of that dreadful dark suit and back into his familiar blue jeans and T-shirt.

"No," she said. "I better not be. I better be dreaming. You better not be sitting here in my room like this."

He tried to smile, but it came out as a wry twist of his lips. "Sorry," he said. "I'm really sitting here."

A host of different emotions flew across her face, but anger won. Her eyes blazed. "Get out."

"Annie, I had to—"

"I don't want to hear it, *Captain Peterson*." She said his name sarcastically, her teeth clenched in barely controlled rage. "You son of a bitch. You set me up. Get out of my house!"

"I didn't know about—"

"You really expect me to believe that?" she seethed. "I know damn well you remember coming into the lab with me when I turned off the lights that night. You *know* that stuff from the English Gallery wasn't there."

"Annie—"

She kicked him, hard, her foot against his back, but the bed covers broke the force of the blow, and he didn't even flinch. "You bastard," she shouted. "The FBI decided that I was guilty five months ago. But they couldn't prove it, so they had to frame me. And you're just going to go along with it, aren't you? Because you're one of them, you creep!"

He gave up trying to explain. He sat there, watching her quietly, letting her vent her anger.

"Tell me," she said, her voice biting, "do you get extra points for sleeping with me, Captain? Four times in one night! You probably got stud points from the other guys for that. Oh, yeah, and once in the morning. A nice touch. Make your buddies wait out in the hall while you make it with the suspect one last time before you arrest her—"

He couldn't hold it in. "I didn't know they had a warrant—"

"Do you *really* expect me to believe *any*thing you say?" she said, as her eyes accused him of terrible crimes.

He looked down at the floor, knowing that he was guilty. He'd kept the truth about his identity from her for all those weeks, even after he knew he was in love with her, even after he knew she couldn't possibly be involved in any kind of crime. He *was* guilty. "No," he said quietly. "No, I don't."

"You were so good," she said, her voice breaking. "All those stories you told about when you were a kid, living out in Colorado, about your Indian grandfather— You probably grew up in the Bronx, right?"

"Not everything I told you was a lie," he said, meeting her gaze. "Those stories were all true. And I was telling you the truth when I said that I love you." He looked down at his hands, clenched tightly into fists on his lap. "I know you don't believe me...."

"Yeah, you're right. I don't," Annie said, watching him close his eyes against the harshness of her words. "What do you want from me? Why are you here?"

Pete stood up and walked across the room. "You're being framed," he said, his back to her as he composed himself.

She laughed, a harsh exhale of air. "Tell me something new, Captain America."

"I want to help you," he said, turning to look at her.

"*Now* you want to help me?" she said, tight anger in her voice. "Yesterday, you could have told them that those things weren't in the lab—"

"Annie, I'm here because you're not safe," he interrupted. "Someone on the inside is in on this frame, and I don't know who it is."

Annie stared at him.

He smiled, a tight, satisfied smile. "Yeah, I *was* there that night, Annie. And I *do* remember. I saw the lab. I know you're being set up."

She kept staring at him, the tiniest seed of hope fluttering in her stomach.

"Why didn't you say something yesterday?" she asked, her voice low. "You could have saved my reputation."

"I thought it was more important to save your life." His dark eyes held her captive. "Until I know how many people are in on this thing, you're safer if they think no one believes you."

"But the FBI? How—"

"All I know is too many things don't add up. How did someone get into the house to put those bats in your room? How did they get in to plant that stolen art? Nobody had the codes to the security system except you, me and Cara...*and* anyone who had access to your case file."

"But what about all those fringe groups the FBI was going to investigate?"

He shook his head. "There's no way one of those groups is responsible for bombing and robbing two

European art galleries—or disarming a professional alarm system to plant bats in your bedroom and stolen art in your lab."

Pete was pacing now. "There's just too much that's wrong about this." He stopped in the middle of the room and faced Annie again. "Why would someone want to kill you? Or why would they want you arrested, in jail, out of the picture?"

Annie stared at him and Pete smiled grimly. "There's a lot of things we don't know. And it's about time we started finding out."

PETE SIFTED THROUGH THE PILE of file folders that were out on Annie's desk. He ran his fingers through his hair, then leaned back and stretched. Man, they were getting nowhere….

"*Here* it is," Annie called from the floor in front of her file cabinet. "June 4, 1989. Back before I started using my computer system. That was the last time I tested anything for the English Gallery. It was a gold ring from ninth-century Wales. Wanna see the file?"

"Sure, why not?" Pete said. He spun in his chair to face her as she brought the folder to the desk. "How come it's been such a long time? Recession hitting them, too?"

Annie shook her head. "No. Alistair Golden's

pretty much got that gallery locked up for sales coming into the United States. They use him exclusively. If it hadn't been for Ben Sullivan, I never would have gotten this job."

Pete frowned. Then reached for the telephone. As Annie watched, he dialed a number. "Yeah," he said, into the phone. "This is Peterson. I need access to a list of all sales of artwork and other artifacts brought into the U.S. via the English Gallery."

"But I've got that information," Annie said.

He looked at her in surprise. "Let me call you back," he said into the phone. He hung up and looked at her questioningly.

"I'm tied into a computer network that keeps track of current sales of artwork and artifacts—anything from a Picasso to a Stone Age ax," Annie said. She came around to his side of the desk and turned on her personal computer and her modem. "It's useful information for art brokers to have. Using this list, I can track down and access a buyer for just about anything. Take your necklace, for instance. If you wanted to sell it, I could find a buyer simply by calling up the names of all the people who have made multiple purchases of Navaho jewelry over the past several months."

Pete leaned back in his chair to give her better access to the keyboard. She narrowed her eyes slightly in concentration as she keyed in the commands to sign on to the network.

"All we have to do is request a specific list where the gallery was the English, and point of shipping equals U.S.A...."

She was close enough for him to reach out and touch her, but Pete didn't dare. Just over twenty-four hours ago, she'd told him that she loved him. But he could still see the look on her face when she found out he was a government agent, sent to investigate her. He remembered her eyes as her love for him died. His heart ached. It was his own damned fault....

"Here we go," she said.

A list of dates and items scrolled down the computer screen. Pete forced his thoughts back to the task at hand and leaned forward for a closer look.

"It's chronological," Annie said, turning toward him. They were nearly nose to nose, and she quickly straightened up. "The most current shipments are at the very bottom."

She sat on the edge of the desk and watched Pete from a safe distance as he moved the cursor down the long list. His handsome face was lit by the amber light from the computer screen. He looked exhausted, overtired, but there was a glint of determination in his eyes. He glanced up, feeling her watching him.

"Why are you doing this?" she asked.

"Because I know you're not guilty," he said, looking back at the computer.

"You paid my bail, didn't you?"

"Yeah."

"Where did you get that kind of money?" Annie asked.

"I borrowed it. If you skip town, I lose everything. My car, my condo…" He looked up at her again, and the familiar glint of humor in his eyes made her heart twist. "Who knows? The guys I borrowed it from would probably even break my legs."

"Why would you risk all that for me?" she asked.

"I'd risk everything," he said simply, squinting at the computer screen. "Even my life…."

"Why?"

Pete looked up at her. "It's not that hard to figure out," he said. "I'm in love with you, Annie."

She stared down at him for several long moments, wishing that he hadn't turned into this stranger sitting before her—a stranger she somehow knew so well. But that was just an illusion. She only thought she knew him. Pete Taylor had been only a cover, a charade. He was gone as absolutely as if he had died. Annie felt a stab of grief so sharp and painful that she almost cried out.

"Is there…" Pete said, then cleared his throat and

started again. "Do I have any chance at all? With you?"

He looked like Pete Taylor. He sounded like Pete Taylor. He even acted like Pete Taylor. But he wasn't Pete Taylor. He wasn't—

Annie pushed herself off the desk, unable to meet his eyes. "No."

Pete nodded, as if that were the answer he had been expecting. With the muscle in his jaw working, he turned his attention back to the computer, as though his last hopes hadn't been dashed to bits.

CHAPTER SIXTEEN

WHEN ANNIE WENT BACK INTO THE office, Pete was on the phone again.

He had printed out a list of names, dates and transactions from the computer, and she glanced over his shoulder, trying to make some sense of it.

He hung up the phone and turned toward her.

"Any luck?" she asked.

"You know this guy Steadman?" he asked, pointing to the list. He was a buyer, and his name appeared repeatedly.

Annie shook her head.

"He buys things from the English Gallery like it's a K mart end-of-the-season sale," Pete said. "There are also a couple of other partnerships and corporations whose names come up frequently."

"But these were all legitimate transactions," Annie protested, looking at the list again. "Some of these pieces are well-known, and these prices are all fair…."

Pete spent the rest of the morning and most of the afternoon on the telephone, trying to gather more information.

Annie went upstairs and cleaned the last of the mess the bats had made out of her bedroom and tried not to think about Peterson. But as she scrubbed the floor, she kept hearing his voice as he asked her if he still had a chance with her. No, she told herself over and over. Absolutely not. She didn't love him. She refused to love him. Sure, she still found him physically attractive....

She closed her eyes for a moment, remembering the night they'd spent together, the night they'd made love. Had it been only two nights ago? It seemed as if a million years had passed since he'd held her in his arms....

"Are you all right?"

Startled, Annie opened her eyes to find Pete standing in the doorway. "Yeah," she said, attacking the floor with renewed vigor. "What did you find out? Anything?"

Pete squatted down next to the bucket, pulling out a second sponge and going to work beside her. "Something," he said. "I'm waiting for a few more calls that should give me the rest of the information I need. Apparently, Mr. J. J. Steadman is buying most of the stuff that comes out of the English Gallery one way or the other. He's an owner or a partner in every single one of the companies on that list of buyers."

Annie stopped scrubbing the floor. "Quite the busy little collector."

Pete smiled and Annie had to look away. "Quite. And quite the mediocre one, too, it seems. He rarely holds on to the pieces for more than a couple of months after he buys them, and he often sells them at a small loss."

"Big deal," Annie said. "There's no law that says that rich people can't be stupid."

"Yeah," Pete said. The muscles in his back and arms rippled as he rubbed the sponge across the dirty floor. "But get a load of this." He smiled at her as he rinsed the sponge in the bucket. "Guess who else owns a piece of J. J. Steadman's companies. Give you a hint. Funny green eyes, gold bracelet, kind of like a rattlesnake in a tux?"

Annie had to smile at him. "Let's see... Could it be Alistair Golden?"

They smiled into each other's eyes; then Annie looked away, her expression suddenly guarded, distant.

They scrubbed for several minutes in silence; then she leaned back on her heels. "You know, Peterson, I don't even know your first name."

Pete looked up. "Kendall," he said. "But nobody calls me that. Everyone calls me Pete."

"Even your mother?" Annie asked.

"She calls me Hastin Naat'aanni."

Man Speaking Peace, his Navaho name.

"That really happened?" Annie said. "It was true, that story you told me, about your cousins, when your aunt died?"

Pete threw his sponge in the bucket and sat cross-legged on the floor, his elbows around his knees. "With the exception of my name, my career and my college, I lied to you only by omission," he said. "Everything else I told you was the truth. I just didn't tell you enough."

Annie was quiet for a moment. "Why did you lie to me about going to New York University? Where *did* you go to school?"

"I didn't," Pete said. "I went to Vietnam. I was drafted when I turned eighteen."

"*That's* where your grandfather didn't want you to go," Annie said, sudden comprehension lighting her eyes.

Pete nodded, looking into the bucket of soapy water. "He didn't understand why a kid named Man Speaking Peace had to go fight a war on the other side of the ocean. He didn't like war," he said. "I didn't, either." But he smiled, and Annie was chilled by the hardness in his eyes. "I was good at it, though. I was good at staying alive, too. And I was good at search-and-rescue raids. I spent most of my time in enemy territory, finding the guys who'd been shot down and bringing them out of the jungle. In '75, after they pulled the troops out, I was asked to stay behind."

"Stay behind," Annie repeated, horror in her voice. "Why on earth would you want to do that?"

"I didn't *want* to. But they asked me to become part of an agency team that was working to locate and free POWs and MIAs," Pete said quietly.

"So you stayed."

"I stayed. I spent about four more years in southeast Asia, doing what I did best," he said. "Making war."

"You were saving lives," Annie protested. "How many men did you help set free?"

Pete looked at her in surprise. She was actually defending him. His heart skipped a beat and he tried to control it. It didn't mean a thing…. "I never knew the exact figures," he said. "But it was in the hundreds."

"After that you joined the CIA?" she asked.

She wanted to know about him. Was it mere curiosity, or… Pete couldn't dare to hope. He nodded. "As a field operative."

"So you've spent most of the past two decades risking your life," she said, shaking her head.

"Not all the time—"

"Oh, I suppose you get a weekend off every few years or so," she said. "How can you live that way, with your life always in danger...?"

"Look at it from my perspective," Pete said. "If I'd stayed in Colorado, I would never have met you."

Annie's eyes narrowed. "Then you definitely should have stayed in Colorado," she said sharply. She stood up suddenly and carried the bucket into the bathroom, flushing the dirty water down the toilet, watching it swirl away.

Pete followed her. "In my life, with my job, I have to get things right the first time around," he said, his voice low and intense. "If I don't, I'm dead. Every now and then I'll blow it, though. I'll make a really bad decision, make a major mistake. After I get over the surprise that I'm still alive, I grab that second chance and I don't let go. And I'm damn sure I don't mess up the second time around."

She was looking at him, her eyes so wide, so blue. He couldn't help himself—he took a step toward her, and then another and another. Before he could stop himself, he'd taken her into his arms. She was shaking, but at least she didn't pull away. "Annie, give me a second chance," he whispered. "I love you— God, please, I need you in my life...."

And still she didn't pull away. Her breasts were rising and falling with each breath she took, as if she had just run a mile. Pete felt his own pulse pounding as his fear of driving her away wrestled with his need. Need won, and he kissed her.

Her mouth was soft, warm and as sweet as he remembered. He felt her arms tighten around him as she responded to him, and he prayed—hell, he *begged* the gods for that second chance.

She opened her mouth under his, and he nearly wept—until she struggled to break free. He released her immediately, and she stared at him, her eyes accusing.

"No," she breathed. "I can't."

Annie ran from the room, leaving Pete alone.

THE PHONE RANG SHRILLY, QUICKLY pulling Annie out of a restless, uneasy sleep. The clock on her bedside table said it was after 2:00 a.m., but there was a light on in the kitchen, shining in through her bedroom door. She could hear Pete talking on the phone, his voice lowered so as not to disturb her.

He was on the phone, sitting at the kitchen table, writing in his little notebook. His T-shirt was off and his hair was rumpled. His eyes were rimmed with red, as if he still hadn't gotten any sleep.

"Yeah, I got it all," he said into the telephone, looking up at Annie. She stood in the doorway, squinting at him, letting her eyes adjust to the bright light. "Thanks, I owe you one."

Pete stood to hang up the phone, and Annie saw that he wore only a tight pair of white briefs. She looked away, embarrassed at her body's instant reaction to his masculinity, afraid to be caught staring.

He immediately noticed her discomfort. "I'm sorry," he apologized quietly. "I was lying down when the phone rang. I wanted to answer it before it woke you."

Annie went to the stove, putting on a kettle of hot water for tea. "What did you find out?" she asked, her back to him.

"Let me put on my jeans," he said. "Then I'll tell you."

"Do you want a cup of tea?" Annie asked as Pete came back into the kitchen, tucking his T-shirt into the waistband of his jeans. Now *she* felt under-dressed, standing there in her flannel pajamas.

"Thanks," Pete said gratefully.

She got a second mug down from the cabinet and dropped a tea bag into it, then leaned against the counter, arms folded across her chest, waiting for the water to boil.

Pete took a lemon from the refrigerator, grabbed the cutting board from the shelf and opened the knife drawer. He was at home here in her kitchen, Annie realized. He knew where everything was; he knew where to find the plates and the glasses, he even knew where she hid a chocolate bar for those times when nothing else would substitute. *He* knew all those things. Captain Kendall Peterson, formerly of the U.S. Army, currently of the CIA, knew all sorts of private and personal things about her. Because everything that Peter Taylor had seen and heard, Kendall Peterson remembered.

"How do you do it?" Annie asked.

He glanced up at her, then finished cutting the lemon neatly into eighths. "Do what?"

"How can you take on someone else's identity for such a long period of time?" Annie asked. "Don't you start to lose your own self?"

Pete shook his head. "Annie, it's not like I'm an actor," he said. He turned toward her, trying to make her understand. "I just take a different name, a different label. It doesn't matter whether you call me Captain or Peterson or Taylor or Hastin Naat'aanni, or whether my driver's license says I'm from Colorado or New York City. I am always the same man. I am me—I'm Pete."

"You think of yourself as Pete," Annie said, "not Hastin Naat'aanni, Man Speaking Peace?"

Pete was silent for a moment, looking down at his bare feet against the black-and-white tile floor. "I *am* Hastin Naat'aanni. I always will be. But in Vietnam, the men in my platoon called me Machine—short for War Machine. I'm that, too."

The teakettle whistled, and Annie turned toward the stove, shutting off the gas. She filled both mugs with steaming water, then set them down on the table. Pete brought the plate of lemons over and sat down across from her.

Annie bobbed her tea bag up and down in her mug, watching as the hot water was slowly stained brown.

"Want to hear what I found out?" he asked.

"Is it good news or bad news?" she countered.

"It's strange," Pete said.

"Fire away."

"Okay. So far, we've got J. J. Steadman—whoever he is—and Alistair Golden as partners in some pretty lame art-collecting companies. And we already know Golden authenticates everything that comes out of the English Gallery—everything except for this one artifact, the death mask." Pete thought for a moment, and then asked, "Does it make any sense that Golden should fly to England *before* every single transaction?"

"Hardly," Annie said, taking a sip of her tea, testing to see if it was strong enough. "But Golden isn't exactly what I'd call sensible. Apparently he insists on packing the artwork or artifacts himself. I think he's kind of anal retentive."

She was silent as she fished the tea bag out of her mug and put it in the garbage. She squeezed a piece of lemon into her tea, then took another sip. "I called Ben Sullivan and told him about this mess I'm in," she said, taking a sip. "I told him I'd be shipping the death mask back to him, and he asked me to recommend another authenticator besides Golden. Seems Golden threw a little bit of a fit when he found out he wasn't going to do the work, and he called up Ben and screamed in his ear. Ben was not impressed."

Shipping the death mask back.

The death mask.

Somehow it was connected to Annie's being framed.

And although Pete couldn't say why, returning the death mask to Sullivan seemed even more dangerous than keeping it.

CHAPTER SEVENTEEN

THE NEXT DAY, ALISTAIR GOLDEN called.

"He said that he wants to come by and discuss taking over some of my work," Annie said. "Since my license has been revoked, *some*one has to do the jobs. And suddenly he's my best friend…."

Pete listened silently.

"He says he'll pay me a referral fee," Annie continued, "and, of course, he'll get all the necessary approvals."

Pete nodded. "Squeaky-clean."

Annie shrugged. "I told him it was okay with me. I mean, I've got to do something with all this work I'm supposed to be doing. I can't just sit on it until my trial."

"Yeah, I know." Pete stood up. "When's he coming?"

"Sometime around three this afternoon."

"I'd like to talk with him when he gets here," Pete said. "On the record."

AT AROUND NOON, ANNIE WATCHED as Pete carefully taped the tiny microphone to his chest, just under his collarbone. Then he buttoned his shirt back up and shrugged on his heavy leather jacket. He picked up the set of headphones he had placed on the desk in the office and handed them to Annie. "This whole surveillance unit is mobile. You can hook the recorder to your belt and carry it with you wherever you go. If you want to hear what's going on, just listen in on the headphones."

"What do you expect him to do, confess to framing me?" Annie said. "We don't even know he's involved."

"Maybe he's not, but maybe he is," Pete replied. He headed downstairs, and Annie followed. "I'm going to go outside and walk around the house to check the range on this thing. When he comes, I want to meet him outdoors and see if I can find out anything before we let him in."

He accessed the alarm system bypass and opened the front door.

"I'll keep talking as I walk around outside," Pete said. "You keep the headphones on, and if you can hear me, flick the outside floodlights on and off."

She looked up at him and said, "I know it's silly, and Alistair Golden is probably about as dangerous as a worm, but this cloak-and-dagger stuff really gets me nervous."

Annie stared into Pete's bottomless dark eyes, searching for what, she wasn't sure. Dishonesty, maybe. Or deceit. But all she could see was love. He loved her. He really, truly loved her. He looked away, as if embarrassed by her scrutiny.

"I'd better get out there," he said.

"Pete," she said.

He stopped and turned back, his face carefully revealing no emotion. "Yeah?"

"No matter what happens, you're going to be careful, right?"

He didn't answer right away, but his heart showed in his eyes as a seed of hope took root and bloomed all in the space of a few short seconds. "Yeah," he finally said, his voice huskier than usual. "You bet I'm going to be careful."

She looked so worried, her blue eyes darkened with anxiety. He reached out and pushed a lock of hair back from her face, stroking her soft cheek with his thumb. "Everything's going to work out," he said gently.

Annie's blue eyes filled with tears. "Everything but us," she said. "I just can't forgive you, Pete."

"Have you really tried?" he asked softly.

ANNIE SLIPPED THE HEADPHONES over her ears.

"Okay, I'm out here," Pete said as he stepped off the porch. He turned to see the floodlights switch on and then off again. "I'm heading around to the side of the house now."

The lights flicked on and off steadily as he made his way around the house, talking all the while. When he got to the front of the house he went onto the lawn and said, "I'm in the front yard now, and believe it or not, it looks like the lawn could use another raking." He looked back at the house, and for a moment, the lights did not come on. Then they did, and quickly went off again. He then spoke softly. "And I'd very much like to help you rake it, Annie." And again the lights stayed unlit for several moments, finally flashing on for a brief second before being extinguished again.

Finally Pete squared his shoulders in the middle of the yard and faced the house head-on. Looking directly into the darkened floodlights, he tried to speak, but his voice broke. He bowed his head, looked up again at the big house he had come to think of as his home, took a deep breath and said, "I'm talking really quietly now, I can barely hear my own voice. Can you hear me? I love you, Annie. And I'm going to win you back if it's the last thing I do."

The floodlights never came on.

ANNIE BRUSQUELY WIPED AT THE tear that had escaped and was running down her cheek. She was about to pull the headphones off when she heard Pete curse under his breath, and then say, "Annie, our guest has arrived three hours early. How rude of him. Of *them*."

At that, Annie hurried to the front of the house to look out the window. Golden, impeccably dressed in a dark blue suit and a maroon tie with accent hand-kerchief, was getting out of his car, and that broker, Joseph James, or James Joseph, or whoever he was, wearing jeans and a light jacket, was getting out of the other side of the car. Pete was running across the lawn toward them as they came up the porch steps. Pete was whispering to her as he ran.

"Annie, lock the door and don't open it, *no matter what happens*. Turn on the alarm, get the death mask out of the safe and hide it in the attic somewhere. Then get out the back door, and get to a safe place. Do you understand me?"

Even as he said the words, she was locking the door, turning on the alarm. As she ran to the safe, got the death mask and hauled the heavy box up to the attic, she muttered under her breath, while another tear ran down her cheek, unchecked, "You be careful, do you understand *me?*"

"WELL, LOOKEE HERE, IF IT ISN'T FIDO," Joseph James said to Pete, an unpleasant smile on his un-pleasant face.

"You gentlemen might want to get someone to check your watches. You appear to be a little early." Pete smiled. "What's the rush?"

"We decided to come for lunch," Joseph James said, folding his arms across his broad chest with a smirk. "On account of our busy schedules."

Joseph James.

It came to him in a flash.

Pete eyed the two men and decided to take a chance. If he was right, he had to keep them talking and out of the house. If he could get them to say something stupid, the tape would prove Annie was innocent, even if he messed up and they killed him.

Pete smiled broadly at the taller of the two men. "Well. We were expecting only Dr. Golden, not you, Mr. James. Or is it Mr. Joseph? Or maybe… Mr. Steadman?"

At that, the man took a step toward Pete, until his face was inches away. "Maybe you should shut up," he snarled.

Jackpot.

Pete looked steadily at Steadman, unperturbed. "My mistake. Your name is undoubtedly Grumpy." He turned to Golden. "And that must make you Sleazy."

Pete was banking on Steadman's anger. He knew that Joseph James Steadman wanted to take a swing at him, to get back at Pete for having been roughed up the last time he was out here. That was good. Angry people didn't think clearly. Angry people weren't careful about what they said, and the mike inside Pete's jacket was ready to pick it all up....

"We're here to see Dr. Morrow," Dr. Golden said, his green eyes a little too bright in his face. "I'd like to get this over with."

"That's a pity," said Pete. "She just went into town. She said she wouldn't be back for a few hours."

Golden smiled, and Pete was reminded of a lizard. "I don't think so," he said. "Her car is still in the driveway."

Inside the house, Annie had called Whitley Scott at the FBI. Scott had said they were on their way. They'd arrive in twenty minutes, maybe less. She now stood at the top of the stairs, listening through the headphones to the conversation outside.

"In fact, I'll bet she's standing on the other side of these windows, listening to us talk," she heard Golden say.

"Maybe," she heard Pete drawl, his Western accent more pronounced than usual. "Maybe not. Why don't you just tell me what you want, and then maybe I can help you." He paused. "Maybe."

Outside, Steadman was starting to lose his cool. "Maybe you'd better be quiet before I use this to blow your head off your neck, smartass," he said as he reached into his jacket pocket and pulled out a huge automatic pistol. He jammed it under Pete's chin.

A vein bulged in Golden's forehead, and Pete thought the man was going to have a stroke.

"It's certainly big enough," Pete said with a cocky smile. "Fire this sucker, and the entire neighborhood will come running to see what happened."

"Keep the gun under your coat," Golden snapped nervously at Steadman.

Inside the house, Annie's fingers clutched the banister. They were threatening Pete with a gun! *Where* was the FBI? According to her watch, they were still over fifteen minutes away. For the first time in a long time, she found herself wishing they would show up early. Slowly she crept down the stairs, closer to the front door.

"Why don't you tell me what you want," Pete offered. "I'm listening." Me and the FBI, he thought. "Maybe we can make a deal."

"You give us the death mask," Steadman said, "and we don't kill you. How's *that* for a deal?"

Pete pretended to think about it. "I guess you're going to have to try to kill me," he finally said. "Though, I've got to warn you, I don't die very easily."

Oh, Pete, what are you doing? thought Annie.

"Or, you guys could crawl into whatever hole you came out of," Pete said. "And come back when you're ready to make a real deal."

Steadman pulled the gun away from Pete's head. With an angry look, he began to attach a large silencer to the barrel.

Unconcerned, Pete sat down on the top of the porch steps and looked up at the two men. "Using a silencer is illegal, you know," he said. "Shame on you."

"Tell Morrow to open the door," Golden said.

"Tell me," Pete said pleasantly. "Do I look that stupid?"

"I would really like to shoot you," Steadman snarled.

"Gee, what a coincidence. I'd like to shoot you, too," Pete said to Steadman, still in the same pleasant tone.

"Put your hands on your head," Steadman snapped, a touch of panic in his voice. He glanced at Golden. "Check his pockets. He's carrying."

Golden was nervous as hell, but he pulled Pete's gun out of his jacket pocket, holding it like a dead mouse.

"I'm not cut out for this," Golden said. "Let's get that crate and go."

"Dr. Morrow," Steadman called, his voice angry. "Open the damned door."

"Annie, I know you're not even in there, but if you are, don't open the door," Pete said calmly.

From inside the house, Annie watched as Steadman backhanded Pete across the face. With a gasp, she saw Pete skid along the porch, hitting the side of the house with a solid thud.

"Open the door, Annie," Steadman called. "Or I'm gonna kill this bastard."

Pete came up smiling. "I hate to break it to you guys," he said, "but I'm Navaho. And you know what happens when a Navaho dies. Sure you do—you did your research before you made those threatening phone calls to Annie. But in case you need a refresher course, I'll tell you. A dead Navaho returns to avenge the wrongs made against him in life. Kill me, and my evil spirit will kick you straight to hell."

Steadman didn't look worried. "I'm gonna count to three, *Annie*," he said, "and then I'm going to shoot him. One…"

"She's not going to open the door," Pete said. "She knows that you're bluffing."

Annie stood at the door, her hands on the deadbolt. His leather jacket was lined with a bulletproof vest, she reminded herself, trying to force back the panic that threatened to overpower her. Even if they shot him, he'd be okay, wouldn't he? Oh, God, unless they shot him in the head. If they shot him in the head, he'd die. The panic was back full-force. If she didn't open the door, and Pete died, she'd never be able to live with herself, knowing that she could have saved him.

"Two," shouted Steadman. "I'm not bluffing."

She didn't want Pete to die. She desperately didn't want him to die....

"Yes, he is," Pete said. "Annie, don't open the door!"

Because, dammit, she loved him. She yanked the headphones off her and pushed the alarm system's front door override.

"Three!"

Annie jerked the door open.

"No!" Pete shouted. God, no! He'd told her to keep the door shut no matter what!

Steadman's gun swung toward Annie.

Pete moved fast, letting his backup gun drop from his sleeve into his hand. He blocked Annie with his body, shooting Steadman cleanly in the right arm and in the leg. Steadman's shots went wild, hitting the roof of the porch, the side of the house.

Then three more gunshots rang out. Bullets from the gun Golden was holding hit Pete, the force knocking him back into the house and slamming him into the foyer wall. He fell like a stone onto the floor.

Annie slammed the door shut and threw the deadbolt, leaving Golden and Joseph James Steadman out on the porch. They pounded on the door, and it strained beneath their combined weight. Much more of this, and they were going to break through, taking the old door right off its hinges.

Pete didn't move.

"Pete," Annie said. "Get up!"

She'd seen the bullets hit him in the chest. That meant he was all right, because his jacket was bullet-proof.

But he still didn't move.

"Pete!" she shouted. It was only natural that he be dazed. He probably had the air knocked out of him. He probably needed to lie there a minute and catch his breath. But she was starting to get scared. Golden and Steadman were going to bust through the door any second....

"Pete, come *on!*" she yelled, turning to look at him.

Blood.

Pete's blood.

Bright and red, it seeped out from underneath him, running in the cracks on the hardwood floor....

With a cry, she ran toward him. Oh, God, he was bleeding. "Please don't be dead. Please, God, don't let him be dead!"

She turned him over onto his back, oblivious to the

door breaking open, oblivious to Golden and Steadman as they shouted and waved their guns at her. Annie was only aware of Pete, of the blood.

There was so much blood, leaking out from underneath the waistband of his jacket, staining the front of his jeans.

He wasn't breathing. God, he wasn't breathing....

"Pete," Annie cried, touching his face, his hair, his arms. Arms that had held her, lips that had kissed her... "No! God, no! Pete, I love you, don't be dead—"

Rough hands pulled her up, off the floor, away from Pete's body. She struggled, sobbing his name, trying to get back to him, uncaring of her safety. Golden hit her, and she fell to the ground, not feeling the pain, not feeling anything but grief. Oh, God, Pete was dead....

He was lying sprawled on the floor, one arm trapped underneath the weight of his body, the other flung out, his fingers spread wide as if he were reaching for something, reaching for her....

"He's dead," Golden said, nudging Pete with his foot. His green eyes looked almost feverish in his white face. He looked frighteningly inhuman, his nervousness frozen away by whatever coldness now inhabited him. "Open the safe, or you will be, too."

Annie sat very still. She didn't care. By killing Pete, Golden had already killed her.

Swearing, Golden began to drag her into the laboratory.

"For crying out loud, give me a hand," he finally said to Steadman.

"Which hand do you want, Al?" Steadman said, his voice pinched with pain. "I got a bullet in my right arm, and I think it's broken, and I'm bleeding like a stuck pig from this gash in my leg—"

"Shut up," Golden said, finally pushing Annie down in front of the safe. He held the gun to her head. "Open it."

Woodenly, she pulled herself up and began to open the safe. He was going to kill her. She knew he would, as soon as she gave him the death mask. He'd killed Pete, and he was going to kill her.

But he wasn't going to get away with it. If she stalled, Whitley Scott and the FBI would come. If she stalled long enough, she might even live to see Golden and Steadman rot in prison....

"You set me up, Golden," she said, suddenly feeling almost deadly calm, turning to look at him. "Didn't you?"

"Open the safe," he hissed.

"The death mask isn't in there," she said.

Steadman cursed loudly.

The panic in Golden's eyes deepened. "Where is it?"

"Tell me why you set me up," Annie said.

"Because it was so easy to do," he said. "The FBI was already investigating you. I just played into their hands."

"What are you talking about?"

"Do we really have to get into the details? The incident at Athens was just your bad luck. We didn't have anything to do with that—you came under suspicion because they couldn't find anyone else. So we staged a similar little event in England after you left. And then we planted the stuff in your lab. Are you satisfied? We gave the FBI what they needed, and now you're gonna give me what I need. Then I'm gonna burn this place down." Golden cocked his gun, pressing it against Annie's head. "Now, where is that crate?"

"Upstairs," she said, curiously unafraid of the gun, its cold metal barrel bruising her temple. "In the attic." Something still wasn't clear. What was the big deal about this artifact? Why did they have to frame her? She'd probably never know....

"I can't handle the stairs," Steadman complained. "You take her. And leave her up there, will you?"

Golden forced Annie's arm back behind her, twisting it upward so that she should have cried out from the pain. But the numbness was surrounding her so completely, she didn't make a sound.

Pete's body lay in the foyer with all that blood, and the grief tore through, slicing into her, cutting her in two. He never knew that she loved him. He had died before she had a chance to tell him. No, that wasn't true. She'd had plenty of chances, she had just been too pigheaded, too stubborn, too *selfish,* and now he was dead and he would never know.

Tears spilled down her face, and she stumbled on the stairs, looking back at him. His face was probably already growing cold to the touch. The puddle of blood had grown. There was even blood on the knees of his jeans....

Annie froze. Outwardly, she made herself keep going, but inwardly, even her heart had stopped beating.

Pete's fingers had been spread, reaching, but now they were clenched, his hand in a tight fist.

Breathe, she told herself. *Breathe.*

Around her, everything snapped into tight focus. She tried to appear to move at a normal speed, and still stall their inevitable climb up to the attic. They were walking up the stairs in slow motion. The light was on in the kitchen, and the black-and-white tiled floor became almost three-dimensional. There was a cobweb hanging from the light fixture in the hall. The banister at the edge of the second-floor landing was in serious need of dusting. And the secondary burglar alarm control panel that had been installed next to Annie's bedroom door was flashing green.

Green. The system had been shut down.

The motion detectors had been turned off. But when she opened the front door, she'd activated only the override, leaving the rest of the system on-line. If *she* hadn't turned off the alarm system, then...

Pete.

Pete was alive.

She started to shake, and Golden pushed her harder. "Scared?" he taunted her. "You better be. If that crate isn't up here, you're dead."

But she wasn't scared. She was happy, thunderously, joyfully happy. Pete was alive! God was giving her a second chance....

His clenched fist had been some sort of signal to her. He knew that she would notice—he knew she always noticed details.

He was trying to tell her something. But what?

They reached the top of the stairs and she pointed to the attic door, unable to speak. Golden motioned for her to open it.

The attic stairs creaked as they went up, up to the attic, up where Golden intended to leave her. Permanently.

Annie's heart was pounding.

She strained her ears, but she heard no sounds from downstairs. No struggle, no scuffle, nothing.

What was Pete trying to tell her?

Golden released her arm as they stepped up into

the attic. He held his gun steady with both hands as he aimed it at her. "Get it."

Behind the old TV. She had put the crate behind the...

The crate!

In a flash she remembered picking up a similar heavy package at the airport. Pete had lifted it up, realized he would need both hands to carry it and refused. *She* had ended up lugging it all the way out to the car because, he said, if something threatening happened while he was carrying it, he wouldn't be able to properly protect her. He wouldn't be able to go for his gun.

He couldn't carry the package and hold a gun at the same time!

And if *Pete* couldn't...

With a silent heave, Annie picked up the crate and placed it solidly in Alistair Golden's outstretched left hand. And she watched as he brought his right hand, his gun hand, over to support the bottom of the heavy crate.

Annie wasn't sure if the look of surprise on Golden's face was from the unexpected weight of the crate, or from the sight of Pete, covered with blood and looking as if he'd risen from the dead, crashing through the attic window, a gun in each hand.

"Freeze," Pete shouted. "Annie, get down!"

Annie dove for cover as Golden lunged toward Pete, futilely throwing the crate at him. She heard the sound of gunshots.

Then there was silence.

"You stupid son of a bitch," Annie heard Pete say. "I *told* you to freeze."

Slowly she poked her head out. Golden lay on the floor, his sightless eyes staring up at the rafters, but Annie could see only Pete.

Pete!

Standing in front of her, breathing, living….

"You're alive," she said, unaware of the tears that coursed down her face. "My God, you *are* alive."

She moved toward him, held by a gaze she'd thought she'd never see again, beautiful dark eyes filled with life. And pain.

"Careful," he said, "I'm covered with glass."

"I don't care," she said, touching his face, wrapping her arms around him. "I love you. I'm never going to let go of you again."

He kissed her, sweetly, softly.

Downstairs, a team of federal agents poured into the house.

"Well, if it isn't the cavalry," Pete said, swaying slightly in her arms. "About time." And then his knees gave out.

The next few seconds blurred together as Annie

caught him, shouting, screaming for help. She didn't have the strength to hold him up, but she kept him from hitting the floor with force, lowering him gently down.

Whitley Scott was there in an instant. "Agent down!" he shouted. "We have an agent down! Get those paramedics up here—"

Someone unzipped Pete's jacket. There was a huge stain of bright red blood on his lower left side.

"The bullet went in under his jacket," Scott's voice said, "and angled up...."

Pete looked up at Scott. "Steadman—" he croaked.

Scott nodded. "We found where you left him," he said. "He hasn't come to yet, but he's cuffed."

"What's this on the floor?" someone asked. "Whoa, these aren't your everyday, average foam chips...."

"Peterson's lost an awful lot of blood," someone said.

Another voice swore softly. "How the hell did he manage to climb up the outside of the house in this condition? It's unreal...."

"Had to," Pete whispered. "Stairs creak...."

"Cocaine," Annie heard someone say. "This entire crate is *filled* with cocaine...."

"Hang in there, Captain," another man's voice said. "Paramedics are on their way."

"Get him downstairs," Scott ordered. "Lift him up and get him down and into a car. There's no time to wait. We can meet the ambulance halfway—"

This couldn't be happening, Annie thought, letting go of Pete's hand as five men lifted him. She couldn't get him back only to lose him again.

Miraculously, the ambulance had arrived, and the paramedics were in the foyer with their stretcher. The other agents laid Pete gently on it.

"Annie," he whispered.

She leaned over him, touching his face. His skin felt so clammy. "Don't you dare die on me, Peterson," she said fiercely. "Not twice in one day. I won't let you!"

"I have no intention of dying," he said, his voice little more than a rasp. His eyes were glazed with pain, his fingers gripping hers. "No way...."

"I love you," Annie told him. "You better not forget that."

Somehow he managed to smile. "I won't."

CHAPTER EIGHTEEN

PETE WOKE UP.

Intensive care, he thought, staring at the massive array of monitors and machines that surrounded his hospital bed.

He was alive.

Yes, he was definitely alive. The pain in his gut was proof of that.

His throat was dry, his mouth was gluey and tasted like old socks. He tried to swallow, but it was a lost cause.

He had an IV tube in the back of his right hand.

His left hand was stuck in some kind of vise....

No, that was no vise grip, that was Annie! She held his hand tightly as she sat next to his bed, her head resting on the edge of the mattress, her eyes closed, her breathing even. She was asleep.

Gently he pulled his hand free, then touched the silky smoothness of her hair.

Her eyes opened slowly, and she sat up, looking

at him. "I was starting to wonder if you were ever going to wake up," she said, her eyes filling with tears. One escaped and slid down her cheek.

"Don't cry." Pete couldn't make his voice any louder than a whisper. "Everything's gonna be all right—"

Her eyes blazed with anger. "You should have told me that you were going to try to provoke Golden and Steadman. I had no idea what you were doing—I thought you'd lost your mind. And when Whitley Scott told me that you had intentionally been making them angry, that you wanted them to try for you, that you were fast enough to disarm them both by winging them and that *I* was responsible for your getting shot because I opened the door and distracted you—"

Huge tears fell from Annie's eyes, faster and faster. Pete reached out to touch her hand, but she jerked away. But then, as if on second thought, she took his hand, bringing it up to her lips, then pressing it against the side of her face.

"I'm really mad at you," she said.

"It wasn't your fault," he whispered. "I underestimated Golden, didn't think he would have the guts to shoot me—"

"If I hadn't opened the door, he *wouldn't* have," Annie said, "but, God, Pete, I was so afraid you were going to die."

"I didn't," he said.

"I love you," she said.

"I remember."

PETE RODE IN THE WHEELCHAIR DOWN to the lobby. Outside the big double doors, he could see the flash of Annie's shining hair in the bright autumn sunshine.

The nurse pushed him through the doors and out onto the sidewalk. The morning air was cold, bracing. He took a deep breath, then smiled up into Annie's dancing blue eyes.

"Okay, Captain," the nurse said. "You can take it from here."

Pete stood up, still moving slowly, carefully. It would be a few more weeks before he was running any laps.

Annie was watching him carefully. "You talked to Whitley Scott this morning?" she asked.

"Yeah."

"Did they find out who was the inside contact?"

"Collins," Pete said. "He had access to the security codes—he got Steadman and Golden into your house."

"So this whole thing was about smuggling drugs?"

"That's it," Pete said. "Steadman put up the money to buy the art, and Golden would take on the task of authenticating it. But what he really did was fly out to England and pack the piece using special foam packing peanuts that he'd picked up wholesale in Colombia. The peanuts were loaded with cocaine, sometimes tens of millions of dollars' worth. Golden would bring the cocaine into the U.S. via England. He figured—correctly—that anything brought in from Colombia would be carefully searched, whereas England's not particularly known for its drug trafficking, so Customs tends to be more lax. As for the artifact, Steadman would turn right around and sell it—usually at a loss. He didn't care if he lost a few dollars on the art, he was making a bundle distributing the coke.

"When Ben Sullivan specifically called for you to authenticate the death mask, Golden had already packed it—gotten it ready to ship," he said. "He and Steadman stood to lose the whole shipment of cocaine." They had reached the car. Pete looked at the woman he had risked his life for, the woman he would gladly risk his life for a hundred times more. "They stood to lose millions. Or worse. You could have found the coke. So they made those threatening phone calls, trying to set up a Navaho group as the fall guy when they stole the piece from you. When *I* made the scene and security got too tight, they got desperate. They tried to kill you, and when that didn't work, they resorted to their back-up plan—they framed you. They were willing to do *any*thing to get Golden named as the authenticator again. Because then the crate—with the coke—would go back into his possession."

Annie shuddered. "I'm just glad the whole mess is over."

Pete let her help him into the car, then watched as she slid behind the wheel.

"Ready?" she asked.

"Very ready." Pete leaned over, pulled her toward him and kissed her, long and hard. They were both breathing heavily when he finally let her go. "Guess what I want to do first thing when we get home?"

Annie frowned in mock seriousness. "You promised the doctor no strenuous exercise."

"Who said anything about strenuous?" He smiled, tugging on her earlobe with his teeth.

She pulled away. "No, Pete, really," she said, all teasing gone. "You better ask the doctor first, make sure it's okay…."

"It's okay," he said, playing with her long, brown hair, running it through his fingers. "And I didn't even have to ask. The doctor brought it up himself. I think he noticed the way I look at you."

The way Pete was looking at her right now… It was heat, steam, fire, his eyes glowing with flames.

He bent to kiss her again, and Annie closed her eyes, losing herself in the conflagration....

"Let's go home," he whispered.

Heart pounding, Annie pulled out of the driveway and onto the main road. After a mile or two, her pulse had finally returned to near normal, and she glanced over at Pete. "Jerry Tillet got funding for his Mexico project," she said. "Ben Sullivan came through."

"That's great news," Pete said. "Can't you drive any faster?"

Annie laughed. "We're five minutes from home," she said.

Pete's eyes told her that five minutes was five minutes too many.

"Cara's going to Mexico with Tillet," she said, trying to distract him—trying to distract herself. Would this traffic light *never* change? "Now I've got to find another research assistant."

"I thought you were thinking about going along," Pete said as the car moved forward. "You know, get your hands dirty for a change, do a little camping...."

Annie didn't answer, didn't even look up from the road. *What are your plans?* she wanted to ask. *When do you have to return to work?* But she didn't. She couldn't get the words out.

"I have a great idea," Pete was saying. "We can go out to Colorado first, then head down to Mexico—"

"We?" She couldn't hide her surprise.

Pete smiled at her. "Yeah. We. You. Me. You know. We could make it our honeymoon."

Annie pulled sharply off to the right, into a department store parking lot. She stopped the car, then turned to look at him. "Are you asking me to marry you?"

There was a spark of uncertainty in his eyes. "I thought I already did," he said slowly. "In the ambulance. On the way to the hospital?"

"You remember that?" Annie said in disbelief. "Pete, you were delirious."

"Well, yeah." He grinned. "Because you said yes...." His eyes were intense and his smile disappeared as he watched her. "*Will* you marry me, Annie?"

She moistened her lips. "I'm not sure I want to be married to someone who works for the CIA," she said softly. "I'm not sure I could handle it...."

The silence in the car stretched on.

Who was she fooling? Annie thought. It wouldn't be easy; she'd spend all her time worrying that he would be hurt, shot, killed even. She'd hate the long hours, the weeks away. But she loved him, and she was willing to take whatever he was willing to give.

"Yes," she said, at the exact same moment he turned to her and said, "I'll retire."

They stared at each other for a long time, then Pete said again, "I *will* retire."

"You don't have to," Annie said quietly. "I'll marry you anyway."

"But I want to," he said, taking her hand in his and kissing the tips of her fingers. "I've been thinking about it for a while. I just never had a good enough reason to retire before this."

"But what will you do?" Annie said. "You're awfully young to retire."

Pete smiled. "I've been thinking about a career change," he said. "I heard there's this really terrific position open—someone's looking for a research assistant. I don't have a whole hell of a lot of experience in a lab, but I'm really good at camping and digging in the dirt, or whatever it is you archaeologists do."

Laughing, Annie kissed him. And kissed him, and kissed him.

When they drew apart, her hands were shaking. "Well," she said. "I'm glad *that's* settled."

But Pete touched her chin, tugging her face toward him. "Wait," he said. His eyes were serious. "I need to ask you…" He looked down for a moment as if gathering his courage. "I know you love me." His eyes met hers. "But have you forgiven me?"

"Forgiven? Yes," she said. "Forgotten? Never. I'm not going to make *that* mistake twice."

His eyebrow moved slightly in the tiniest of frowns. He didn't understand....

"I'm *never* going to forget that you love me," she said, and put the car into gear. "Let's go home."

* * * * *